W9-AKT-234

HIDDEN COVE

This Large Print Book carries the
Seal of Approval of N.A.V.H.

HIDDEN COVE

MEG TILLY

WHEELER PUBLISHING
A part of Gale, a Cengage Company

GALE
A Cengage Company

Copyright © 2019 by Meg Tilly.
Solace Island Series.
Wheeler Publishing, a part of Gale, a Cengage Company.

LIBRARY OF CONGRESS CIP DATA ON FILE.
CATALOGUING IN PUBLICATION FOR THIS BOOK
IS AVAILABLE FROM THE LIBRARY OF CONGRESS

ISBN-13: 978-1-4328-7258-8 (hardcover alk. paper)

Published in 2020 by arrangement with Berkley, an imprint of Penguin Publishing Group, a division of Penguin Random House, LLC.

Printed in Mexico
Print Number: 01   Print Year: 2020

I'd like to dedicate this book to my husband, Don, with love. Thank you, honey, for all that you do and all that you have done. You are my rock. xo

PROLOGUE

The sole meunière was cooked to perfection, moist, and the brown butter sauce with hints of lemon and parsley was flawless. However, he was able to swallow only a few mouthfuls. Wasn't able to do justice to the lamb chops. Didn't even bother attempting the passion fruit pavlova.

The chef appeared like a shadow at his shoulder, worry etching deep grooves around his mouth, on his forehead. "Sir," he said hesitantly. "Dinner? Was it not to your liking?"

"Dinner was fine, Jacques. Feeling a little distracted is all. You know how I am." He lifted his shoulders in an elegant shrug. "So emotional."

"Of course. Forgive me. I should have known." His chef inclined his head, giving a modified bow as he backed silently out of the room.

He plucked the white linen napkin from

his lap and daintily dabbed the outer corners of his lips. His butler, Fredrick, rushed forward and pulled out his Gothic throne chair — circa 1850, obtained from a private castle in France — as he rose to his feet, grace in motion.

He took a few steps, then paused. "I thought I saw Tati on the way home," he told his long-faced butler. "Followed her discreetly in the limo for a while, keeping a half-block distance at all times, but then she slipped into a fur shop. I instructed Bob to pull over, got out, and entered the shop. In a matter of minutes I found her. She was standing before a three-way mirror modeling a gorgeous Russian sable coat. I have to tell you, my heart was racing, until she turned around and we were face-to-face. It was then I realized my eyes had been playing tricks on me again. Her nose was the wrong shape and her irises were brown." He sighed.

Fredrick cleared his throat. "Well, sir," he said cautiously. "Always, at this time of year . . ."

"Yes. Yes, you're right, of course. Such a disappointment, though, to have one's hopes so high and then dashed like that. I was tempted to break her nose for being the wrong shape. Gouge out her eyes." He laughed. Fredrick didn't. No sense of humor, poor fellow. "That will be all, Fredrick," he said as he passed his butler standing like a sentinel by the dining room door. "I shall put myself to bed tonight."

"Very good, sir."

Once settled in his Italian leather armchair, he thought on the fur shop encounter further. The reminder of Tatiana was a sign. It was as if she had descended from heaven and whispered in his ear, "Enough time has been spent, my love, setting the stage. The muse is hungry. Requires sustenance. You must, once again, step into the light." After two pours of brandy — Emperador, of course — his nerves had calmed sufficiently to pick up the phone and make the call.

"Alexus, darling," he crooned when she answered the phone. Sweat dampened his underarms and the back of his ecru silk shirt. "I was wondering if I could interest you in a little pre-exhibit champagne tomorrow night before the doors are opened to the masses?"

ONE

Gabriel Conaghan skimmed over the day's work and then heaved a sigh of relief. Some days the writing went fast and the words flowed. This had not been one of those days. He had been unable to settle into the world of his novel. His protagonist had felt flat and one-dimensional. He'd gone online to do research only to look up an hour and a half later with the realization that he'd fallen down a rabbit hole and was reading stuff that had nothing to do with what he had initially looked up. It wasn't until he'd disconnected the Internet and turned his cell phone to do not disturb that he was able to dive fully into Troy Master's world.

As Gabe saved his work in his documents folder on his desktop, in the cloud, and on a flash drive, he became aware of the stiffness in his shoulders, neck, and lower back. Once again he'd sat at his computer for far too long. Night had fallen, and what did he have to show for it? A few more pages added to his latest manuscript.

He pushed back from his desk and stared out his study window. Not much to see, just the brick wall of the neighboring building. He leaned his face against the smooth surface of the cool windowpane and tilted his head back, as this enabled him to see the smallest scrap of night sky. Suddenly he longed for more. What was "more"? He had no idea, but lately he had noticed a pervasive feeling of emptiness niggling at him, as if something intangible was missing. The air in his sleek loft apartment seemed stale, as if the oxygen had been depleted. He'd been holed up in there for a couple of days, writing, eating, sleeping, and then writing some more.

He grabbed his cell phone off the desk, got a coat from the hall closet, and slipped it on. On his way through the kitchen he poured himself two fingers of whiskey and then climbed the circular stairs that led to his rooftop terrace.

The slap of frigid air had him turning up the collar of his overcoat; however, he enjoyed the sharp bite of it. Found it invigorating after being glued to his keyboard all day.

What time is it? he wondered. He huffed

out a laugh. *Forget what time . . . what day is it?* That was the disadvantage to being self-employed. One day blurred into the next. He pulled out his cell phone and clicked the home button. *It's 9:38 p.m.? Wow. Who knew it had gotten that late.* He swiped up on the screen and turned off the do not disturb. Instantaneously his phone started to buzz with incoming messages and e-mails.

He took a slug of his whiskey and savored the heat as it traveled down his throat, then glanced down at the phone. What he saw had his heart thumping hard in his chest with worry.

There was a profusion of missed phone calls from his mom. Something must be terribly wrong.

Fergus Conaghan looked with satisfaction in the mirror that his wife, Alma, held before him. "Looks good," he said. "Perhaps a dab more shadow under the eyes."

"I will not, Fergus," she replied with a touch of tart lemon to her voice. "You already look like death warmed over. If I add any more, the poor boy will think you're on your deathbed."

"Good!" Fergus roared. "I want to scare the crap outta him. I'm sixty-five years old.

You turned sixty-one last week. Why isn't he married? Where are our grandchildren? We should have been gifted with half a dozen by now. But has he done his duty? No! None of the children have."

"Give him time. He's only thirty-six."

"When I was his age, our fourth child was in your belly."

"It was a different era, Fergus."

"He's wasting his life, hunched over that keyboard of his. How many blasted murder mysteries must that boy write?"

"He writes crime fiction, honey."

"How's he ever supposed to meet anyone when he never goes out? Refuses to socialize. Has his nose to that computer all damned day. The boy needs a good boot in the rear end, and I'm just the man to give it to him. We're going to send him to Solace Island. No one on God's green earth could resist the siren's lure of that gorgeous landscape." Fergus rubbed his hands together gleefully. "It will lull him away from his keyboard and out into the world."

"And what if it doesn't? Fergus, this is a crazy scheme . . ."

"Never you mind." He waved away her objections. "You didn't marry this wily guy for nothing. This head here?" He rapped his gnarled fist on his temple. "It's stuffed with high-quality brains. You'll see, my dear. I've also devised a devilishly clever backup plan." He grinned triumphantly. "What the landscape doesn't accomplish, the task I give him will. He'll be forced to talk and interact with people. *Real* people. Not the make-believe ones that populate those darn books of his."

The bedside phone rang. Fergus grabbed it. "Yup?"

"Mr. Conaghan," the doorman said. "Your son is on his way up."

Fergus hung up the phone and leapt into action. "Draw the curtains!" he yelled. "Turn off the TV. We gotta set the stage!" While she closed the curtains, he dimmed the lights. *Oh sweet Jesus!* Her makeup was lying on the bed. He snatched it, ran into the master bathroom, and shoved the makeup in a drawer. While he was there, inspiration struck. He quickly stuck a washcloth under the tap, wrung out the excess water, and then rubbed the wet washcloth in his hair. The moisture was a good touch. Made him look like he was feverish and sweating. He scrubbed his fists against his eyes to make them bloodshot and slightly swollen. Dabbled a little water on his brow and on his upper lip. *Should have been a damned actor.* He chortled to himself. *I belong on the stage!*

The elevator chimed, marking his son's arrival to their Park Avenue penthouse.

Fergus sprinted back into the bedroom, his hip giving him only minor trouble, dove into bed, and yanked the covers over his shoulders. He could hear Alma greeting their son at the door as Fergus sank his body deep into the bed and rattled out a feeble cough.

Let the games begin!

"Not to worry, Dad," Gabe reassured his father. "I'll take care of it."

"I . . ." His father dissolved into a racking coughing fit. "Water . . . water . . ."

Gabe grabbed the glass of water off the bedside table and placed it in his dad's shaking hand. "Here you are."

His dad took a tiny sip. "Thanks, son." Fergus's eyes drifted shut as if wearied by the bout of coughing, the glass resting on his chest. "I feel bad . . . laying this burden on you," his father croaked feebly.

"It's not a burden," Gabe lied. "I was just thinking I wanted to get out of New York for a while. You're doing me a favor. I'll be your eyes and your ears. I will check the place out and send you a report." Gabriel removed the glass of water from his father's limp grip and set it back on the bedside table. "And I want you to focus on resting up, regaining your health. Before you know it, you'll be back on your feet, irritating the hell out of all of your loved ones." Gabe's voice was a whisper now, a peaceful lullaby that had lulled his father to sleep. A soft snore was rumbling forth. He was having good dreams apparently, because there was a hint of a smile gracing his father's lips.

Gabe crossed the room on quiet feet and exited, gently closing the heavy oak door of the master bedroom behind him. He felt as if he'd been run over by a Mack truck.

His mother's hand alighted on his forearm. "Are you all right, son?" she asked in her soft, lilting voice. Her family had immigrated to New York when she was six years old, but traces of the old County Cork accent still lingered in times of stress.

"He looks terrible," Gabriel said. It was an effort to keep his voice from cracking. "I knew he was fighting a cold last week." He shook his head. "How could he have deteriorated so quickly? Dad mentioned the doctor ordered a chest X-ray?" His mother was wringing her hands, which was never a good sign. "That Dad might have pneumonia or possibly something worse?"

"I said *walking* pneumonia," his father bellowed from behind the closed door. He must have woken up. The man had the ears of an elephant.

His mother bit her lip, her face flushed with emotion. "Don't you concern yourself too much, Gabe. He's a hardy old fart." Her voice was a little sharp. The stress and worry must be getting to her.

He patted her hand. "Don't worry, Mom. It's no problem. I'll throw a few things in my suitcase and catch a flight out."

"But your manuscript. I know you have a deadline coming . . ."

"It's not a problem," he said, pulling her in for a hug and dropping a gentle kiss on the top of her graying hair. She felt slighter than before, more fragile. His parents had gotten old while he wasn't looking. "I can write anywhere. It will be nice to get away from New York for a while. I was supposed to take Nora to lunch tomorrow —"

"Not to worry. I'll let your godmother know it will be lunch with me instead."

"Thanks," he said. "Give her my love."

"Will do."

He kept the reassuring smile firmly on his face until the elevator doors closed behind him. *Shit.* He rolled his shoulders, trying to dispel the tension that had settled there. His father's request was a massive inconvenience. It would disrupt the flow of his writing to hop on a plane and fly to the Pacific Northwest.

Never mind. Family first, he told himself. *You'll go to this Solace Island. Check out the Mansfield Manor for Dad, then return, back home in four or five days, maybe less.*

Two

Gabe missed the last ferry to Solace Island by six minutes. He arrived at the terminal in time to see the ferry pulling away from the dock carrying only a handful of trucks and cars. Light was spilling out of the boat's windows, leaving shimmering reflections trailing on the ocean's dark, inky surface.

"Guess I won't be arriving tonight," he said as he watched the ferry recede in the distance. He swung the SUV he had rented at the airport in a tight U-turn and headed up the road toward the motel on the outskirts of the small town he'd passed through moments earlier.

After an unsatisfactory fast-food dinner of dried-out, greasy fried chicken and a biscuit that could have been put to good use as a hockey puck, he set his laptop on the spindly desk and tried to write. He'd managed to get a couple of pages in on the plane, but as he read them over, he realized they were shit. He deleted the day's work and took a slug of soda that had been part of his meal package, grimacing. The soda had no fizz — just like his writing.

He woke early, his phone vibrating on the nightstand. He picked it up, glanced at the screen. It was his dad.

Typical.

Normally, when his dad phoned him at the crack of dawn he'd let the call go to voice mail, but yesterday had shaken him.

He swiped the screen. "Yup?"

"What do you think of the place, boyo?" His father sounded much better than he had yesterday, full of vigor.

"Not there yet. Luggage took a while. Missed the last ferry."

"Well, you're in for a treat. Can't believe I managed to snag the property." His dad chortled gleefully. "Of course, McCall had to croak first. Bought it from his widow for a song."

"Good going, Dad," Gabe said, knowing full well that his dad had probably overpaid. McCall had been one of his best friends, and he would have used the excuse of the purchase to make sure his widow was well taken care of.

"Call me when you've had a chance to

walk through the place."

"Will do. You're sounding good. The antibiotics must be kicking in."

"Yes. Well —" His father's words were cut short by an extended coughing fit. His dad made a valiant effort to continue the conversation, but finally Gabe convinced his father it was best he not overexert himself. "Right —" *Cough . . . cough . . .* "I'll hang up then —" His dad blew his nose long and loud. Gabe pulled the phone away from his ear, but not fast enough. He could have lived quite happily without hearing all that moisture trumpeting through his dad's nose at such close range. "I look forward to hearing your thoughts on the place, Gabe. A piece of heaven, Solace Island is. A little piece of heaven."

Gabe hung up, catching sight of the digital clock on the bedside table. It was 5:26 a.m. His dad must have forgotten to factor in the time difference. He considered trying to grab a couple more hours of sleep. After fifteen minutes of staring at the dark ceiling, he got up.

The motel room was damp and smelled of mildew, the beaten-up linoleum floor cold under his feet. He didn't need to open the curtains to know that it was still dark outside. He gathered up his belongings and

22

checked out.

The early-morning ferry to Solace Island was surprisingly full. A lot of large trucks, some long haul, some short distance. Gabe got out of his vehicle and stretched in the brisk air. The edges of the night sky were starting to soften as he weaved his way between a commercial dairy truck and a beat-up vehicle that — from the smell emanating out of the back — was used for hauling either garbage or manure.

He entered the small ferry lounge. With the exception of two straggly haired back-packers leaning against each other and catching a few more moments of sleep, the place was empty. There was a coffee/espresso/hot chocolate/tea vending machine. *How bad could the coffee be?* Gabe thought, rummaging in his pocket. He pulled out a handful of change and fed it to the machine. He made his selection and watched as a paper cup dropped down and a thin stream of watery brownish-gray liquid began to dribble into his cup. It did not look promising.

He took a sip anyway.

One was enough.

He tossed the coffee into the gray garbage bin and went back out to his vehicle, reclined his seat all the way back, and shut his eyes.

THREE

Zelia Thompson shoved her chair away from her dad's old mahogany desk with its light walnut inlay. The large desk dominated the small office space she had commandeered for herself in the back room of her gallery, but she didn't care. Whenever she felt frazzled she would smooth her hands across the gold-embossed green leather writing surface and think of her father working at that very desk, and it always soothed her. At the moment, however, there was no soothing to be had. She needed distance from the unsettling image on her desktop computer screen.

Nope. Moving my chair back isn't enough. She stood and took a half step backward. The soft underbelly of her knees bumped against the seat of her chair. Her fingers pressed against her lips in an almost praying position as she stared at the painting displayed on her glowing computer, unable to tear her eyes away.

She stepped forward, clicked the mouse, and then hastily retreated again.

Another painting was now on the screen, a slightly different palette, but equally disturbing. Gone were the green tones representing . . . foliage, perhaps . . . ? The browns and steel gray were also absent, but the varying shades of rust that seemed to spill outward like a septic wound were present in this painting as well. The brushstrokes the artist had used to lay down the paint created an optical illusion. The dark, deep reds seemed to seethe and bubbled outward, merging with a thick, almost-black darkness. Both of the paintings were abstract, yet it was clear they were portraits of some kind, some features missing, others out of place, with the artist's signature, Dattg, scrawled in the lower-right-hand corner.

"Clearly the artist has talent," Zelia murmured. "But my God . . ."

Something about the paintings made her feel slightly nauseous. She stepped forward to click to the next painting in the portfolio but found herself putting the computer to sleep instead.

"I'm going out," she called up to where her employee, Mary, was carefully unpacking Kendrick's bronze and glass *Water Lilies* sculpture. "I'll need you out front while I'm gone."

"For sure," Mary replied. "Be right there." A second later she appeared at the top of the stairs, stopping to untie her work smock and hang it on a hook. As Mary descended the stairs she smoothed back into submission the few flyaway wisps of her mousy brown hair that had escaped her bun.

Zelia still couldn't believe the good fortune that had befallen her on that rainy February day three years ago when the inimitable Mary Browning walked through the door and inquired about a job. She couldn't have been more than midtwenties at the time and yet she'd seemed much older, as if life had knocked her around a bit. She was soft-spoken, self-contained, very knowledgeable about art, plus she had organizational skills that blew Zelia's mind.

Zelia was not about to quibble with the fact that Mary didn't have a social security number and needed to be paid in cash. To pacify her need to pay her fair share, Zelia figured out how much would've been paid in taxes and once a month she wrote a check for that amount to the Solace Island Community Services, which provided food security to the locals, shelter and housing, mental health outreach, services for developmental disabilities, and more.

She knew it was wrong to pay an employee under the table, but there had been something in Mary's eyes that had made Zelia's decision a no-brainer. Beyond Mary's calm exterior, Zelia had felt waves of quiet desperation emanating from her pores, and underneath that, suffocating, bone-deep loneliness, and isolation. Having been orphaned at nineteen, Zelia knew what it was like to be a young woman alone in the world.

Was it an idealistic, risky thing for a small business owner to do? Perhaps, but she didn't regret her decision. Solace Island was a beautiful place to live, but finding reliable year-round employees had proven to be a challenge. In the three years before Mary had arrived, it had been a constant revolving door of employees. Most of the hires were decent people, but they were more transient, their priorities not career-based. They would work for a few months and then drift off to climb Mount Kilimanjaro, go to a yearlong yoga retreat or a work-study at Esalen. Once Zelia had come back from lunch to find the gallery unattended. The young man she'd hired had a blanket spread out on the roof. He'd been enjoying the view, smoking a joint, and working on his *all*-over tan.

At least when Mary dropped off the radar it would be for only a day or two. She'd always return, no explanations offered, but she'd work with a vengeance and within hours the gallery would be running smoothly again.

"Is everything all right?" Mary asked.

"Mm-hm," Zelia replied, wrapping her cashmere shawl around her. She'd splurged on it when she'd traveled to England about a year after her husband, Ned, had died. She'd rescheduled the trip several times before she'd finally made it to London. Grief had had a way of sucking her down back then. The slightest task had seemed to require a colossal effort to accomplish: brushing her teeth, showering, wearing something other than Ned's oversized clothes.

Finally, she'd managed to pull herself out of the gray fog that had enveloped her. She'd gotten on a plane, flown to England, and met with the talented young Welsh artist she had been tracking.

Yes, Zelia thought as she picked up her purse, the shawl she'd purchased six years ago had cost an arm and a leg, but it was totally worth it. The baby's breath softness of the shawl comforted her, and when she'd wrap it around her shoulders she was filled with happiness. It was as if a master weaver had woven an angelic song of joy into the very fibers of the yarn.

"I won't be long," Zelia told Mary. Then she slipped out the door to enjoy the brief patch of sunshine that had forced its way through a gap in the dark, fast-moving clouds. She inhaled deeply, arching upward, face to the sky, and filled her lungs with the crisp, late-February air. She glanced at her watch: 4:45 p.m. Too much to do, too little time. "Fifteen minutes," she murmured. "Then I'll return."

She cut across the park to the boardwalk that followed the ocean's edge, glad she'd worn her Frye boots. They were stylish, yet comfortable enough to allow her to indulge in one of her long walks at a moment's notice. She lengthened her stride, legs happy to stretch out. The sound of her boot heels hitting the wood walkway reminded her of horses. *A two-legged horse,* she thought with a smile. She shook out her arms. The natural swinging momentum that accompanied a vigorous stride didn't satisfy them, so she let her arms have their way and did a couple of complete circles, as if her arms were propellers on a seaplane preparing to take off.

"Ciao, bella!" Nicolò Rossi called from the doorway of his pasta shop.

When he and his sister, Sofia, had opened their shop four years ago, Solace Island residents had celebrated. What a luxury it was to have access to authentic homemade pastas, sauces, and hefty chunks of Parmesan, Romano, and pecorino cheeses imported from Italy. Their store also sold fresh mozzarella and ready-prepared foods like lasagna, eggplant Parmesan, and tiramisu.

Zelia waved, but she didn't stop. He was a lovely man, single, and apparently attracted to plus-size women, if his pursuit of her was any indication. He wasn't bad-looking. However, she'd already dipped her toe in that water. Went on a date. Had a goodnight kiss. No sparks. At least on her end. Unfortunately, he hadn't arrived at the same conclusion.

The boardwalk gave way to concrete steps that led across a small path, through a postage stamp of a park, and up another flight of steps, which spit her out on the road. She followed the road, deep in thought. *What should I do? The artist is talented, but . . .* She shook her head, her hands, too, as if she could shake the disquiet off like raindrops from a tarp. She strode past the marina, where boats bobbed on the water,

31

then cut through the pub parking lot.

Her friend Alexus had exquisite taste in artists and had mentioned in her e-mail that she was including three of Dattg's paintings in her exhibit that was opening tonight at her gallery, Feinstein & Co., in Greenwich, Connecticut. That Alexus had managed to carve a name for herself amongst that crowded, competitive art scene was impressive, and even more remarkable, her business was thriving.

Zelia started up another long flight of stairs that climbed the rocky cliff face and would eventually lead to the giant sculptures that stood in Mansfield Manor's back field. Mansfield Manor was consistently on *Le Monde*'s Gold List. Gullible tourists with more money than sense would arrive, year after year, to pay ridiculous sums of money to stay in a smattering of rather dated, gray-shingle-clad country cottages.

I guess the real question is, Zelia thought, taking a break to catch her breath before ascending the last flight of stairs, *why is Alexus pushing me so hard to do an entire exhibition for him?*

They had become fast friends over the years — two women running their own galleries — becoming successful each in their own right. She liked Alexus's quirky sense of humor and infectious laugh. They'd bumped into each other a few times at various art fairs at Frieze, in Miami. Then they'd been seated next to each other at a six-course tasting menu dinner in Basel. Wine pairing had been included. The food and wine pairings were sublime. By the end of the evening the two of them were laughing, perhaps more than they should have. A long-distance friendship ensued. Every now and then there would be a flurry of texts, some about work, some bemoaning the shortage of desirable men, and sometimes it was just a brief *hello, how's it going?* If Zelia's flights transferred through JFK or LaGuardia, she'd book a day between flights and grab a shuttle to Greenwich for a nominal fee. She'd sleep on Alexus's sofa bed. They'd stay up late talking and ingesting copious amounts of fine chocolate and red wine. Alexus had even made the trek to Solace Island once, after which she'd declared, 'It's quaint, my dear, very rustic. But my God, Zelia, what the hell do you do for fun?"

Just thinking about the look on Alexus's face when she'd said that made Zelia smile, but just as quickly the smile fell away. Yes, they were friends — *But for her to ask me to put on an entire exhibition for this unknown artist seems a bit bizarre.*

"There is something I'm not seeing," she murmured. She took hold of the wooden banister and headed up the last flight. It felt good to move, to feel the slight burn in her legs. The cold wind blowing off the ocean nipped at her fingers and face, causing Zelia to wrap her fluttering shawl more tightly around her body.

Alexus has never asked me to show a single artist's work before. Sure, sometimes in conversation an artist's name might come up, but usually it was tied to an outlandish story about something the artist had done or said. *This wasn't that. This was a demand cloaked as a request.*

The stairs were behind her now. She paused for a moment and scooped up the hem of her velvet dress. She tied a large knot in the rich jewel-toned fabric to protect the bottom from getting soaked by the coarse strands of uncut grass that had survived the winter. Then she was off again, striding through the field. The smell of damp earth and crushed grasses rose like a gentle strand of music, keeping her company as she strode toward the towering sculptures. There was something about the dark, faceless figures that comforted her. Hooded, yet somehow peaceful as they stood patiently with their gently sloping shoulders and bowed heads.

She stood for a moment among the sculptures, her head bowed as well, eyes shut. "I can't do it," she said aloud. Suddenly she felt lighter.

Gabe was at the window in the Hampstead Cottage, a mug of coffee in his hand. He was taking a break from writing at his computer.

He'd decided on the ferry ride over not to let the management know he was there on behalf of the new owner. He'd get a better idea of how Mansfield Manor was run if he wasn't getting preferential treatment. So far he had spent the morning tromping around the property. The exteriors of the manor and cottages were very picturesque. The site couldn't have been situated better. The interiors were the problem. They were extremely dated. Appeared to have been renovated in the early 1980s and not touched since.

However, the grounds were lovely. Stunning, really. The gracious front lawn gave way to a private beach, where a nestled, hidden cove was flanked by towering Douglas firs, red cedars, and a sprinkling of dogwood, maple, oak, and aspen trees. The views across the smattering of smudged-purple shadowed islands were glorious and far-reaching. If one wanted an even broader horizon, the guests could take the path on the right side of the property, along the water's edge, to the wooden bench resting on the farthest point of land. From there the world opened up. One could see the bobbing boats in the marina, and beyond that to the lovely town of Comfort, which was only a seven-minute amble away.

The hotel didn't have a gym, which would've been nice. The lack of a gym wasn't an issue for Gabe personally. Early in his career he'd realized that if he wanted to stay healthy while on book tour he'd need to be creative. While gyms were de rigueur in many of the North American hotels his publisher put him up at, internationally, it was touch and go. He'd devised a series of high-intensity exercises based on the tae kwon do discipline he'd discovered as a teen and continued to practice for much of his twenties. He had adjusted a few of the forms so they could be completed in a hotel room using minimal space.

However, he'd recommend to his father that they put a gym in. State-of-the-art equipment was expected in a five-star resort. Didn't matter if the guests rarely used it. They would want to know they had the choice. Steam rooms, chilled ice water with cucumber slices, fresh rolled white hand towels, and a basket of crisp apples for an impromptu after-workout snack.

He wrote for a couple of hours, then sampled the "high tea" in the manor house. The tea had been hot and strong, but the baked goods and the little tea sandwiches had been uninspired and stale. The glass of port was a stingy pour and of mediocre quality.

Gabe returned to his room, added his observations to the notes for his dad, then settled down to write for a few more hours, making sure to get up and stretch every thirty minutes or so. He would wander to various windows and take in the 360-degree views. Sometimes it felt as if that were his life, married to his computer as the days flipped past, catching glimpses of other people's lives from behind the safe confines of his window.

On one of his stretch breaks, he noticed a woman in the back field. She stood among the wooden sculptures, almost as if she were one of them. He was too far away to make out her features, but there was something about her that drew his eye, captured it. Perhaps it was her stillness, or the splash of color against the tall beige grasses.

Suddenly she moved. As if she were a wild deer awakening from a dream. She took off at a rapid clip, strode across the field, and disappeared down a flight of wooden stairs.

Gabe stayed at the back window awhile longer, but she didn't reappear. He hadn't thought she would. Her stride had been determined and purposeful, her body leaning forward as if her mind had already arrived at the place she was headed.

He poured more coffee into his mug, his thoughts still lingering on her. He unwrapped a complimentary cookie from its plastic wrap, then returned to the desk, where his manuscript was mocking him.

FOUR

LOOKED AT OUR UPCOMING SCHEDULE, ALL BOOKED UP. THX 4 THINKING OF ME THO.

It surprised her how long it had taken to find the right words. Zelia glanced at the time at the top-right-hand corner of her computer screen, 4:37 p.m. Alexus, on the East Coast, would have closed shop for the day. Zelia read over the text message one last time, then hit send.

The reply was almost instantaneous.

WHAT ABOUT LATER IN THE YEAR?

Jesus, Zelia thought, staring at the screen. *She must be working late.* She chewed on her lower lip. *What now? Alexus knows I'm at the computer because I just sent her a text.*

WE'RE BOOKED SOLID. SORRY, she typed.

NEXT FALL THEN?

What the hell? Zelia thought, but she must have said it out loud because Mary came in from the next room.

"What's going on?" Mary asked.

"Ick . . ." Zelia said, pushing back from the computer and rubbing her face. "Alexus Feinstein wants me to do an exhibit for an artist she's championing and I don't want to."

Mary shrugged. "Then don't. You've worked hard, built a name for yourself. You and your gallery are highly respected in the art world, which puts you in the catbird seat."

"She's advocating pretty aggressively, which is out of character for her. Maybe she's been drinking — I don't know, but it's making me uncomfortable." Zelia blew out a frustrated breath. "The thing is . . . I feel defensive, too. The artist is talented. I would even venture to say enormously so . . ."

"And yet . . ." Mary said. The woman would have made a damn fine therapist.

"And yet I don't want to have these . . . these paintings in my beautiful gallery. Don't want to be surrounded by his art. I don't know why, but I feel almost nauseous when I look at it, scared, like my breath can't get past my throat." Zelia scooted her office chair back toward her workstation. "Here," she said, clicking on the file. "Take a look. Tell me what you think."

Zelia vacated her chair, and Mary sat down and started clicking through the images. Zelia watched her assistant closely. Mary had an uncannily correct intuition when it came to art. She could tell in a flash where talent lay, what would sell, and what price people would be willing to pay.

Mary's face didn't change as she studied each painting one by one. She was systematic in her perusal, carefully considering each one before clicking to the next.

"Well," Zelia said with a half-hearted laugh, trying to break the tension that was building in her gut. "You've gotten a lot further than I did."

Mary didn't respond, just went to the next painting and the one after that. When she reached the last one, she closed the file and turned to face Zelia.

"You're right," Mary said, her forefinger sliding the frames of her charcoal-gray glasses back into place on the bridge of her nose. "It doesn't matter how gifted the artist might be. You can't have these paintings here. It would damage your heart. Anyone who knows and cares about you wouldn't ask you to do this." She turned back to the computer and pecked out a few words.

NOT NOW. NOT EVER. DON'T ASK AGAIN.

Mary looked up at Zelia, who was standing next to the chair. "Okay?" she asked.

Zelia couldn't help but laugh. It was rude, but there was something that felt right about it as well. "Okay," Zelia said, nudging Mary out of the chair. "I get it. I need to grow a pair." Zelia sat down and softened the edges of Mary's text.

AS MUCH AS I RESPECT AND ADMIRE YOU, LEXI, THESE PAINTINGS ARE NOT RIGHT FOR ME OR MY GALLERY. NOT NOW. NOT EVER. PLEASE DON'T ASK AGAIN.

She glanced over at Mary, who nodded. "Send it," she said.

Zelia sent the text, a slight ache in the pit of her stomach.

The reply was immediate. SCREW YOU!

"That went well," Zelia said with a nonchalance she didn't feel. She shut down the computer, went into the bathroom, and washed her hands. Used lots of soap, hoping the warm water would help disperse the anxious adrenaline that was zinging through her, unwind the knot that had settled in her gut.

FIVE

Zelia woke to her cell phone ringing. *Damn.* She'd forgotten to switch it to airplane mode before she went to sleep. She glanced blearily at the clock on her bedside table as she reached for the phone. *Who in the world would be calling me at 7:23 in the morning?*

She'd had a terrible night's sleep. Felt guilty about the dismissive text she'd sent to Alexus and sick about the aggressive reply she'd received in return. *Screw you . . . What the hell was that about?* Screw you . . . From Alexus, who, until last night, had never been anything but an absolute sweetheart. *Maybe she was joking?* But even as Zelia thought it, she knew she was clutching at straws. *Look, everybody's entitled to an off day. So Alexus was pushy. You could have been kinder in your refusal. You don't know what kind of stress she might be under that caused her to respond like that. Maybe she'd been drinking. Maybe she's having financial difficul-*

ties. It's hard enough being a small business owner. Add on to that the art world, which is so darn finicky . . .

Around and around her thoughts chased one another. Sleep had arrived only once she'd promised herself she would reach out to Alexus in the morning.

Bzzzz . . .

She peered at her phone. *Not a local number,* she thought as she swiped her finger across the screen.

"Hello?" She knew the minute her voice escaped from her lips that there was no way in hell she was going to be able to pull off the fairy tale that she hadn't just been woken from a dead sleep. Her voice was way too husky and sleep-filled.

No one replied.

"Hello?" she said again.

She heard a slight *click.* "Hello there," a cheery recorded voice chirped. "I hope you are having a fabulous day! I'm Jane from Ackerman's Air Duct Cleaning Company —"

Zelia pressed end, switched her cell phone to airplane mode, then plopped it on the bedside table. Briefly, she wished that it had been an actual human on the phone, so she could let them know how inconsiderate it was to cold-call people early in the morning.

She pulled the covers over her shoulder in an attempt to grab another forty-five minutes of sleep. After twenty minutes she realized it wasn't going to happen. Trying to sleep with a deadline clock ticking was an impossible task.

She got up, took a shower, and dressed before making a travel mug of tea and a slice of buttery cinnamon-sugar toast. She pulled on her jacket and boots. Out on her driveway she gave Old Faithful, her 1992 Volvo sedan, her daily pat on the hood. "Hey there, old girl. Blue skies, so I think I'm going to hoof it today. Don't get up to any mischief while I'm out." Old Faithful didn't reply. She never did, but Zelia liked to imagine it made her happy to be acknowledged thusly.

Zelia took a path through the woods, munching happily on her cinnamon toast. She'd drink the tea on the smoother terrain of the boardwalk, which bordered the bay and led to her gallery and beyond.

Gabe leaned against the boardwalk railing, tipped his head upward, and shut his eyes, enjoying the early-morning sunshine on his face. He could hear the seagulls behind him,

45

wings flapping, and the occasional shrill caw. They were flying into the air with clams in their beaks, dropping them onto the rocks and then swooping down to eat the contents. Sometimes a wily seagull would lurk below and snatch the prize from the broken shell. Made him laugh. Reminded him of his dad.

When they'd spoken this morning, his dad had sounded much improved, eager to pick Gabe's brains about the place. "Take your time, boyo. No need to rush back. Enjoy all that the island has to offer. Beautiful women, hikes, biking, art galleries, artisan cheese makers, bakers, beautiful women . . ." His dad had repeated the last one with a laugh. "It's all those damned yoga studios populating the island, keeps them healthy — and flexible, too. Important for a woman to have flexible hips, makes birthing easier. You're gonna love Solace. We sure did."

Gabe wasn't going to touch that crazy birthing theory with a ten-foot pole. "You've been here?" His dad seemed so conservative. It was hard to picture him flinging off his suit and tie and rubbing shoulders with the tree-hugging free spirits that appeared to populate the island. "Doesn't seem like your kind of place."

46

"What do you know about my kind of place? Hell yeah, I've been there. Was on a fishing trip. Met your mother when we came ashore to stock up on supplies."

"Wait a minute. Family folklore is you and Mom met at a pub."

"Which we did. That little pub down by the marina, right there on Solace Island. Toby's. You should check it out. I came through the door, and there was your mom wiping down a table, her face shining bright like a button. She was on the island for the summer on a farm stay. Was picking up extra dough waiting tables in the evenings. Love at first sight. For me, anyway. She took a little convincing. Thought I was a rogue." There was laughter in his voice, as if he was pleased that she'd sussed him out so well. "Came back to Solace for our honeymoon, where, I am proud to inform you, you were conceived —"

"Dad —"

"Yes siree, I planted you in your mother's womb right there in Mansfield's Elsworth Cottage —"

"Seriously. TMI."

His dad cackled happily. "Yep. If you think about it, a love for Solace Island is probably embedded in your DNA. It's a magical place, my son. A game changer. You'll see."

Along with the feeling of vertigo that arose from the unwanted image of his dad and mom having intimate relations, a flicker of irritation flared. The latent teenager inside him wanted to snap that he was perfectly happy with the status quo of his life, thank you very much. Was in no need of a damned game changer. He managed to suppress the temptation. He was working on establishing a more mature relationship with his dad and not giving in to the knee-jerk responses that made him feel like a shit heel afterward.

He steered his father's attention to the weather, asked about the nor'easter that the news channels were having a field day with, made a few appropriate comments, and then hung up. He decided to take advantage of not being buried under a foot and a half of snow and grabbed his jacket, heading out.

It was a glorious day, forty-two degrees Fahrenheit with a crisp breeze blowing off the ocean. He breathed in. Could almost taste the salt from the sea. He imagined the soot and pollution from the city leaving his lungs and floating away as he exhaled. The air was different here, crystal clear; it renewed and refreshed.

He heard the sound of footsteps approaching. Sounded like a woman, wearing boots with a slight heel. He contemplated keeping his eyes shut, but the writer in him was curious if what he imagined was correct.

He cracked his eyes open, slanting a quick look at the feet, and was glad that he had. She was wearing boots, but they didn't look like he'd imagined. They were deep blue velvet with clear amber heels, an impractical purchase for the West Coast's rainy climes. Intrigued, he brought his gaze up from her half boots, past her voluminous charcoal-gray dress, which — with the aid of the strong headwind — clung to her voluptuous curves. The whole ensemble was topped off with a forties swing jacket, the top two buttons secured, allowing the rest of the fabric to flutter behind in her wake. Unexpected lust slammed through him. His gaze moved up her graceful ballet dancer's neck to a heart-shaped face surrounded by a mass of soft brown curls that shimmered with honey-blond highlights. Her eyes were downcast. The woman was clearly deep in thought, seemingly troubled about something. He wanted her to glance up, but she didn't. Her lush red lips were parted slightly, as if a word or a breath were resting between them, waiting to be released.

And then it hit him. She was the woman who had been standing among the sculp-

49

tures yesterday. But that wasn't all. There was something familiar, a sense of déjà vu. The wispy fragments of a long-forgotten dream.

He straightened and opened his mouth to speak, but she'd already passed him, leaving a trailing scent of cinnamon sugar, breakfast tea, and a fragrance that was uniquely hers.

He watched her briskly stride along the boardwalk, a travel mug in her hand. Then she veered left and cut through a parking lot. She stood in front of the Art Expressions Gallery, rummaging through her jewel-toned purse, then transferred her mug into her left hand and unlocked the door. She had the buttons of her swing jacket undone by the time the door closed behind her.

SIX

Zelia read Gunter Möller's artist statement and groaned. "Seriously?" she said, scrubbing her hands across her face. "This took you a month and a half to write?"

She reread it, hoping somehow a second reading would bring clarity.

My work embodies the chaos within and reflects the outward disorder of the world, like a broken mirror found in the heart of the forest. Always striving to capture a modicum of light that has long been denied. Decades lost. Decades denied. I achieved this result through carefully applied and thought-out brushstrokes, which represent the slow, plodding footsteps of time. — Gunter Möller, Artist

Nope. No clarity. "Good Lord," she murmured. "I have no idea what this jumble of words means."

She clicked reply and typed:

Hi, Gunter. I received your artist's statement. Thank you. It's a good start. However, I feel it needs another draft in order to make your thoughts more accessible to the viewer. If you are deep in the throes of the work, no worries. I'd be happy to do a polish for you. — Zelia

"Please let him be deep in the throes of work," she said, hitting send.

She glanced at the time. It was two forty-five. That meant that on the East Coast Alexus would be closing shop in fifteen minutes. Zelia had left a message on her cell voice mail, but Alexus hadn't returned the call. Hadn't replied to the e-mail she had sent that morning or the midday text.

Zelia stared at her computer, willing Alexus to respond.

Two more minutes passed.

"This is ridiculous," Zelia muttered, picking up her phone. "I am not losing another night's sleep over this." She scrolled through her contacts and tapped Alexus's office landline.

Brrrring . . . brrring . . .

"Good afternoon, Feinstein and Company. How may I help you?" It was Alexus's assistant. He sounded a bit run-down.

"Hi, Tristan," she said. "Zelia here. You okay? I hope you aren't coming down with that dreaded flu."

"No, I —"

"Oh, thank goodness. You do *not* want this flu. I just got over it. The darn thing lasted for three weeks. Ugh. Hey, I need to talk with Alexus for a moment. Could you patch me in, please?"

"I'm sorry, but —"

"Look," Zelia cut in. "I get it. She's pissed off. Told you not to put me through, but it's very important that I —" Her voice petered out because it sounded like he was crying. "Tristan?"

He didn't answer, but she could hear hiccuping gasps on the other end of the line.

"Hey, Tristan, don't worry about it. Truly. I didn't mean to put you in an uncomfortable position. Please let Alexus know that I called. If you would tell her I'm sorry I was abrupt last night and to call me back when she gets a —"

"It's not that —" He started sobbing bigtime now. "I'd put you through if I could — I wish that was a possibility — but she's . . . she's dead —"

"Wha . . . ?" Zelia felt as if she had been slammed into a brick wall. "I'm sorry, what did you just say?"

"She's dead," he choked out. "She was found here last night, sprawled on the sofa. Needle in her arm. Overdose. Heroin." Tristan's words tumbled out like water through a breached dam. "It was awful. I don't know if you've ever seen a dead person before, but oh my God. The image is imprinted in my brain — the police were here. I didn't know what to do. Still don't. Am I supposed to come to work tomorrow?"

Zelia knew all about grief. She let him talk, made comforting noises, while her mind spun in overdrive, trying to make sense of what she'd just heard as waves of shock, loss, and guilt crashed through her. Also present, in the whirlpool of emotions, was a faint niggling feeling, but she couldn't quite identify or grasp on to it. Like the wispy tail end of a dream, it hovered just beyond her ken.

SEVEN

Zelia discreetly massaged the back of her neck, trying to dispel the tension that seemed to have lodged there. She rolled her head from the right to the left.

Still tense.

She sighed. Snuck a quick glance at her watch. Twenty-two minutes to go. Then she would go home, get in her baggy pajamas, and indulge in a generous pour of Syrah, along with a wedge of chocolate cheesecake left over from her birthday. Thirty-four years old. How the hell had that happened? No children. No husband. Not even a possible candidate on the horizon. This was certainly not how she'd envisioned her life turning out.

Alexus had longed for children as well. Was always on the prowl for Mr. Right, via dating apps, through friends, family, her synagogue. She was vigorous about her search.

A new wave of grief swept through Zelia. It was hard to get her mind around the fact that Alexus was gone. Had their last interaction been the thing that had pushed Alexus over the edge? She certainly hadn't seemed herself last night. *I should have picked up the phone after receiving her text. Sorted things out.* Now calling her was no longer an option. Zelia shut her eyes and exhaled. *I miss her already. I miss listening to her spout her no-nonsense sermons about life.* Alexus was always lecturing Zelia about something. That she was a soft touch with the artists, that she was forgetting how to have fun, that she was wasting precious years away grieving Ned.

She was right, I guess, but I wasn't ready to date. Figured when I was, the right guy would magically appear. Zelia sighed, peeling off another red dot and placing it on the artwork label next to the painting *Ripe Peaches* to show that it had sold. She gave herself a mental shake. *Enough with this melancholy. Count your blessings. Lord knows you have multitudes.*

Zelia turned and scanned the room. The Three Artists February's Folly was going well. The gallery was swamped with people, many of them buying. The majority of Michael's paintings had been snatched up within the first half hour, which wasn't unexpected. His paintings always flew out the door. Only three remained: a charcoal sketch of a nude, a watercolor, and a lovely twelve-by-nine-inch painting of a stormy ocean just after dusk. It was a departure from his usual style, but still, she was surprised it hadn't been purchased, as *Below the Surface* was one of her favorites. She was secretly hoping it wouldn't sell. Then she could justify splurging on it for herself.

Nils had sold four folk art paintings, and there were yellow stickers on two others. Yellow stickers Zelia was hoping she would be able to switch out for red before the night drew to a close. Her next-door neighbor, Lori, was considering *Red Barn* for over her fireplace. It would look good there.

Two of Otto's were spoken for, but then Otto — a lesser-known artist — had insisted on nosebleed prices, so it was a happy surprise any of his paintings had sold at all. Although, the buyer of the most expensive one, *Sandstone Dreams,* had a similar nose and jawline to Otto, not to mention the same disappearing hairline and last name.

Yes. The show is going well. You need to shake this disquieting feeling, this oppressive sadness.

57

A hand alighted on her forearm, causing a jolt of panicked fight-or-flight to surge through her. *What the hell is wrong with me?* Ever since Alexus died she'd been having these little panic attacks.

"Sorry," Mary said. "I didn't mean to startle you. I've got a buyer on line two, a Mr. Guillory."

"Guillory . . . Guillory . . ." She combed the recesses of her mind for a second but couldn't place a face with the name. "What painting is he interested in?"

"*Below the Surface.*"

"Figures," Zelia said as she made her way toward the office.

"Are you okay?" She could hear the concern in Mary's voice.

"Yeah."

"Zelia?"

"It's just —" She shook her head. "I had one of those 'aha' moments. Not in a good way. I'm fat and I'm old —"

"That's the most ridiculous statement I've ever heard. You are a gorgeous woman —"

"Mary. I'm fat —"

"You're zaftig."

"Zaftig. Full-figured. Call it what you like. I've packed on an average of five pounds a year ever since Ned died. According to the charts, I sailed past the normal threshold and landed firmly into the overweight category sixteen pounds ago. I am not exactly a man magnet."

"You are a beautiful, curvaceous woman, and if some stupid man can't see past a few extra pounds —"

Zelia snorted derisively as they stepped into the office. "A few?"

"Then he doesn't deserve you," Mary said defiantly, talking over Zelia, her eyes blazing.

"Anyway," Zelia said, suddenly feeling subdued. "I was doing the math, and in eleven months and eighteen days my ovaries will have reached the past-due date, and every subsequent year that passes, my chances of conceiving and having a healthy baby diminish." She laughed sadly. "I always figured by this age I would have a couple of rosy-cheeked children tugging at my skirts." She turned toward the phone on the desk so she wouldn't have to see the answering sorrow in her friend's eyes. "You'd better go out and watch the floor," she said before Mary could wrap her in a hug. She didn't want the melancholy to overwhelm her. Needed to keep it together until she got home.

Once Mary exited the office and closed the door behind her, Zelia picked up the phone receiver and pressed the flashing red hold button. "Zelia Thompson, how can I help?"

Mr. Guillory was fine enough, but she found herself wanting to get off the phone. *Maybe I need to take a break. Get my mojo back. I'm burnt out.* She forced herself to be present, answered a few questions, keeping her voice pleasant and breezy. His voice seemed familiar. Perhaps he had purchased from her before, or she had met him at some art fair or another. She managed to bluff her way through the conversation. The gentleman made the purchase via a corporate numbered bank account. Didn't need her to ship as he was planning on visiting the island in a few weeks and would pick it up in person.

Well, that was easy enough, Zelia thought as she hung up the phone. She was sorely tempted to stay, hide from the crush of people. Enjoy the peaceful solitude of the back office. Just for a few minutes.

She didn't.

The artists were counting on her.

She stood. Smoothed her hands down the silk fabric of her dark cerulean dress, then squared her shoulders and returned to the fray.

She was instantly aware of an atmospheric

shift in the gallery, as if an earthquake was coming and she alone could sense it. She scanned the crowded room, trying to find the cause, and then her gaze screeched to a stop.

A tall, dark-haired stranger was standing in the doorway. He didn't have the air of someone contemplating an art purchase. He seemed bemused, as if he'd stepped inside to get out of the driving rain and was surprised to find the space occupied.

He had a commanding presence. Zelia was astonished the other occupants in the gallery hadn't rotated to face him as well. It seemed as if his smoldering gaze was locked on her, as if he had been waiting for her, knew her already. It was a ridiculous, fanciful thought, which she immediately discarded. Even from across the crowded room she could see the piercing intelligence that sparked from his eyes.

He smiled, sending lazy heat coursing through her. His hand pushed the dark, windswept hair back from his face. He was wearing a gray T-shirt under a beat-up black leather jacket, boots, and faded jeans that clung in all the right places. The man was built just like she liked them. With a hard body that was long and lean.

"Who the hell is that?" she heard Mary

murmur from behind her. *Of course,* Zelia thought. *That's who he was looking at. You were just blocking his eye line.* Even though Mary tried to camouflage it, she was a looker, tall and slender with flawless skin. There was something about her friend that radiated old money and class.

"Looks as if we're about to find out," Zelia replied, watching him make his way across the room, the other occupants instinctively moving out of his path like the parting of the Red Sea.

"Zelia." She felt a tap on her shoulder. "Zelia." A little louder, breaking the hypnotic draw of the stranger's presence. She turned reluctantly. Otto was looking at her, excited anxiety spewing out of his pores along with the scent of the garlic cleanse that he was three days into.

"Yes, Otto?" she said, taking a casual half step backward in an attempt to create a little distance from the pungent vapors emanating from his body.

It didn't help. He just scuffled closer.

"That woman over there —" Otto gestured to Beth Parsons, who was standing in front of his *Sandstone Nights* painting and gazing at it as if somewhere hidden in the painting she would find the meaning of life.

"She's interested in purchasing my painting."

Zelia felt the stranger arrive beside her. She didn't have to look. Could feel his force field tingling along her skin, tickling the tiny hairs along her arms. "That's wonderful news. I'll be over in a minute —"

"No. Please, Zelia," Otto entreated, tugging her arm. A sheen of sweat had taken up residence on his forehead and around his nose, the perspiration intensifying and expanding the reach of his potent eau de garlic. "What if she changes her mind?"

"I'd be happy —" Mary started to step forward, but she froze midstep. Her eyebrows shot skyward, her nose crinkling. She blinked.

Zelia bit down on her lip to keep the laughter from bursting forth. Clearly this was Mary's first time in close proximity to Otto tonight.

Mary straightened her spine and cleared her throat. "To assist —"

She sounded a little nasally. Must be breathing through her mouth. Now that *is a true friend, offering to walk away from a mouthwatering stranger to deal with the very pungent Otto.*

"No, no, no. Too important," Otto said, shaking his head like a wet dog. "Zelia's gotta come. Make sure this sale closes. I really, really need this —" His voice was rising.

"Okay, no worries," Zelia said soothingly, suppressing an internal sigh. "I'm happy to talk with her. That's what I'm here for." And she was. No point sticking around, mooning. Watching from the sidelines as sparks flew between the mysterious stranger and her dear friend and colleague. "If you'll excuse us." She tossed the comment over her shoulder, then discreetly sucked in a deep breath of untainted air and allowed Otto to lead her away.

It took much longer than anticipated to nail down the sale for Otto. Not because the woman was unwilling, but because Otto's fan wanted to discuss every brushstroke with "the *artiste.*" Otto was more than happy to indulge her. He launched into a verbose dissertation; unfortunately, his death grip on Zelia's arm refused to loosen — not until Zelia insisted she needed use of both hands in order to take possession of the woman's check and to write down delivery instructions and a receipt.

When the three of them emerged from the office, the art show had concluded. The place was quiet, the gallery cleared of people. A few die-hard partiers were still chatting in the parking lot, doing their final hugs and good-byes.

Otto started to veer toward the makeshift bar. "Would you like a final drink to toast —"

"Oh, Otto. So sorry," Zelia said. She hastily took a large diagonal step, effectively cutting him off at the pass. "But we're closed. The two of you will have to take your party elsewhere."

Otto glanced at his watch, then looked at the flushed Beth. "Would you be interested in some Cajun-style chicken wings and a beer at Toby's? We'd have to hustle to get our order in before the kitchen closes, but it's doable."

"Otto," she cooed. "But what about the cleanse you're partaking in?"

He wiggled his bushy gray eyebrows at her. "I'm dropping it, effective immediately. I find I am feeling rather carnivorous."

"Oh, Otto." Beth slapped him playfully on the arm. "You're so naughty."

"You up for it?" Otto smirked.

"If you are," Beth purred, her gaze dropping to the crotch of Otto's sagging faded black jeans. "I'm feeling rather ravenous myself . . ."

"Wonderful. Have fun you two," Zelia said as she ushered a triumphant Otto and his giggling middle-aged fan through the front door, then locked it firmly behind them.

"We had a good night," Mary commented. "I got Sasha Tancred to commit to Nils's *Languid* before she left." She swept the napkins and scattered toothpicks off a cocktail table and into the wastebasket in her hand, then moved to the next one.

"Thanks, Mary. I'd planned on locking that sale down, but . . ." She shrugged. No need for words. They both knew that she had taken one for the team. Zelia got the black bus box from under the backroom kitchen sink and started gathering the wineglasses.

"It would be so much easier if you'd use disposable wineglasses."

"I know," Zelia said, smothering a yawn. "But every time I start to reach for them in the supermarket, I think about the fish and plant life in the ocean that is being suffocated by all the minuscule plastic particles . . ."

"Yeah, yeah, yeah, I get it," Mary said, laughing. "You're such a good person —"

"No. Seriously. I'm not. If I were *truly* a good person, I wouldn't have begrudged Otto the time it took to close the deal. It's my job, for crying out loud. And I definitely wouldn't have negative thoughts, like, 'What the hell were you thinking, Otto, going on a raw garlic diet cleanse right before your major show?' And 'No, I really don't want to hear the minutiae about the antiviral, antibacterial, anti-parasitic properties that will reduce toxins and parasites from your large intestine. And I have *NO* desire to hear about the importance of cleaning the' — and I quote — 'hardened older feces from the colon'! Good Lord."

"Ew . . . ew . . . ew . . ." Mary was clearly grossed out, batting her hands in front of herself as if trying to dispel the imagery, but she was laughing, too.

Zelia shook her head with a what-are-you-gonna-do-with-these-crazy-artists shrug. "Luckily, his fan was a huge fan of garlic colon cleanses as well."

"No!" For some reason this made Mary laugh even harder.

"I kid you not. Perhaps she found the stench surrounding him to be an aphrodisiac. Oh, I'm a terrible person. He's one of my artists. I shouldn't be laughing about him behind his back. There is no hope for me."

"Me either. Guess we're both going to keep Beelzebub company come Judgment Day," Mary said, still laughing, wiping moisture from her eyes. "Because I was super happy you didn't take me up on my generous offer. Speaking of Beelzebub, Mr. Tall, Dark, and Handsome wasn't just glorious eye candy. The man's got a brain and a wicked sense of humor."

"That's great, Mary," Zelia said. She was happy for her. Truly. It was just —

"Unfortunately, he wasn't interested in me . . ."

"Of course he was —"

"Nope. No tingles. Had the feeling he was waiting for you to reemerge from the office."

Zelia stamped down hard on the flicker of happiness that comment inspired. "Must be a wannabe artist."

"Wrong again. He's an author. Writes crime fiction. Gabe Conaghan."

Zelia shrugged, pretending nonchalance. "Never heard of him." Of course, she wasn't a reader of crime fiction. She preferred women's literary fiction, with a healthy dollop of romance novels thrown in for pure reading pleasure. *An author. Figures. With his looks, all he'd have to do is show up at a reading and the women would be snatching his books off the shelves like warm, buttery hotcakes.*

Later that night — February's Folly concluded, the garbage bagged and tossed in the dumpster behind the mews — Zelia was home and grateful to be submerged in a hot lavender and Epsom salt bath. She was on her second glass of Syrah when she figured out what had been niggling at her. Like an invisible splinter under her skin, the hot water and wine loosened it. Allowed a fuzzy, almost-forgotten memory to push its way to the surface.

A conversation she and Alexus had at Frieze four or five years ago. They were walking back to the hotel, arm in arm, tipsy from too many strawberry margaritas. Both of them wore sundresses, enjoying the warm and sultry Miami night air, barefoot, heels in their hands, sweaty from dancing at the after-party. Zelia had still been in the "healthy" weight range then. Curvier than when Ned had died, but guys seemed to appreciate the extra pounds and she'd been fending off horndog offers all night. However, Zelia had just wanted to dance, to blow off steam. Had no interest in hooking up, even less in pursuing a relationship. It had felt too soon for that.

They'd passed a junkie slumped beside a garbage can, her hair matted, her skeletal clawlike hand extended, tremors coursing through her. "Please," the woman moaned.

"Please can you spare some change? Any-thing will help." She had open sores on her face. "I'm hungry. Haven't eaten in two days." The woman's eyes were sunken, tortured, desperate.

Zelia dug in her purse, pulled out a five, and handed the bill to the woman. Alexus watched, shaking her head.

"You know she's going to spend that money on drugs," Alexus said as they continued on their way.

Zelia shrugged, slightly embarrassed. "I know. I just . . ."

They walked on, but the carefree tone of the evening had dissipated.

"I might drink too much," Alexus had said, breaking the silence that had de-scended between them. "Might have smoked the occasional joint in high school. But I would never, *ever* use chemical drugs. Can you imagine being that woman? Pre-pared to do anything for a fix. No way. Thank you very much. Not for me. I value my brain too much. Enjoy being smart."

Suddenly the hot bath was no longer soothing; instead it made her feel claustro-phobic. Zelia bolted from the tub, caught an accidental glimpse of her face leached of color, her large breasts swinging as she lunged for a towel. She wrapped the thick terry cloth tightly around herself, her heart thumping way too fast in her chest as Alexus's words ricocheted in the empty space around her.

"I would never, *ever* use chemical drugs . . ."

EIGHT

"Zelia," Mary said. "You've got to stop pacing. You're making me dizzy."

Zelia turned and stared bleakly at her friend. "I don't know what to do." She was exhausted. Hadn't been able to sleep all night. Every time she lay down and tried to relax, Alexus's words would start to play on a continuous loop.

"Come sit down." Mary patted the metal folding chair next to the little card table in the back room. "I've made you a nice hot cup of tea." Mary opened the cupboard, got out the box of short-bread cookies, and put a couple of them on a saucer. "We're going to go over this rationally."

Zelia dropped into a chair. She inhaled, then blew the breath out slowly. Her mouth was dry, as if she had spent the last five minutes with her lips scotch-taped around a blow-dryer. She took a sip of her tea. Too hot. It scalded her taste buds, made her eyes smart. "I don't believe" — she swallowed hard — "Alexus overdosed on purpose."

"Honey," Mary said gently. She placed the cookies on the table and took the other seat, her hand covering Zelia's. "No one ever means to overdose. They just do. It was a terrible, terrible accident."

"No. That's not what I mean." Zelia turned her hand over and gripped Mary's hand. "I'm not being clear. My mind is a bit fuzzy from lack of sleep. What I'm saying is . . . I think Alexus was murdered. The overdose was a cover-up."

Mary stared at her as if she'd sprouted a second head.

"Say something," Zelia finally urged.

"And you . . . believe this . . . why?"

"She didn't use hard drugs."

"You don't know that."

"I do *know* it. We had a conversation about drugs when we were at Frieze. Took me a while to remember. My only excuse is it was a while back — before you came to work for me."

"Well, I've been here three years." Mary wasn't looking at her as she rearranged the buttery cookies on the saucer. "So, if you had this conversation before then —" She caught her lower lip between her teeth, clearly troubled. "A lot can happen to a person in that amount of time."

"Forget it." Zelia got to her feet. "You think I'm crazy."

"No," Mary replied. "I think you're grieving. Big difference. You're feeling bad because of how your last interaction went down. Which I have to tell you, if anyone was being a bitch that night it was Alexus, not you. You have *nothing* to feel guilty about. For what it's worth, I believe you are trying to find answers when maybe there are none."

"I just . . ." Zelia didn't know quite what she was feeling. "I know" — she thumped her clenched fist over her heart — "something is off with the whole 'overdose' picture. You know what?" She snatched her cell phone off the table. "I'm gonna —" Zelia typed "Greenwich Police, Connecticut" into the Google search bar and tapped the call button before she could lose her nerve.

"Zee? What are you doing?"

The phone was ringing. "I'm —"

"Greenwich Police Department."

Zelia held up a finger, listening hard.

"If this is an emergency," the recording said, "please hang up and dial nine-one-one. If you know the extension for the person you are calling, please dial it now. For all other calls please stay on the —"

There was a click on the line. "Greenwich Police, how may I help you?"

"Hello." Her heart was pounding. She tried to steady her breath. "My name is Zelia Thompson. I'm calling because a friend of mine, Alexus Feinstein, died three nights ago in the back office of her art gallery, Feinstein and Company, located in Old Greenwich. I'm not sure if you are familiar with the case? The newspapers said it was an overdose. But I've been turning it over in my mind and it just doesn't feel right. I'm pretty sure Alexus didn't use hard drugs." Suddenly her words dried up. She just stood there, her face hot, her cell phone plastered to her ear.

"Give me your name and phone number. I'll pass your concerns on to Detective Hurley, who was at the scene." The woman on the other end of the line sounded weary.

"Thank you." Zelia gave the woman her name, her number, along with Alexus's information, and then hung up feeling slightly embarrassed, like the woman on the phone thought she was wasting valuable police time.

"What did they say?" Mary asked.

"That she'd pass my concerns on." Zelia flopped into a chair. "I got the feeling that she thought I was a hysterical female, jumping at shadows." She shrugged. "Maybe I am." She could feel her face was still flushed.

"Do you feel better for having called?"

Zelia shrugged. "I don't know." She didn't feel better. Not one iota.

"Look. You've done what you can. You voiced your concerns. Now it's up to them to follow through."

"But what if they don't?"

"That's not your responsibility."

"It sucks. It's so frustrating." Zelia scrubbed her hands across her face. "I wish there was someone I could talk to who could help me figure this thing out. Nothing about it makes any sense to me."

Mary nodded. Leaned back in her chair and took a sip of her tea, watching Zelia with a considering expression on her face.

"What?" Zelia snagged a shortbread cookie and bit into it.

"I just had a thought —" Mary paused, then shook her head. "Nah."

"Mary, you had an idea. Spit it out."

"Well, that author from last night. I Googled him when I got home —"

"I knew you liked him," Zelia said, placing her cookie on her saucer and scooting it away.

Mary shook her head. "Not in that way.

The way his gaze followed you, made me curious to know more about him. Apparently" — Mary was looking way too pleased with herself — "Gabriel Conaghan went to your alma mater. What are the odds of that? Huh? Maybe it's a sign that you're meant to be." Mary smirked, then wiggled her eyebrows.

"You're nuts."

"Seriously, I'm not making this up. You overlapped. Graduated three years apart. Does the name ring a bell? Maybe you knew him, had a one-night stand? Because I'm telling you the heat that was smoldering off that man as he watched you . . ." Mary fanned herself.

"Number one." Zelia held up a finger. It was best to nip this flight of fancy in the bud. "I don't know the man. Never met him before in my life. Two." A second finger joined the first. "I've never had a one-night stand."

What?" Mary looked as if Zelia had confessed she could fly.

"Never," Zelia said firmly, sticking another finger in the air. "And three. I was *with* Ned."

"The whole time?"

Zelia nodded. "Even if I hadn't been in a happily committed relationship, the Berkeley campus is e*nor*mous. Different majors. We could have attended the entire four years and never crossed paths once."

"Really?"

"Let me put it this way. The student population is substantially bigger than the entire population of Solace Island, *including* the weekenders."

"Oh." Mary gave a rueful laugh. "You would not believe the happily-ever-after fairy tale I concocted last night. He was an old flame, maybe a one-night stand who never got over you. Tracked you to Solace and wants to get married and have two-point-five babies. Ah well. The start might be different, but that doesn't mean the ending can't be the same. Mr. Conaghan is super successful. His novels hit the *New York Times* Best Sellers list with great regularity —"

"She says, apropos of nothing." Zelia took a bite of shortbread. "You and your match-making —"

"Hear me out," Mary said with a Cheshire-cat grin. "Matchmaking aside, the guy writes *crime* fiction. A heavy-hitter author doesn't operate in a vacuum. He's got *people.* I bet he has access to police, FBI profilers, et cetera. You should meet with him and tell him your concerns about

78

Alexus. See if he thinks murder is a likely possibility."

"Yeah. I bet that conversation would go over well. Hey, you, famous writer. I'd like to pick your brain . . ."

"You won't know unless you try."

Zelia shook her head. "I have no idea where he lives. Don't have his phone number . . ."

"He mentioned he was staying at the Mansfield Manor." Mary reached behind her and snagged the phone. "You can call him right now." Zelia stared at the phone in Mary's outstretched hand. "Take it," Mary said, a hint of laughter in her voice. "It's just a phone, not a cobra. You should call him. It might help settle some of your worries about Alexus."

NINE

Zelia stood across the street from the Intrepid Café. She wore the hood of her deep-ruby-red cape coat up to help keep the light, misting shower at bay. Deciding to wear her favorite boots for added courage was a mistake. Weather forecasts for clear skies and bright sunshine meant diddly-squat in the Pacific Northwest. Her beloved indigo velvet boots with their darling clear amber heels were now getting speckled from the rain.

Well, she told herself as she squared her shoulders and headed determinedly across the road, *at least this meeting is forcing you to get over your ridiculous avoidance of this café.*

Solace Island residents had been abuzz ever since Intrepid had opened its doors. Sometimes Zelia felt that if she had to listen to one more person rave about the amazing baked goods to be obtained there she would scream. Enough with the chatter about flaky crusted pies and lemon pound cake drizzled with a mouthwatering citron icing. Who cared about a delicious chocolate cake with broiled nut topping, the sides slathered with high-quality Belgian chocolate?

So, the two Harris sisters who had descended on Solace like a plague of man-hungry locusts could *cook.* Big deal. Not only could they cook, but they were skinny and gorgeous as well. And if local gossip was to be believed, Maggie and Eve were also kind and charming and lovely and blah . . . blah . . . blah . . .

Okay, fine. Zelia could forgive them for being so perfect. But the younger one, Maggie, had marched into town and promptly scooped up Luke Benson from under Zelia's nose. Zelia had spent the previous year trying to encourage the delicate blossoming friendship into something more. *She's just here on vacation, looking for a holiday fling,* Zelia had told herself. But Luke had married the damned woman, and according to all sources, they were very, very happy. *Barf.*

Luke was the first man Zelia had been attracted to in the seven years that had followed Ned's death. *It's been almost eight years now, but who's counting.* Her eyes suddenly felt hot. *This is stupid. I shouldn't still be missing Ned so badly.*

Zelia knew the whole being-pissed-at-Maggie-Harris-now-Maggie-Benson for the Luke thing was unreasonable. The man was never meant for her. She knew that now. She was glad he'd found happiness. Even though it was with someone else. She just felt a little less than was all. She'd been prepared to offer him her heart, but it wasn't enough.

So, she'd avoided the Intrepid Café. It had been easy with so many nice eateries to choose from on the island. She hadn't planned to boycott it forever. Just until the sharp pang of disappointment subsided. But then one month led to two, which led to four, and here it was, more than a year later and still she hadn't gone in.

No time like the present. Zelia reached the front stoop of the café. She felt a little embarrassed, but relieved, too, that Gabriel Conaghan had picked the Intrepid and the jinx was going to be broken.

A tiny bell, which was attached to the door hinge with a lilac ribbon, jingled as Zelia swung the door open and entered. Instantly, she was enveloped by the delicious smells of home-baked food. She inhaled deeply. *Umm . . . not just sweet baked goods, but savory, too. And what is that . . . soup? A rich tomato soup from the smell of it. Coffee, tea, and . . . Oh. My. God!*

Zelia was suddenly frozen to the spot. *Where did they obtain these gorgeous, gorgeous paintings?*

Someone bumped into her. "Sorry," Zelia murmured, moving away from the doorway and out of the flow of traffic, her gaze still entrapped by the beauty and lush power of the artwork on the walls. Each piece stood on its own, and yet clearly they were all created by the same artist. Landscapes, all of them. Outwardly simple things — a tree arching upward, a cliff's edge, the ocean's surface, a storm rolling in — and yet so much more. Passion and longing and sorrow, too, in every brushstroke. Zelia felt as if the artist had ripped herself open, captured the very essence of her being, and put it down on canvas for the world to witness.

Gabe had woken early. He'd stayed up late typing the report on Mansfield Manor. It had felt good to e-mail the file to his dad, get it off his plate. Then he'd gone to bed tired, planning to book his return flight. But instead of sleep he'd spent a good portion of the night digging through the winding corridors of his brain, trying to figure out why the gallery owner felt so familiar, where else he'd seen her and when. Then, right as he was hovering on the threshold of sleep, an image came to him. A much-younger woman, barefoot, with flowers in her long, lush hair. She looked glorious in the vintage sleeveless white cotton day dress from the twenties, which she must have found at a garage sale or in a thrift shop. The woman had been quite a bit thinner than Zelia and hadn't had her magnificent breasts, but the face, the length of her body was the same. He hadn't known either the bride or the groom. Ron, his roommate at Berkeley, had dragged him to the wedding. "Knowing Ned, it's going to be super informal," Ron had assured Gabe. "They won't mind another body."

It had rained during the ceremony. The grass was wet, but as they all trooped out of that beaten-up old house and down the weathered steps to the backyard, the sun had forced its way through the clouds. A partial rainbow had appeared overhead. It was only for a minute or two, and then it flickered out. Nobody else had seemed to notice it, their eyes on the happy couple taking their vows.

Once the vows were spoken and the register signed, the bride had started to turn to face the assembled motley crew of fellow

84

students and friends when Ned tipped his head toward hers. There was a mischievous smile on his face as he murmured something to her. Gabe was at the far end of the yard, couldn't hear what Ned had said, but the young woman had burst into joyous, infectious laughter. Gabe had never seen anything as beautiful as her face in that moment, her whole being lighting the world around her. The groom, laughing, too, had swung her into his arms and whirled her around and around in an enormous hug.

Someone turned on music, and people started dancing among the battered grass and the mud. Someone lit up and started passing a joint around, and wine and a homemade chocolate cake were brought out.

Gabe made his excuses to his friend and slipped away. Too much happiness. He didn't want to taint it with his inexplicable longing and lust for her. The bride. Someone he had never laid eyes on before that day.

Was the gallery owner the same woman? That joyous bride of ten years past? If so, there was a sorrow in her eyes that hadn't been present before. A weight. Not just physical, but emotional as well.

Wouldn't that be an interesting synchronicity? Life looping around on itself like a labyrinth walk.

If it was her, is she still married? was his last conscious thought before sleep claimed him.

He'd been well into his morning pages when the phone had rung. He'd turned his cell phone to airplane mode but had forgotten there was a landline. He was tempted to not answer, but knowing his father, he'd keep calling every five minutes until he got Gabe on the phone.

It was a pleasant surprise when he picked up the receiver and heard Zelia's voice. She had spoken only one sentence last night before she was whisked away, but her smoky, sensuous rasp was incredibly distinctive. The second she said hello, he *knew* it was *her.*

She'd sounded shy and a little wary, but she had tracked him down to see if he'd be open to meeting up for a coffee, so maybe things were different now. Maybe he had a chance.

He arrived at the café early and claimed the corner table. Used the waiting time to daydream about possibilities. His notebook was out so that if the muse knocked he'd be prepared. He sat with his back to the wall, even though he doubted it was necessary on sleepy Solace Island. The biggest danger to one's body appeared to be the soggy, multi-colored umbrellas that many of the gray-haired set seemed to be wielding. Black, navy, or dark gray umbrellas were what generally populated the city streets on a rainy day, but Solace clearly marched to its own tune.

He could feel the corners of his mouth kick up. *Maybe I'll put that detail in my next book. Troy Masters striding alongside the wife of one of his Washington, DC, clients. She is carrying one of these colorfully painted pieces of whimsy, which is an annoyance throughout the book. However, when Masters is dis-armed, he grabs the umbrella and fashions it into a makeshift lethal weapon.* Gabe reached for his mug to take another sip of the piping-hot, well-brewed cup of coffee. It was amazing how soothing he found this island. There was something about the peaceful rhythms of the daily life that was a balm for his weary spirit.

Then he saw her standing in the middle of the café, staring at the walls — she must have arrived while he was jotting down notes. Zelia. Zelia Thompson, she had told him on the phone. Was Thompson Ned's last name? He couldn't remember. Her given name suited her. It was exotic, unique, and rolled out of the mouth in a lush, satisfying way.

He followed her gaze, curious what had captured her attention. *Ah. The artwork on the walls.* He hadn't noticed the paintings before. They really were quite remarkable.

He looked back at Zelia and watched her turn slowly, taking in each painting, her cheeks flushed. Her hands rose, as though she were sleepwalking, and drew back the hood, revealing her heart-shaped face, the soft tumbling mass of golden-brown curls.

He was aware of an unreasonable longing to cross the room and bury his hands and his face in her hair and inhale her scent. He'd had the same urge all those years ago at the wedding and again last night at the gallery, where he'd found himself striding across the room like a madman. But she'd slipped away before he'd had a chance to introduce himself. If she was the same woman, Ned hadn't been there last night. Was he seeing to the business side of things in the office? At home taking care of their children? Were they still together? Divorced? Or maybe Zelia wasn't the woman at the wedding. Maybe his writer's mind was playing games with him, leading him on a fanciful chase.

A family dashed in through the doors,

laughing merrily as they brushed the rain off their umbrellas and coats. The sound and their energy appeared to pull Zelia back to the present. She shook her head slightly as if to clear her mind, then crossed the room to the woman manning the register. When they spoke, Zelia's face flushed even more. *Do they know each other? There is a slightly cautious distance to their body language.* Then the cashier smiled, a warm, genuine smile, as she bent and scribbled something on a scrap of paper. She straightened and handed the paper to Zelia, who took it as if it were something precious. She folded the paper once, twice, and then opened her purse, placed the paper in an interior pocket, and zipped it shut.

He was curious what was written on the paper that caused her to treat it with such care.

After the cashier had rung in her order and Zelia paid, she turned and scanned the café. Her gaze met his, and once again he felt as if he'd been struck by lightning, every cell in his body surging to attention.

TEN

Zelia made her way to the corner table where he was lounging, sensual awareness sparking through her like Fourth of July fireworks. *That's odd,* she thought. Even Ned hadn't triggered this type of visceral reaction in her.

"Gabriel Conaghan?"

He nodded and rose to his feet. His movements appeared slow and languid, like honey spooned out of a jar, but Zelia knew that that was an illusion. Just because a large predatory member of the feline family has been caught dozing on a sun-warmed rock does not mean the animal can't move fast when it wants to.

He was long and lanky. Tall. Very tall. She had to tip her head back, almost as if she were accepting a kiss, to take him in. Her gaze traveled across the hard angles and planes of his face, chiseled cheekbones, the days-old stubble unable to soften the strong lines of his jaw. There was a slight upward tilt of his lips, as if something amused him, laugh lines fanning outward from the corners of his eyes.

How long has it been since I laughed — really laughed — with a man? And for the second time that day Ned's dear face rushed to the forefront. Laughing this time in her memory, that deep hooting laugh that he had, head thrown back —

"And you're Zelia." Gabriel Conaghan's voice tugged her reluctantly back to the present. Memories of Ned had been less frequent lately, more viscous, not as defined. It made her feel panicky. Like soon she would lose even the wisps she had left of him. As if she were stuck on the shore and he was rowing out to sea in a little dinghy with the fog rolling in. Now barely a faint shadow in the mist. Sometimes she wondered if she was remembering him clearly. Was she saving only the good bits, discarding all the rest? Mary had hypothesized that Zelia had built the memory of Ned to such monumental proportions that there was no room left in her life for any other man.

"Yes." Zelia nodded. The sounds of the café surrounded her now, people talking, the clank of dishes and silverware, the air filled with delicious smells of home cooking.

Her gaze rose to meet his. The piercing awareness in his eyes belied his casual posture as he reached out and clasped her hand in his. She could feel the controlled strength radiating from his lean, muscular body the second he grasped her hand. The feel of his skin, of his warm calloused hand enclosing hers, made her knees grow weak. *How did I not see him,* she wondered, feeling slightly dazed, *the second I entered the room?*

She liked that his dark brown hair wasn't slicked back with gels or product. It had a tumbled, windswept quality, as if he'd just ridden into town on his horse.

He was wearing a heather-gray T-shirt with the long sleeves pushed up, a titanium watch with a black dial face. She shook her head. Even the man's forearms had nice muscle tone. Tan with a light dusting of blond hair. *He must have been blond as a baby —*

"You can call me Gabe," he said, his baritone rumbling through her, jolting her eyes back up to his.

"All right," she said, keeping her voice brusque and businesslike. This was not the time to get gaga about some man. Particularly one who lived — where did he live?

No matter. It was bound to be far away. She had no time for foolish crushes. There was important business to attend to. The unexpected heat that was thrumming through her was not a reason to turn into a gibbering pile of mush. "I appreciate you meeting with me."

"My pleasure," he murmured, pulling out a chair for her. His voice was low, husky, and trickled through her like brandy warmed over a flame.

She looked at the chair, a little surprised. Nobody had ever pulled out a chair for her. "Thank you." She sat and gestured to his coffee. "I was planning on treating you."

"Next time," he said as he returned to his seat. She knew there wasn't going to be a next time, but still, the promise of it sent a tingle of pleasure through her.

He swept his notebook and pen into a leather satchel that rested on the floor beside him, then straightened and looked at her. Really looked at her, as if he could see inside to all the places she kept hidden from the world. His eyes were a deep espresso, the color of his irises so dark it was hard to distinguish where the iris left off and the pupil began. "I feel like we've met before . . ."

She felt her face flush. "No. We haven't.

I'm sorry. I know this is probably a little unusual" — she tried to shrug off her feeling of self-consciousness — "a strange woman contacting you out of the blue. You met my colleague, Mary Browning, last night, and she mentioned you wrote crime fiction."

He nodded. He opened his mouth as if he were going to say something, but apparently thought better of it. Understandable. How was the poor man supposed to respond? *Yes, half the modern world is not only aware of my occupation, but is waiting with bated breath for my next bestseller to hit the bookstore shelves?*

Zelia cleared her throat. "I didn't know where to turn. I was hoping you might be able to help settle my worries — perhaps shine a bit of clarity and perspective on a situation that has arisen. You see, my friend Alexus has died and I . . ." She suddenly had a lump in her throat and her eyes felt hot. "And I —" *What am I doing here? This is madness.* "I'm sorry," she said, standing abruptly. "This was a mistake. I'm so sorry to waste your time —"

"Don't go," he said, his voice gentle. "Sit down. Please. I won't bite. Promise." She sank back down, but she could feel the heat in her cheeks, her throat. His hand covered hers briefly, warm and comforting. "I'm sorry for your loss."

She nodded, unable to meet his eyes. Knowing that if the compassion in his eyes matched what she could hear in his voice, she would lose it. "It's no bother. I'm happy for you to pick my brain," he continued. "Or to be a sounding board. Maybe I'll be able to help, maybe not. Won't know unless you tell me what the problem is."

He was right of course. Action was called for. Whether she came across as foolish or not was irrelevant.

"Well . . ." Zelia puffed out a breath, her insides feeling jittery as she dug into her purse, removed her tablet, and placed it on her lap. "I'm not certain if there is a problem or not." She unbuttoned her cape and hung it on the back of the chair. She could feel him watching her even though she was angled away. It was a little unnerving to be the sole recipient of his laser-like gaze. "It might just be I'm seeing connections where there are none —" She broke off because she could see Luke's fresh-faced wife approaching their table.

"Here you are," Maggie said with a cheery smile. She set down a pot of green tea, a sturdy mug, and a slice of Intrepid's famous lemon pound cake.

"Thank you," Zelia replied, busying her hands pouring the steaming tea into her mug.

"Would you like your coffee topped up?" she heard Maggie ask Gabriel.

"I'm fine for now, thanks," he replied.

In her peripheral vision she could see Maggie move away. Zelia tipped her head toward her cake. "Feel free to dig in. I've heard it's quite good."

"The food here is amazing," he said. "Discovered this café fresh off the ferry three days ago. I was ravenously hungry, and the quality of the food was a revelation. Coming here has become a daily ritual."

"The art on the wall is remarkable," she said. It was. But that wasn't why she was here.

He nodded.

She exhaled a slow, steadying breath. Braced herself, then dove in. "I brought a couple articles about my friend's death. I was hoping you would take a look at them? Let me know if anything jumps out at you?" She didn't mention her last interaction with Alexus. The thought of sharing that conversation with him made her feel hot with embarrassment and a dollop of guilt.

"Sure."

The act of placing her hand on the tablet

on her lap — knowing she was inviting a stranger into the dark labyrinth that had taken over her mind — reactivated the shakes she'd managed to battle into submission on the walk over.

She pushed the saucer with the lemon pound cake to the side, placed her tablet on the table, opened her Dropbox, then passed the tablet to Gabe.

She watched him read the articles she had accumulated. The panic fluttered inside her as if a gray sparrow were trapped, ricocheting around, attempting to escape the confines of her chest.

ELEVEN

It didn't take Gabe long to scan the news articles — the *Hartford Courant,* the *New Haven Register,* and the *Connecticut Post.* Different approaches to the same information: One Alexus Feinstein, age thirty-eight, found dead of a heroin overdose in the back office of her art gallery, Feinstein & Co., which was located in Old Greenwich, while a party was taking place downstairs. Her dead body was discovered when a couple, Marla Warren and Kenneth Oakley, "got lost" trying to find the bathroom. *Clearly the couple were looking for a place to hook up. Finding a corpse must have been a bit of a mood buster.*

He handed the tablet back to a tightly wound Zelia, who was watching him intently.

"Well?" she said, her teeth worrying her lower lip. "What do you think?"

He took a slug of his coffee, sorting

through his thoughts. "A gallery owner. Deceased. Drugs were involved."

"Do you think there is a possibility of foul play?" She was watching him closely, as if he had all the answers. He wished he did. It would be nice to be the one to eradicate the anxiety that was reverberating off her like a multitude of silver balls in a vintage pinball machine.

"Do you?"

She caught her lip between her teeth again, her brow furrowed. "I don't know." Her eyes had grown dark with worry. "I hope not, but I need to make sure. See, my friend, Alexus" — Zelia scrolled back and tapped on the *Hartford Courant* article — "she didn't use hard drugs."

"Sometimes it is difficult to know if someone is using —"

"Why does everyone keep saying that?" she said, clearly frustrated. "I *know* her. She would *never* voluntarily touch the stuff."

Gabe sat back in his chair. "So, you believe there was foul play. That someone killed her and staged it to look like an overdose."

Zelia nodded, her gray-blue eyes large. "Perhaps . . ." Her voice cracked slightly. "It's a possibility. I think there's reasonable doubt about what actually happened to her."

"Have you gone to the cops with your concerns?"

"Yes. I called the Greenwich Police Department. A detective called me back. He felt my concerns were unfounded. They had done an investigation. Found no evidence of foul play. The doctor concurred with their findings. Declared Alexus's death an accidental overdose and signed a death certificate saying so."

"And you're hoping I will . . . ?"

She leaned forward, her face focused, intense, her hand on the table, clenching into a tight fist. "I was hoping through your writing you had access to specialists in the field who could help me dig a little further. Help me clear her name."

"And if you can't?"

"Fine. I'll deal with that. I just need to know for sure."

"Why?"

"It's hard to explain. I feel like a rock has been embedded in my chest. It's not big, but it's there, cold and uncomfortable —" She broke off, glanced down for a second, then met his eyes again with her chin set. "You think I'm crazy, don't you? Seeing shadows where there are none."

He shook his head. "To be honest, at this point it's impossible to draw a conclusion one way or the other. However, doing this type of investigative work takes time and money . . ."

"I already thought of that. I have some savings put aside that I can use —"

"And more often than not, the answers one gets aren't the answers one was hoping for —"

"I don't care," she cut in, her flushed face determined as she thumped her clenched fist against her magnificent chest. "I *need* to know. My friend might have been murdered. I *can't* just sit here and do nothing."

TWELVE

"I really appreciate you looking into this," Zelia said as they left the café. The misting rain had let up. The sidewalk was dark from the recent dampness. There were a few puddles to step around, and the world smelled fresh and clean.

"I'll do a little digging," he replied. It felt right walking beside her. "We'll see where it takes us. I can't promise I'll be able to uncover anything."

"Thanks." She smiled. Glanced at him. He could see a trace of vulnerability in the gray-blue depths of her eyes. Well hidden, but there, like the flash of a silver fish and then gone.

He liked the way she moved. Long strides, an easy flow to the swing of her arms, the rotation of her torso. *Did she take dance as a child? Perhaps.* There was something about the way she held herself, as if leaning into the world like a racehorse ready to run.

But there was a slightly braced quality as well, as if she'd vowed not to stagger in the headwinds that were buffeting her.

"This is going to seem like the weirdest conversational segue ever, but I've got an image in my head that I just can't seem to shake. Did you go to Berkeley?"

"Uh-huh," she said, still facing forward but tilting her head slightly, as if trying to capture a melody slipping past on the wind. "Why?"

"You remind me of someone. I attended a wedding with a friend, maybe ten or eleven years ago. It was a casual affair, students tying the knot in the back garden of an old wooden house, saggy porch, paint peeling. It had been raining earlier, but the weather cleared up. The bride was wearing a white cotton dress from the twenties, barefoot, flowers in her hair —"

She stopped, her hand alighting on his forearm as she turned toward him. Eyes wide. "That was me," she whispered. "Oh my God. Were you a friend of Ned's?"

He'd dropped her off at the gallery, but the memory of her still walked beside him. The sorrow in her eyes when she told him Ned had passed on impacted him. *What would it feel like to be loved so deeply? To be missed?*

Would anyone miss me? he wondered as he cut behind the pub and headed for the wooden stairs that led to the back field of the Mansfield Manor. His family, sure, but who else? His readers? Momentarily, but there were a million other crime fiction writers to fill in the gap. His friends? He had colleagues, but who could he count as his friends these days? His *true* friends. A wave of melancholy swept over him. *My parents are right. I've lost sight of what is important. So busy building a career, I forgot to build a life.*

THIRTEEN

Gabe stared at his computer screen, then pushed back from his desk. "Shit." He rose to his feet, raking his hands through his hair. "Damn. Not good." He paced the room once, twice, scanned the articles onto his phone, then headed out the door.

It wasn't until he arrived under the awning of Art Expressions Gallery that he realized the polite thing would have been to call first. Oh well. He was already there.

He tugged on the door handle.

The place was locked.

"Great."

"Can I help you?"

He squinted in the direction of the voice. An upstairs window was cracked open, and he could make out the shape of a woman standing there. He couldn't see her features, as the window was awash with color from the reflection of the setting sun. He knew it wasn't Zelia. The woman had a pleasant

105

enough voice, but it didn't cause the visceral internal reaction that Zelia's voice created on his senses.

He shaded his eyes with his hand. Still difficult to see, but he was pretty sure it was Zelia's co-worker. *What was her name?* "I was hoping to speak with Zelia. Is she still inside?"

The woman opened the window wider and leaned out, a friendly smile on her face. "No. Just me. Wrapping up. Zelia left a couple minutes ago. If you run thataway" — she gestured with her hand — "you might catch her. She usually walks home via the boardwalk."

Zelia heard rapidly advancing footsteps. Either someone was in a hurry or they were up to no good. *Always better to face trouble head-on,* she thought. She tightened her grip on her shoulder bag. She kept her body language casual and her gaze mild as she rotated, bending her knees slightly and dropping her center of gravity, her feet planted.

When she saw Gabe jogging toward her, relief rushed through her, temporarily making her legs feel wobbly. "Oh. It's you." Or maybe her jelly knees were caused by how hot he looked, with his long legs gobbling the distance between them, windswept hair, and the intense look in his eyes. "Thank goodness."

"You looked ready to rumble."

"Really? I thought I hid it well."

He smiled. The crinkles at the outer corners of his eyes spread outward like sunbeams. The warmth that washed over her caused a fissure in the fossilized barrier she had erected to protect her bruised and weary heart. She had to look away before he saw how much he affected her.

The sun had started its evening's descent into the welcoming embrace of the ocean, painting the world with a magical glow. A flock of black oystercatchers skimmed low across the sparkling water.

"Yeah," he said. "Perhaps from a normal person, but we writers are suckers for noticing the minutiae, the small contradictory details."

She nodded. "Makes sense." The oystercatchers made a sweeping semicircle, then landed on the water, sending ripples outward. Zelia faced Gabe again. "Where were you headed in such a hurry?"

The lingering traces of his smile fell away. The seriousness of his expression caused a dropping sensation in her stomach. "I did some digging," he said.

"I had a feeling it might be something like that." Zelia shut her eyes for a second, needing to gather her thoughts. She didn't know why she wanted to put off hearing what he'd discovered. Just knew she wasn't ready yet. "Have you had dinner?"

"You okay with sitting on the deck?" Zelia asked him. "This time of year can get a little chilly."

"It's snowing in New York," Gabe replied.

"Right. The deck it is. Hi, Shirley," she said, nodding to the frizzy-haired waitress who was deftly steering her way through the crowded interior with a seafood platter and two plates of fish and chips. "I'll grab some menus. We can seat ourselves."

"Thanks, love," Shirley replied, casting a quick smile Zelia's way.

Zelia plucked two battered menus from the wooden box by the cash register, then led the way through the small dining room of the Seaside Shanty.

The restaurant was right off the boardwalk and perched over the water on spindly footers that would never pass building code now. The place looked to have been built in the 1940s, and the decor hadn't been touched since. On the walls were the obligatory wooden ship's steering wheel, old

108

photos, and brass nautical instruments for measuring rain, temperature, and wind speed.

"Don't let the smell fool you," Zelia said, snagging a few blankets from the large basket near the door leading out to the deck. "The food is a little old-fashioned, but it's super tasty."

She must have read his mind. The smell of decades-old fry oil and fish permeated the interior of the small building.

He followed Zelia onto the deck, enjoying the crisp bite of the fresh air as the screen door swung shut behind them. The last sliver of the sun disappeared into the ocean as they sat at a table in the far corner. The sky was streaked with color. She handed him two of the blankets. "One to sit on, because as picturesque as these wrought-iron tables and chairs look, they are hard on the ass."

"The other blanket?"

"Is for your pleasure: wrap it around your shoulders, drape it over your legs — user's choice."

Gabe snorted. He'd be damned if he was going to huddle under a blanket like an infirm old man. No way. He did, however, follow her suggestion and use one to cushion his butt.

The only other customer on the outer deck was a weather-beaten fisherman who looked as if he had been eating at the Seaside Shanty since the place opened. No blanket in sight. His false teeth, however, were resting on the table before him as he chowed down on a large bowl of seafood chowder and slurped a thick chocolate shake.

"What do you recommend?" Gabe asked, perusing the menu.

"Nothing fancy. Where they shine is in the traditional fare. Fish and chips. The coating is nice and light, not greasy." She managed a halfway believable laugh. "Well, I guess 'not greasy' is relative. If you really want minimal grease, go for the pan seared or baked. Their halibut is fresh. I prefer it over the cod. The bucket of steamed spot prawns is good. All the chowders are great. Old-fashioned milk shakes. Crab cakes to die for. Stay away from the pasta, or anything with a sauce . . ." Her voice petered out, as if the nervousness she'd been trying to outrun had finally caught up with her.

"Stay away from pasta and sauce. Duly noted," he said.

"We'll place our orders and then you can — ah, here's Shirley now. Do you need more time?"

"Nope." Gabe shut his menu. "Hi, Shirley. I'll have the fish and chips. Halibut please — two pieces — and a chocolate shake."

"Spoken like a local," Zelia said. She ordered spot prawns and locally brewed elderberry cider.

Shirley bustled off. Dusk had fallen, the sun's farewell celebration smothered by the encroaching darkness. He took a sip of the ice water Shirley had left at the table. "Ready?"

Zelia gave a short nod, her face calm, but the energy pulsating off her reminded him of a cornered animal.

He removed his cell phone from his pocket and opened the document containing the articles. The information was in his head, but the physical action gave her a moment of privacy. There was no easy way to dispatch this news.

"While looking into Alexus's death, I stumbled across this."

He slid his phone across the table. It didn't take Zelia long to read the articles that appeared in the *Oregonian* and the *Register-Guard* four months ago, as both were brief: Winnie Efford, forty-nine, owner of Windsongs Gallery, located at the core of the Pearl District, Portland's thriving art and design area. Previous mental health is-

111

sues. Heroin overdose. Possible suicide.

He heard her suck in her breath. Didn't hear the exhale.

Zelia laid his phone back on the table and pushed it over to him, her movement cautious. "Do you think it's a coincidence?" she asked.

"Perhaps." His spidey sense was saying no, but they needed to be careful. He earned his living writing fiction. He couldn't completely trust what his instincts were encouraging him to believe. "We need to do some more digging. It's best to take emotional thinking out of the equation. To deal with cold, hard facts." He opened the next document he had scanned. "There was also this." He handed her his phone. "Not an overdose, but another unexplained gallery owner death. A male this time, however. If these deaths are not accidental, this particular 'murder' doesn't follow the modus operandi of the other two. Once I started reading, I remembered the case. It was splashed all over the newspapers a couple years ago. Richard Rye, thirty-eight, had just opened a new gallery in Chelsea three months prior to his disappearance. His mutilated torso was discovered along the Hutchinson River in New York State by a hiker and his dog. They were able to identify him due to the distinctive tattoo across his left shoulder that spiraled down his spine to his buttock. His right foot was found farther down the riverbank, his Salvatore Ferragamo driving shoe still attached."

Zelia winced.

"Sorry. That was thoughtless of me. Odd details fascinate me."

"No worries. I imagine you get immune to the gross-out factor in your line of work."

"Still —"

Shirley arrived with their drinks. "You okay, sweetheart?" she asked Zelia. "You're looking a little pale."

"I'm fine, thanks," Zelia said, glancing at Shirley, a slightly strained smile on her face.

"When did you last eat? Maybe you're hypoglycemic, like me." Shirley lit the small candle in the red glass container on their table. "I had to start carrying little baggies of nuts and dried fruit in my purse for when I feel tired." Shirley patted Zelia on the shoulder. "Well, not to worry. Your order is up next. It will be here in a jiffy." She moved to the fisherman's table, reached for his candle, but he waved her off. Gabe was too far away to hear what he said to Shirley, but it made the waitress cackle loudly. She was still chuckling as she exited the deck, the screen door banging shut behind her.

"I have a vague memory of someone talking about the Richard Rye death at a dinner party." Zelia's voice drew Gabe's gaze back. "They were farther down the banquet table. Their conversation was quite animated, but Alexus and I had just arrived in New York for the SCOPE Art Show. She was dating someone new, so we . . ." Zelia trailed off, seeming to draw into herself.

"Did you know Winnie Efford?" Gabe asked gently.

"No." Zelia shook her head as if to clear her thoughts. "But I'll call Feinstein and Company in the morning. Alexus's assistant would know if Winnie was a friend."

"Good idea. I'll call my brother in New York. Rick's an NYPD homicide detective. I'll see what he can dig up."

FOURTEEN

He slowly returned to his body, unsure of the time or where he was.

He was lying down, but he wasn't in bed with his smooth silk sheets that cooled and caressed his sensitive skin. He was chilled. Could feel rough, textured fabric under his cheek and hand. It was stiff, damp, and smelled of blood.

He cracked open an eye. *Ah.* He was home. Lying on the sofa in his studio. Night had fallen. The room was quiet and dark, a solitary moonbeam causing the large oak tree outside the window to cast witchy shadows on the floor. Everything seemed serene.

Thank goodness.

The last episode where he'd lost time, he had come back to consciousness to discover he was naked, the lower half of his body submerged in the muddy swamp at the back of his property. He'd caught a bad chill from being out in the elements for who knew how long. A cough, too, that developed into a bout of walking pneumonia. Missed a couple weeks of work.

He allowed his eyes to drift shut. Weary. So weary. He breathed in deep, taking in the smell of creativity that permeated his studio. There was something so comforting about the scent of his paints, the chemicals, and turpentine. The copper-penny smell of blood was more prevalent than usual. He didn't have to turn on a light to know what he would find. He knew well the consistency and texture of the substance that coated his hands. Not just his hands — his face, his hair, the fabric of the sofa underneath him, and God knew what else.

No matter. No matter.

He would straighten out the mess in the morning. For now, sleep beckoned. Blessed sleep. A soothing sense of peace wrapped around him, cradled him as if he were a newborn babe swaddled in the finest cashmere, tenderly held in a loving mother's arms.

FIFTEEN

Mary smirked when Zelia burst into the gallery twenty-six minutes after opening and a full forty-one minutes later than she usually arrived. "Well, Sleeping Beauty, did you have a good evening?"

"I am *never* late —"

"Ahem . . ." Mary made a show of glancing at the clock on the wall. "I beg to differ. But then, I imagine you have a good excuse." She laughed. "I'm *hoping* you have a good excuse — like hot, sweaty sex between the sheets with Mr. Tall, Dark, and Heavenly."

"How did you know we —"

Mary pounced on her, glee written all over her face. "So, you *did* have sex with him! Way to go, you wanton hussy —"

"No. Good grief, Mary. I didn't have sex with him. We had dinner."

"Aaaand?"

"And nothing. The man's not interested.

117

We talked about Alexus."

Mary deflated. "Damn. When you were late this morning, I was *so* certain. I was glad one of us was getting laid. Ah well. Speaking of Alexus, a package arrived from her this morning. I put it on your desk."

"That's odd." Her friend hadn't mentioned shipping anything to her.

"Want some tea?" Mary asked.

"Sure." Zelia unbuttoned her jacket and slipped it off her shoulders. "You know what I've decided?"

"What?" Mary asked over her shoulder as she walked to the drink station.

"I'm going to have a baby," Zelia said as she hung her jacket in the closet.

Mary spun around, her jaw dropping. "You're pregnant? Oh my God! I didn't know you were dating anyone."

Zelia laughed. "If you could only see your face. No. I'm not pregnant. Not yet. But I'm gonna be."

Mary was staring at her, mouth still agape.

"I was lying in bed last night."

Mary wiggled her eyebrows.

"Alone," Zelia said firmly. "Couldn't sleep. Kept thinking about Alexus and how desperate she was to be a mother. It had been a dream of hers, but she was waiting for Mr. Right. Unfortunately, as we both know,

Mr. Right never showed up. And now she's dead. I am *done* putting off the things that are really important to me. I am *not* going to continue waiting for someone to fall in love with me so I can begin the rest of my life."

"Zee, babies are a lot of work. They're messy and cry a lot. You'd never again get a full night's sleep."

"I know. And I want it all. The mess. The sleepless nights. I want to know what it is to give birth, to nurse a child, to watch him or her grow and mature. Would I rather have a partner so I'm not doing it alone? Yes. But apparently that doesn't seem to be an option for me. So, I'm going to start researching sperm banks and —"

"Sp-sperm banks?" Mary's sputter morphed into a mini choking fit.

"You okay?" Zelia thumped her on the back.

"I'm fine . . . Just breathed in the wrong way," Mary rasped. "Spit went down the wrong tube." She blew out a breath, wiped her eyes, and straightened. "Honey . . . ." Her voice still sounded a little ragged. "I wouldn't be a friend" — she wagged a finger at her — "if I didn't remind you of that old maxim. You are supposed to hold off on all major decisions for six months to a year after the death of someone close to you. You aren't supposed to move" — another finger joined the first — "quit your job, or change your investment strategy." Mary looked at her sternly. "I think deciding to have a baby on your own would fall into the 'major decisions' category."

"Whatever. I'm going to do it." Zelia headed toward her office.

"Wait for six months —"

Zelia whirled and glared at her. "I don't. Have. Time. My biological clock is winding down."

"Two months, then," Mary said, plopping a tea bag into a mug and pouring steaming-hot water over it. "Two months won't make that much difference."

"I'll think about it." She was *so* not going to think about it. She said she was just to shut Mary up.

"Good." Mary topped off her coffee and added a glug of cream from the mini fridge. "By the way, I called Eve Harris as you requested. Arranged for you to go by her studio next week, Tuesday, at one p.m."

"Thanks." Zelia came to a stop in the doorway of her office. A 37-by-4 3/8-by-30 cardboard shipping box lay across her desktop. It looked innocuous enough, wrapped in brown paper and thick 3.5-

millimeter tape, but something about the package made her throat constrict. *Probably because you know she's dead. Feels a little eerie receiving something from her now, like her soul is reaching out from beyond the grave.*

"Here you go," Mary said, appearing at her shoulder and handing her a steaming mug of tea.

The smell of jasmine calmed her. "Thanks." Zelia took a sip of tea to fortify herself, then stepped forward and placed the mug on her desk. "Right. Let's see what she sent."

Zelia removed an X-Acto knife from the top drawer of her desk and slit the tape. The instant she touched the box, a sense of wrongness swept over her. "Given the shape," she said — her voice sounded tight, unnatural to her ears — "I'd say this is probably a painting." She lifted the freed flaps of cardboard and pulled the Bubble-Wrapped object out. "Yep. Looks like one, feels like one —" She was glad she wasn't alone. Grateful Mary was there. Zelia removed the Bubble Wrap, the cardboard pads, the palette tape and wrap that protected the paint. *Why are my frikkin' hands shaking?* Zelia turned the painting over and then she knew.

"No shit," she heard Mary say. "What the hell?"

Zelia placed the painting on the desk, picked up the cream-colored note that fluttered out and turned it over. ALEXUS FEINSTEIN was embossed in HTF Didot font at the top of the card. A word was scrawled across it in Lexi's familiar handwriting.

"What's it say?"

"The name of the painting," Zelia answered as she took a couple of steps back, feeling the need to create some distance between herself and the artwork.

Mary strode forward. "Why on earth would she send you this? She knows you don't like the artist." She plucked the Dattg painting and the packing materials off the desk. "Well, not to worry. I'll rewrap this and ship it back to her."

"Good luck with that," Zelia said.

SIXTEEN

Mary paused. "Oh." She huffed out a breath. "You're right. I forgot for a second that she was . . . Now I feel like a dickhead for the uncharitable thoughts that were clanging through my head." She looked at the painting in her hands. "Well. What do you want me to do with it? The dumpster is right out that door. No trouble at all to toss it."

Zelia shook her head. The painting was powerful. Gazing at it made her feel ill. *Isn't that what art is supposed to do, make you feel something?* "I think I'm supposed to keep it." Just saying the words made her stomach clench.

"Why?"

"I don't know," she said slowly. "I just think I should. Alexus must have sent it for a reason. Maybe there is something I'm not seeing. Maybe she typed out an e-mail explaining and forgot to hit send — Ack!

No. I don't want it on my desk. Let's put it —" Zelia gingerly took the painting from Mary. *If only Alexus hadn't sent it. If only she hadn't died.* Zelia sighed. "I'll hang it in the gallery."

"Really?" Mary looked as if Zelia had just announced she was going to eat the painting for supper.

"She died, Mary. The last conversation we had, she asked me to display Dattg's work. It's the least I can do. Who knows? Maybe someone will buy it."

Zelia hung the painting around the corner in a nook where she wouldn't have to see it too often. She printed a label, mounted it, then affixed the label on the wall by the painting.

She returned to her office, sat down, and pulled up Dattg's CV on her computer. She found the artist's contact info, started to type an e-mail, but couldn't muster up the enthusiasm to find the appropriate words. "Later," she murmured, closing the draft. She felt unsettled. Jangly.

She opened her desk and rummaged around until she found the blue sage smudge stick and abalone shell that she had purchased at the Solace Island Saturday Market last summer. Zelia didn't usually go for that type of thing, but the woman who was selling them had two small hungry-eyed children clinging to her flowing skirts. The woman had said burning the sage would clear out bad spirits and negative energy. Zelia had smiled and nodded, pretending that was exactly what she was looking for. A random act of kindness. However, she was grateful for the purchase now.

Zelia read the hand-printed instructions.

— Focus your energy.

And how exactly am I supposed to do that? Well, here goes. She stared at the dried leaves of sage that were wrapped together with colorful cotton string. The smudging stick had an earthy smell.

— Light the sage. Stay connected to your breath.

Sort of hard not to. Death would be the alternative, she thought. However, just thinking about her breath made her feel more centered. She lit the sage stick.

— Smudge in a clockwise direction.

She carefully smudged her office and the gallery. There was something very peaceful about swirling the sage stick and watching the smoke trailing after. She waved her other hand to disperse the smoke.

"Don't even think about laughing," she told Mary as she entered the main area of the gallery.

"I would never," Mary said, her face serious, but Zelia could hear the faint echoes of suppressed laughter in her voice.

Never mind.

She spent more time than she wanted near the Dattg painting, smudging the area around it. Wasn't sure if it helped or not.

Finally, her arms got tired of circling and wafting. Besides, she didn't want to set off the gallery's smoke alarms, so she extinguished the smudge stick and returned to her office.

Her tea was lukewarm, but she still sipped it. At least she wasn't shaking anymore. *You have dealt with the unexpected,* she told herself, *and now you move on.*

SEVENTEEN

Zelia wasn't all that surprised when she discovered that her walk home at the end of the workday had taken her to Mansfield Manor instead of her intended destination. However, she wasn't seeking comfort in the field communing with the sculptures. She was standing in the lobby at reception. An adorable older couple was completing their check-in. He had a full head of steel-gray hair, hers a wispy soufflé in a softer gray color. While the receptionist finished the paperwork, the couple held hands. The wife's face tilted toward her bantam rooster of a husband, love evident in her eyes.

"Welcome to Mansfield Manor." The receptionist handed the couple a set of old-fashioned brass keys. "The bellman will make sure your suitcases are brought to your room. Lucy will show you the way to the Elsworth Cottage."

"No need." The old guy cackled. "We've

been here a million times before. Know this place like the back of our hands." His hand snuck down and gave his wife's bum a furtive squeeze. "It's a wonderful hotel where magical things happen."

"Behave, Fergus," his wife whispered, giving his shoulder a playful slap.

Zelia quickly switched her focus to the old-fashioned arrangement of peach roses on the low coffee table that sat by the fire between two comfy armchairs.

"We like to think so," the receptionist said. "I hope you have a lovely stay. If you need anything at all, just let us know." The couple moved to the side, depositing the keys in a pocket and purse.

Zelia stepped up to the desk. "I'm here to see Gabe Conaghan," she told the receptionist. The old couple swiveled to look at her. The woman's hand was still half in her purse.

"Is he expecting you?" the receptionist asked.

"No. But I'm a friend." Zelia felt her face flush. She could feel the elderly couple watching her avidly. "I'm not going to his room," she said, making sure her voice was loud enough to carry to their listening ears. Didn't want them to think she was some kind of hotel-frequenting hussy. "If you would be so kind as to call and let him know that Zelia Thompson is waiting in the lobby."

"Certainly," the receptionist said, turning to pick up the hotel phone.

"No need," the old guy chirped. He stepped forward, beaming happily. "We will drop you off on the way to our room." He turned to the receptionist. "Gabe's staying in the Hampstead Cottage, isn't that correct?"

"Yes, sir," the receptionist replied.

"Perfect."

"Really," Zelia said. "I'm fine. I'm happy to wait. If you would just call his —"

"Nonsense," the sweet-faced woman cut in. There was a soft lilt to her voice, the faint traces of an Irish accent. "It's right on our way." She smiled. Her dark brown eyes twinkled merrily. Something about her face seemed familiar. "Please," the woman said, looping her arm through Zelia's. "Indulge an old couple with the pleasure of a couple minutes of your company." And somehow Zelia found herself walking out into the last vestiges of sunshine and heading down a gravel flower-lined path arm in arm with the woman while her grinning husband led the way.

"Hold on a second," Gabe said. "Someone's at the door. Turndown service must be making the rounds early today. I'll send them on their way." He pushed away from his desk, where he'd been making notes, crossed the room, and opened the door.

Shit.

Gabe blinked.

Nope. It wasn't an illusion. His father was standing on his porch, grinning at him like Beelzebub on spring break.

"Dad? What . . . are you doing here?"

"Surprise!" Fergus said, pulling Gabe in for an enormous, back-thumping bear hug. "And look who else is here. Your mom —"

"Hi, honey." His mom wiggled the fingers of her free hand at him. Her other hand was looped through the arm of —

"Zelia?" Gabe shook his head slightly, trying to clear it. What was Zelia doing on the walkway leading to his room? Why was she arm in arm with his mother, who was supposed to be in New York? Were they friends? Did they know each other? And why did it feel so damn good seeing them together?

"Gabe? Everything okay?" He heard Rick's voice pipe from the cell phone in his hand.

"Jesus," Gabe said as he brought the phone to his ear. "Mom and Dad are here. What the fu—"

"Sounds like you're busy. I'll let you go," his brother said.

Gabe heard laughter on the other end of the line right before the phone went dead. He slid the phone in his pocket, then turned to his dad, still feeling rather stunned. "Wow. So you're feeling better. That's great. Uh . . . What are you doing here?"

"We were hoping to have dinner with you. Is that fabulous French chef Marcel still running the kitchen?"

"Only in the evenings —"

"Wonderful! The man's a genius." His dad turned and beamed at his wife and a rather red-faced Zelia, who appeared to be trying to find a polite way to regain her arm's independence. "Of course you're invited to join us, my dear. I'm sorry, what was your name?"

"Zelia," she said, with a trapped-in-the-headlights expression on her face. "Zelia Thompson. Thank you, but —"

"Terrific! I'm ravenous." Fergus jogged down the steps and took his wife's arm. "We'll meet you two lovebirds in the dining room in half an hour. That will give your mom and me a little time to freshen up from the trip."

"But . . . but I —" Zelia stammered as his parents fled down the walk. It was quite impressive how fast the two of them could move when they set their minds to it.

"It's a waste of breath," Gabe said from the doorway. "Trust me. I speak from years of experience. When my father puts his mind to something, there is no dissuading him. Want to come in, have a drink? We can raid the minibar."

She took a step toward him, then stopped and glanced in the direction of his rapidly disappearing parents. "How about a walk around the gardens?" she said.

He felt an internal smile bloom. *Who knew Zelia Thompson was so old-fashioned?* What she didn't know was she could have swung naked from tree to tree and his parents probably would have applauded her free-spirited originality.

"The gardens it is." He stepped off the porch and joined her on the path.

They walked for a few moments in silence. "It wasn't my intention to barge in on your dinner with your folks."

"I know."

"You seemed kind of shocked."

"Not about you joining us. The fact is,

dinner with my parents tonight was a surprise to me as well. I wasn't aware they were planning a visit."

"I'd totally understand if you'd prefer I don't come. You could make my excuses. To tell you the truth, I really should be home packing right now."

"Packing?"

Zelia turned to face him. "Yeah. That's why I came to see you. I wanted to let you know. Tristan was out when I phoned, but the temp who was covering found both Winnie Efford and Richard Rye listed in Alexus's contacts. I've booked an early-morning flight to JFK. Mary can handle the gallery with her eyes shut."

"You're going to Greenwich?" *Is she nuts?*

"Yes. I figured I've been to Alexus's gallery before. Maybe I'll notice something odd or out of place that the police overlooked."

"Let me get this straight. We think it's possible your friend Alexus might have been murdered."

She nodded. Her top teeth snagged her plump lower lip. Which was distracting as hell and not helping matters. He needed to focus, to concentrate on what she was saying. "And we are in agreement that perhaps Alexus isn't the first gallery owner that has

133

been killed. And so you decided it would be a good idea to *jaunt* down to Greenwich, Connecticut, *by* yourself to take a look around?"

Her spine stiffened. "That about sums it up," she said, her voice taking on a breezy air.

"Are you in*sane*?"

"No need to put on that pompous professorial tone," she said, wafting his objections away. "I'm not a starry-eyed acolyte hanging on to your every word. I am a grown woman. Responsible. Who happens to own and run a very successful business —"

"What if the killer is still there? Hmm? Looking for another victim?"

"All the more reason for me to zip down there pronto," she said pertly. "Someone needs to stop this monster. Am I scared? Sure. I'd be an idiot not to be. However, I refuse to let fear deter me."

"Great." He groaned, shutting his eyes for a moment to think. His head was reeling. He felt her hand alight on his shoulder.

"Don't take it so hard." She spoke more softly now, as if he were the one needing soothing. "I'll be careful." She was patting his back as if he were a cranky toddler she was tucking in for a nap. *Jesus.* He sighed. Opened his eyes.

She was looking at him, her gaze troubled. "I was hoping you'd tell me I'm doing the right thing."

The breeze off the water had caused tendrils to escape from the forest-green velvet clasp that held her hair up and away from her face.

He longed to reach out, undo the clasp, and release the rest of her golden-brown hair with its warm, shimmering highlights. Wanted to luxuriate in the feel of those long silky strands pouring through his hands like fool's gold. Wanted to pull her lush body flush with his, wrap his arms tightly around her, and try to find a way to banish the fear from her face.

But he didn't. Couldn't.

He was aware that his impulses where she was concerned were suspect. She thought of him as a friend. Not even that. He was a crime writer who might be able to help her solve the unanswered questions about her friend's death. She was not looking for a relationship. She was a woman who had lost the great love of her life.

He, on the other hand, was a horny bastard who had fallen in lust with a woman on her *wedding* day. A woman he didn't know, who was *clearly* deeply in love with the man she was marrying. What kind of sick fuck did that? To make matters worse, he now realized he'd been carrying some kind of a torch for her ever since.

No. He didn't offer her comfort. He stood there like a stiff cardboard cutout. He opened his mouth, hoping something inspired would come out.

"Give me your info. I'll book the same flight."

Great. It was all he could do not to roll his eyes. *Way to wow her, Mr. Writer. You're supposed to be a goddamned wordsmith —*

"You're going to come with me?"

He couldn't quite read her expression. There was caution there, but there was something else, too. Did she think it was ballsy of him to invite himself? *Doesn't matter. Better she think you pushy than that you politely step back while she dashes off to Greenwich, possibly risking life and limb.*

He nodded. Stiff. Like the primitive robot-man he'd become.

"Oh, Gabe." Her voice was barely louder than a whisper. The furrow that had taken residence between her eyes smoothed, and a slow smile dawned on her face. "Thank you *so* much," she said, like he had just given her a fistful of priceless jewels. "I can't even —" When her voice broke off, her shining eyes looked suspiciously bright. She flung herself in his arms. "I was so scared to go, but I was going to anyway. Oh my God." She was hugging him fiercely. Her soft pillowy breasts smashed against his chest, and the scent of her skin, tea, honeysuckle, and warm woman surrounded him. "It's going to be so much better with you along. Thank you! Thank you so much!" She looked up at him and he was lost. His better self would have stepped away, not taken advantage, but instead he lowered his head. Slowly. Giving her time to turn away or say no. His lips were a heartbeat from hers when he felt the slight pressure of her hand pushing against his chest. He froze, disappointment shooting through him, jagged and sharp edged.

"Someone's coming," she whispered.

The world around him snapped back into focus. He could hear footsteps approaching on the gravel path, along with the murmur of voices. "Sorry," he said, dropping his arms back to his sides. Both of them stepped apart, leaving his body bereft, longing to pull her close again.

"Me, too," she murmured, glancing at him sideways, her cheeks flushed.

His parents appeared around the bend, Gabe's mother's hand tucked comfortably in the crook of her husband's arm. She was laughing softly and his dad was looking pleased with himself.

Gabe jammed his hands in his front pockets in an attempt to minimize the obvious bulge straining against the buttons of his fly. Felt like a goddamned teenager.

"Hey, son. Zelia," his dad called. His free arm swept outward as if the view and all it encompassed were his doing. "Pretty damned spectacular, huh?"

"You got that right," Zelia said with a smile. "Wouldn't live anywhere else."

"Mom. Dad," Gabe said. He gave his mother a kiss on her soft, powdery cheek, and then they all walked to the dining room together, Gabe deep in thought. *What did Zelia mean when she said, "Me, too"? Was she sorry I attempted to kiss her? Or sorry we were interrupted?*

EIGHTEEN

"So, tell me," Alma Conaghan said, covering Zelia's hand with her own. "How long have you known Gabe?" The comforting texture of Alma's skin against hers caused a pang of longing for her own mother.

For a second her mind flashed back to that last summer before she headed to Berkeley. The long, lazy days spent on the boat with her parents, reading, fishing, crabbing. The burst of activity when the wind would pick up and fill their sails, sending the small craft soaring across the sparkling water. She had been bored a good portion of the time. Had wanted to spend the summer with her friends before the gang split up and went off to various universities and gap-year adventures. To enjoy their last carefree summer together, hanging out, going to movies and beach parties, sneaking into clubs, and ordering frothy alcoholic beverages while dancing the night away.

She'd resented that her dad had insisted she spend the summer with them on his new boat instead of letting her stay home. If only she could have known then how precious that time with her parents was. More than once she had wished for the ability to turn the clock back. She would have told her parents how much she loved them. Not been so snarky.

"Where did you meet?" Alma's voice pulled Zelia's thoughts from the past. Her gaze traveled to Gabe's mother's face — she was looking at her so hopefully.

Zelia hated to disappoint her, but sometimes the best way to rip a bandage off was to do it fast. "I'm afraid you have the wrong idea about my relationship with your son. We're just friends." She saw Alma's face fall, making her feel as if she were stomping on fluffy kittens, but she forged on. "Relatively new friends at that. Gabe kindly agreed to help me look into a difficult situation that has arisen." *Why is Gabe scowling at me like that? He should be pleased I'm not misconstruing his kindness.*

"That sounds like Gabe," Fergus Conaghan said, beaming as he rubbed his hands together. "Of course the boy would step up. Help out. A modern-day knight in shining armor he is. He's rich, too. Makes a bloody fortune on those damn books. Now, are we talking about a dangerous situation? That would be good."

"What in the world are you rabbiting on about, Fergus?" Alma admonished him. "We don't want either one of them in a dangerous situation."

"Nonsense! Adrenaline is supposed to do wonders for the libido. You want grandchildren, don't you?"

Grandchildren? Oh, good Lord. Zelia opened her mouth, but Alma beat her to it.

"They are *just* friends, Fergus. Friends."

"For now." Fergus chortled with a delighted gleam in his eyes. "But if we could throw a little danger in the mix, then all bets are off! Would be fight-and-flight," he said, half rising from his chair and striking a superhero pose. "Man against the elements! Something like that can cause a testosterone surge —"

"Dad," Gabe said. He shook his head, his eyes rolling skyward as if saying a silent prayer for patience. "Enough. You aren't helping." A slight flush appeared along his chiseled cheekbones.

Oh my God. Gabriel Conaghan, the hardbitten crime fiction writer from New York City, of all places, is blushing. Zelia blinked, wishing she hadn't noticed, for the sweetness of it, the vulnerability under his tough exterior, made her fall for him even more.

Fergus plopped down into his seat and peered at Zelia over the smudged reading glasses he had donned when the menus arrived. "Are you married?"

"No," Zelia answered. The way the conversation was swooping from one unrelated topic to another made her feel as if she'd fallen down a rabbit hole.

"Boyfriend?" Fergus barked.

"No, but —"

"Do you want children?"

"Of course I do. Who wouldn't?"

"Fantastic. You've got the hips for it. Popping them babies out should be a snap." Fergus turned to Gabe and wagged a finger at him. "You picked a good one. Don't let her get away."

Gabe looked at her, a slight smile curving the outer corners of his lips. He gave an almost imperceptible shrug, and suddenly Zelia found herself having to stuff down an unexpected urge to giggle.

She was *not* a giggler. Never had been. She picked up her menu and ducked her head behind it.

Dover Sole, pan fried, butter lemon

She forced herself to focus on the words.

Filet of Beef Wellington, mushroom
duxelles, foie gras, puff pastry Coq au
vin, farm-raised chicken braised with red
wine, lardons, mushrooms

Any words.

Quail Normande, apples, cream, calvados
Breast of Duck, medium rare with sour
cherries

Anything to keep the laughter that was rising like champagne bubbles in her throat from escaping.

"Are you sure we can't tempt you with an after-dinner brandy? Another cup of tea?" Alma asked, peering at Zelia hopefully.

"No, thank you," Zelia said. "I probably should get going."

Really? Gabe thought, suppressing a smile. *What a surprise. You mean you have a life with places to go and people to see?* Poor Zelia. His parents had kept her hostage for what was likely the longest meal in the history of the Mansfield Manor dining room.

"Oh, wait." Gabe's mom sat up in her seat, waving for the waiter. "We forgot to order a selection of local cheeses. To polish off the meal and balance the sweetness of the desserts."

"Mom," Gabe said, laughter in his voice. "You couldn't cram another morsel in your mouth if your life depended on it. I'll have the check please," he told the waiter, who looked much relieved.

"I could, too." There was a slightly plaintive quality to his mother's voice as Gabe signed the check that the waiter whisked out of his apron pocket. A wistfulness on her face that had Gabe rounding the table and dropping a kiss on her head.

"Love you, Mom," he whispered. "I know what you're doing."

"What?" She was trying to look innocent but was unable to suppress the twinkle in her eyes.

Zelia rose to her feet. "Thank you for dinner. It was such a pleasure meeting both of you."

Gabe gave his mom a quick hug. "And in this instance," he murmured softly, "oddly enough, I appreciate it."

"Gabe will walk you to your car," Fergus bellowed, pushing to his feet, gnarled hands on the table, as if his hip were giving him trouble again.

"Well, that would be a pretty long trek"

144

— Zelia slipped her arms into her jacket — "seeing as how I left my car at home."

"So much the better," his dad replied, looking as if he were about to attempt the Irish fling. "Off you go. We won't wait up."

"Turn right up here," Zelia said. "I'm the third driveway on the left."

Gabe swung the SUV onto Nightingale Road. As he turned into her drive, his headlights illuminated a multicolored vintage lady's bike that was housing a mailbox. "Nice mailbox. It's like it's having its own private party."

"Yeah." Zelia smiled. "It sort of is. I'm a great believer in second chances."

"Second chances?"

"If at first you don't succeed, blah . . . blah . . . blah . . ." Her hand made little circular motions in the air.

"Still not quite clear what you're talking about."

"I discovered the bike at a garage sale a couple years ago. Had hoped to restore and refurbish it so I could ride it to work. Finn at the bike shop informed me it was a lost cause. The rust, he said, had compromised the structure. It wouldn't be safe."

He shifted into park and switched off the engine. Her home was a cozy little shingled cottage with an inviting porch complete with flowerpots and a rocker. They sat in his vehicle in comfortable silence, Zelia deep in thought. "It felt wrong," she continued, "to toss the old bike out, almost as if I'd be tossing out a piece of myself, a part of a dream. So, I marched to Morgan's Hardware and purchased a small metal mailbox and paint colors that spoke to me of happiness. I cut a hole in the sides of the bike basket, slipped the mailbox in, and secured it with wire. Then I went to town with the paints." The moon through the windshield illuminated her face and the soft smile that the memory had called forth, causing his throat to constrict. In all his years, he'd never seen a more beautiful sight.

"The following autumn I filled the remaining space in the bike's shopping basket with potting soil and a plethora of flower bulbs. I topped it all off with a layer of emerald-green moss and a prayer. I'd never had much success with plants before, but to my surprise, the following spring a profusion of flowers pulled off a glorious debut. And their arrival is something I look forward to year after year." She turned to him. The soft smile had bloomed like a summer rose, filling the interior of the SUV and all the empty calcified spaces in his heart with joy. "And every spring as I walk past my mailbox, the sight of the flowers tumbling out of the bike basket causes my heart to dance just a little."

She beamed at him, and he could feel the answering smile on his face as he blinked like a man drunk on moonshine from her beauty.

"Thanks for the ride," she said, the smoky rasp of her voice like liquid fire in his veins, and then she did the damnedest thing. She leaned over and brushed her lips over his, once, twice, lighter than the touch of a dandelion puff, her lips warm, soft. "Night," she whispered, and then she was gone, out of his SUV and up her front porch steps. She turned, waved once. "See you tomorrow morning," she called, and then disappeared into her house.

NINETEEN

"Why did you park? This isn't Alexus's gallery. We aren't even in Greenwich." Zelia glanced around the rather sketchy neighborhood a trifle warily, which perversely cheered Gabe up. Showing a modicum of caution was an improvement from her seeming willingness to plunge into dangerous situations without batting an eye. "Did you put the wrong address in the GPS?"

"Nope." Gabe switched off the engine. "Need to pick up a few supplies." He unstrapped and got out of the car.

Zelia followed suit. "Supplies?"

"Figure if we're going to do this thing, we might as well do it right." He dropped some quarters in the parking meter, then headed toward a nondescript gray building that was in need of a fresh coat of paint.

Zelia looked at the worn black sign with white lettering. Her eyes widened. "A spy shop?" she said. "Whatever for?"

"There's a difference in price, obviously," the retired cop behind the counter was saying. "I'd say the basic black powder and brush will serve you fine for the majority of jobs. However, for intricate lifts off difficult surfaces, personally, I'd go with the magnetic wand."

"Oh my goodness, these are fabulous." Gabe could hear Zelia at the far counter, chatting to the skinny clerk, whose eyes had widened to the size of teacups when Zelia had entered the store. And who could blame him? She was every man's wet dream come to life. But for a nerdy early twentysomething who was attempting to grow some kind of facial hair with little success? Gabe smothered a smile. The clerk would probably remember this interaction until his dying day. The poor guy seemed stunned speechless by the magnificence of her smile and her body. The woman packed a punch. Hell, Gabe's lips still tingled from the memory of last night's barely there kiss. If Zelia ever decided to kiss him in earnest, he'd probably self-combust.

"I appear to be looking at you, but in actuality I'm perusing everything that's going on in the store behind me," Gabe heard her exclaim. He glanced over his shoulder to see a beaming Zelia wearing a pair of mirrored sunglasses. "This is so cool!" The clerk's cheeks were flushed scarlet as he swallowed hard, his Adam's apple bobbing, his head nodding.

Gabe turned back to the objects resting on the glass counter before him. "I'm going to go the magnetic route," he said. He slid the magnetic wand and the jar of black magnetic latent powder to the clerk. "Do you have fingerprint cards?"

"Yeah, but index cards at an office store work just as well and are more cost-effective."

"Thanks for the tip. I'll keep it in mind. However, today I don't have time for the extra stop, so I'll bite the bullet. I'd like some general lifting tape and polyethylene, nitrile gloves, medium and large."

"Very well. Will that be all?" his clerk asked.

Gabe glanced over at Zelia, who was turning in various directions, mirrored glasses still on. "Throw in the lady's sunglasses as well."

TWENTY

"I'm so sorry, Zelia," Tristan said. "You should have spoken with me first. I could have saved you the trip." He was standing in front of the door that led to the back offices, blocking access. "I can't unlock the door for you. No one is allowed to go back there."

"Tristan, I've been in Alexus's office a million times."

"I know." He nodded, his eyes troubled. "And if she were still alive it would be a different story, but —" He broke off, squeezed his eyes shut for a second. When he reopened them Zelia could see that he had gathered his inner resources and wasn't going to budge. "I'm sorry," he said firmly. "I can't let you rummage around in her stuff."

"I'm not going to rummage, Tristan," Zelia said. She could feel a slight sheen of sweat starting to coat her face. "I just want to look around. I flew all the way down

151

here. I'm trying to help. It's possible there was foul play."

"The police ruled that out," he said, his brow furrowing.

"Tristan, you know Alexus didn't use drugs."

"Actually, I don't." He shrugged apologetically. "As an employee, I wasn't privy to her private life." He paused and then brightened. "Wait a minute. I think there's a way around this. Are you the executor of her will?" He looked at her hopefully. "Because if so — and I don't mean to offend — I'd need to see the notarized legal documents. However, if you were, then I'd be able to let you go back there, no problem."

Zelia sighed. "No," she said, trying not to let her exasperation show. It wasn't Tristan's fault that he needed to do everything strictly by the book. "I'm not."

"Oh dear." He shook his head regretfully. "Gosh. I'm so sorry, Zelia. I wish I could help, but the law is the law. I'm not allowed to give anyone access to her private belongings other than law enforcement or her legal representative."

"Well," Gabe said as they exited the gallery. "At least we tried. We have a bit of time before our return flight. Do you want to grab a bite to eat?"

"Oh no, this isn't the end of it," Zelia said. "We've come all this way. I'm not turning back." Something about the tone of her voice jolted Gabe into high alert. He probably wasn't going to like whatever was about to come out of her mouth. "The way I see it, we now have two choices. Both require we rebook our flights for tomorrow."

"Zelia —"

"Option one: we get disguises."

Gabe stifled a groan.

"We reenter the gallery when Tristan is occupied with a client. We hop into the broom closet, which is right next to their public washroom. Once he's locked up and left for the night, voilà! We pop out and look around the gallery with impunity."

"I hope you are joking —"

"Au contraire," she said firmly. "Option two . . ."

He prayed option two was more reasonable than option one.

"We wait nearby until he locks the gallery for the night and *then* we break in," she said with obvious relish. The determination that lit her face conjured images in Gabe's mind of Grace O'Malley, an ancient ancestor who was a sixteenth-century warrior woman and an Irish pirate queen to boot. Gabe was sure

153

she was up there in the afterlife, hooting with laughter at the predicament he was in and applauding Zelia's gumption. He, however, was not.

"I'm hoping," he said, "this pregnant pause is you catching your breath before stating option three? Because options one and two" — the nonchalant tone he was going for was failing spectacularly — "are *clearly* the muttering of a woman who has gone stark *raving* mad!"

Twenty-One

Gabe entered the coffee shop and strode toward the corner table where she was sitting. "Oh good," Zelia said. She could feel her face flush. "You're back." He hadn't mentioned her spur-of-the-moment goodnight kiss. But then neither had she, although she couldn't stop thinking about it, the feel of his lips under hers. "Did you find what you needed?"

He nodded, clearly still grumpy about the coming night's adventure, so it was probably not the best time to start an in-depth conversation about whether he would be interested in kissing her again sometime in the near future.

Gabe tucked a large plastic shopping bag beneath the table. The handles were tied into a knot so the contents weren't visible.

"What did you buy?"

"Stuff," he replied, as if that were answer enough.

"Tristan hasn't left the building," Zelia said, trying to lighten his mood. "How do I know this, you might be asking, since you can clearly ascertain that my back is facing the stakeout building? Aha!" She tapped her mirrored sunglasses. "With my handy-dandy spy glasses I can see everything going on behind me."

Gabe didn't even smile.

She sighed. This stakeout business was not nearly as exciting as it appeared in the movies. She'd been sitting in the coffee shop down the block from Alexus's gallery for what seemed like an eternity. Once Gabe had settled her there, he'd left with the cryptic comment that he had a few errands he needed to run if she was determined to stick to her foolhardy plan for tonight.

She was, of course.

At first she'd opened her mouth to argue about his description of her dashing, daring plan, but then she'd closed it again. No need to quibble over minor details. Besides, as the hours ticked by and the afternoon slipped away, she was starting to get the uncomfortable feeling that he might be right.

"Well, now that you're here, I can take these off," she said as he settled into the chair opposite her. "Since you have a clear view of the place." She removed her sunglasses and placed them in their case in her purse. The wearer might be able to see behind oneself, but they weren't the most comfortable sunglasses in the world. Zelia sighed. Hopefully, now that she had kept the sunglasses perched on her nose for more than an hour, Gabe wouldn't feel his money had gone to waste. "I'm going to get another tea. Want anything?"

He declined.

She swung by the bathroom, which was starting to feel like an old friend. Three large teas will do that to a woman. Then she decided to mix things up with an iced mocha coffee and a Boston cream doughnut.

As night started to fall, Gabe moved them to a different table, tucked in the shadows near the bathrooms. They sat side by side so they both had a clear view of the gallery.

At first she thought he'd moved them because her frequent treks across the coffee shop to the bathroom were starting to embarrass him.

Wrong.

Apparently, Mr. Writerman was a details guy and realized that once it got dark outside, the interior of the coffee shop

157

would be illuminated. Sitting in the window would be like being actors on a stage. "Best at this point to mimic stagehands," he pointed out. "Making things happen, invisible and silent, tucked in the wings."

"Ah," she had said, nodding wisely. "Yes." But that salient fact had never crossed her mind.

Unfortunately, in her indignation over the move, she'd inadvertently highlighted the fact that she was peeing a lot. Which — in hindsight — would certainly qualify as an impress-the-hell-out-of-the-hot-guy misstep.

The idea of breaking into a secured building had seemed like a great idea when she was grouchy about being denied access to Alexus's office, but now she was having second and third thoughts.

"Maybe this is crazy —"

"Maybe?" Gabe said, a little too pointedly for her taste, so she didn't elaborate. Didn't say, *I've chickened out. Let's go home.* Didn't say, *When I said I was going to break into the place, I forgot to mention that I have no idea how one goes about doing that.* Just took another slug of her drink that was now tepid, feeling as if her body was so hydrated it could float away. She checked the time on her phone. Feinstein & Co. should be clos-

ing any minute now.

"Here we go," Gabe said, his large hand covering hers. Tristan had appeared at the front door, accompanied by an elderly couple.

"Ah," she said lightly, as if his touch wasn't causing a jolt of electricity to shimmer up her arm, down her torso, where the sensations settled in a pool of pulsating warmth low in her abdomen.

Zelia sat there, her hand under his like it was no big deal, as they watched the elderly couple chat with Tristan. She exhaled slowly. She hadn't realized how desperately lonely she was. How much her body craved to be touched.

Tristan smiled at something the elderly woman said, then assisted the couple into their waiting limo, a chauffeur shutting the door behind them. The limo pulled into the traffic. Tristan reentered the building, then reappeared seconds later. He locked the door and took off at a brisk pace down the sidewalk, turned right at the corner, then disappeared from view.

"Time to head out." Gabe released her hand and rose to his feet. He slung his satchel over his shoulder. Something metal clanked as the bag settled against his hip. It was bulkier than it had been earlier.

"Is that a gun?" Zelia tipped her head discreetly in the direction of his satchel.

"No." Gabe picked up the large plastic shopping bag from under the table and tucked it under his arm. "If I were packing, I wouldn't have it banging around in my bag. That would be asking for all kinds of trouble. Ready?"

She nodded, pulled on her sweater, picked up her purse, and followed him out into the cold night air. She *wasn't* ready. Would *never* be ready. Her breath was shallow and her mouth felt as if it had been stuffed with cotton batting. They were making a terrible, *terrible* mistake, and it was all her fault.

The weird thing was that for all of Gabe's doomsday mutterings, as the time for action grew closer, it was as if something in him shifted. The man seemed calm and filled with a laser-like focus.

"Gabe?" She had to scamper slightly to catch up. "I was thinking — *mmrrph.* What the hell are you doing?" she squawked, because he had suddenly pivoted, grabbed her arm, and pulled her into the darkened arched doorway of an old brick building.

"Shhh . . . keep your voice down," he whispered. His warm breath was fanning softly against her temple. Because it was dark, it was hard to make out individual features, but she could feel the height and strength of him. Could smell the warm, clean male scent that emanated from him, wanted to lean into and be surrounded by his essence. "We don't want to attract attention."

Ah . . . She smiled, a frisson of excitement tingling through her. *He's in super-spy mode. My own private 007 has pulled me in here for a "good-luck" kiss.* She tilted her head back in anticipation of the sensuous warmth of his lips taking possession of hers. But instead of pulling her closer, the contrary man stepped away.

She heard the rustle of plastic and then he pushed something soft into her hands. "Put this on."

"What is it?" Zelia asked, a little embarrassed and grateful for the cover of darkness.

"A hoodie."

"Oh. Thanks," she said, attempting to return it. "That's really kind of you. I *am* cold. That is true." Her teeth were chattering slightly. "But I'm not *that* cold."

"Zelia —"

"I don't do hoodies," she said kindly.

He sighed. "Zelia. The illegal act of breaking and entering would not be classified as a fashion-forward event. Put the damn

161

hoodie on and make sure that the hood is pulled over your forehead so your face is obscured."

"But it's dark. You said we were going to attempt to enter through the back alley. Who's going to see us?"

"Hopefully, no one. However, from the time we enter the alley until I can black out the security cameras —"

"Security cameras . . ." She swallowed hard.

"There will be an approximate five-second gap," he continued dryly. "During that time, it would be best if your face was covered so you aren't easily identifiable as the person who committed said crime."

"Yes. Of course." Zelia hastily donned the sweatshirt and pulled the hood down low over her forehead. The extra layer did add a welcomed warmth. "Good heavens. I had no idea Alexus had a security system. It seems like such a safe area. How did you figure that out?"

"Walked by, kept my phone down by my side, finger on the video button." He pulled a second hoodie out of his plastic bag and put it on. "Once I was around the block, I took a look, zoomed in, and *bingo.* Security cameras. One over the back door, a second overlooking the alley."

"Wow."

"There's also a discreet one over the front door."

"There is? Unbelievable. How many times have I walked through that door and never noticed?"

"I wouldn't be too hard on yourself. Prior to this there would've been no reason to clock it. Do you have something you can tie your hair back with?"

She glanced down at the curls that were tumbling out from under her hood. "Yes, I see what you mean. Would be a dead give-away." She dug into her purse, found her tortoiseshell clip, pulled her hair back into a makeshift French twist, and secured it. Then she replaced the hood over her head. "Better?"

He nodded. Slung his satchel back over his shoulder. "Let's head out."

Head out?! A wave of panic engulfed her. She grabbed his arm. "But if there's a security system, even if you 'black out' the camera, won't an alarm go off?"

"And that, my friend," he said, pulling his hood down to cover his face, "is the million-dollar question."

"You know," Zelia whispered as Gabe sprayed black paint over the second camera

163

above the back door, "I feel kind of sorry for Tristan. His boss died, and the gallery's future and his job are uncertain. Of course he's going to try to micro-control the things that he can — where are you going?"

Instead of scaling the fire escape or jiggling the door handle, Gabe had moved farther down the building. She quickly followed. "Wh-what are you *doing*?"

"You're the one who —" Gabe had donned rubber gloves, pulled a screwdriver out of his satchel, and was removing the screws in a panel on the back of the building that was almost invisible in the darkness.

"Jesus," she muttered. "You have eyes like a bat."

"Ah. Please. Stop with the romantic talk. I might get a fat head. Here, hold this for a second." He handed her the screwdriver, dropped the screws in the front pocket of his jeans, and then removed the metal panel. "As I was saying before I was so rudely interrupted, you're the one who wanted to look around her office, so I'm doing my damnedest to get you in." He flipped open the lid of the plastic box nestled inside. "Not sure if the alarm is attached to the phone line or the Internet. Best to disable both," he said.

"You know what? I've been thinking, and I don't know if we should —"

He gave a hard yank on a thick black cable line and a thinner phone line to disconnect them both, the loose wires dangling in his hand. "There we go." He flipped the box shut and moved to the back door. "Put these on," he said, withdrawing another pair of gloves from his satchel and handing them to her.

Her heart was pounding so hard she could hear the blood rushing in her ears. "I'm not sure this is wise." She could already see the news headlines blaring: *Art Expressions Gallery Owner Caught Red-Handed with Famous Crime Author Gabriel Conaghan Breaking into Colleague's Office. Murder! Sex! Sin!*

"It's up to you," Gabe said, facing her. "We can turn around right now. Go home. Drop the investigation. Or we can take advantage of the building being empty and look around. Your choice."

Twenty-Two

They made their way up the back stairs. Zelia had a death grip on his arm. He didn't blame her for being scared; he was a little freaked out himself. The only place he'd ever broken into was his godmother's house. That had been with her blessing and with her alarm system's password safely stowed in his pocket. Disarming the Feinstein & Co. system felt like he was attempting a high-wire act with no safety net below.

The alarm wasn't blaring. Hopefully a silent signal hadn't been triggered at the monitoring station.

The beams from their flashlights created bobbing orbs of light on the concrete stairs and the lower part of the walls. They'd left the light switches off. Best not to draw unwanted attention to the building. Zelia hadn't spoken a word since they had stepped over the threshold. Probably shocked at how easily he'd broken into the building. *Showcasing your misbegotten skill at breaking and entering is probably not the best way to wow a woman.*

"Where's her office?" he asked as they reached the top of the stairs.

Zelia paused, then jerked her head toward a door that was ajar on the right side of the hall. She let go of his arm, wrapping her arms tightly around her chest as if she had contracted a sudden chill. Clearly, she was scared. Best to dive in. Dread only made things worse.

"Ready?" he asked, keeping his voice calm and matter-of-fact.

She nodded.

As they entered the office, he heard Zelia's sharp intake of breath. Didn't blame her. Tasting death on the air was difficult in the best of times. That it was her friend who had died made it even worse. Gabe had ridden shotgun with Rick several times, walked through crime scenes, the morgue, the courthouse, jail. It had disturbed him in the beginning, but with repeated exposure he'd developed some sort of psychic callus, because he barely registered it anymore. Just slipped into writer mode and focused on the idiosyncratic details that made each situation unique.

Although, in this instance, it was he who

would be attempting to collect evidence rather than watching his brother and his partner do it. Also, there was the inescapable fact that if he and Zelia were caught they'd soon be residents *in* the jail rather than ride-along visitors.

Until this moment, he hadn't been sure if this was a wild-goose chase. Thought perhaps his subconscious was using the reason for the trip back East as an excuse to spend time with Zelia, hoping to get closer. But once he stepped into Alexus's office and felt the cold slap of nausea-inducing violence shimmering around him, he was certain. Zelia had the right of it. Alexus had been murdered.

Facts, he reminded himself. *You must deal in facts, not suppositions.*

"Anything look out of place?" he asked.

He watched as Zelia braced herself, squared her shoulders, and scanned the office. "No. Not at first glance. It looks like it always does. It's just —" She shook her head. Her exhale was shaky. "It's almost as if . . ." She hesitated, her lower lip caught between her teeth. "I can feel her presence here. Like she's waiting, can't . . . can't move on." She squeezed her eyes shut, but she wasn't quick enough to stop the sudden tears from escaping. She turned her back to him, shoulders shaking, her breath coming out in ragged, shallow gulps.

Should I offer her comfort? Give her a hug?

He stepped toward her.

Paused.

I don't want her to think I'm using her vulnerability to hit on her. Shit. Troy Masters would totally know what to do in this situation. Damn it all. Life is so much easier when lived on the page.

"Do you need a hug?" His voice came out gruffer than he'd wanted, as if he were reluctant to touch her. In actuality, he wanted nothing more than to scoop her into his arms and kiss away her tears.

"I'm fine."

"You're not fine, Zee. You're crying."

"Oh, what the hell." She whirled to face him. "You're right. I'm not fooling anybody. Yes. I'm crying. My heart is hurting so bad, but I'm angry, too, that she's not here and I'm left with all these frikkin' questions." Her arm slashed out as if it were a sword, and then the ferocity drained out of her and all that was left were tears. "I miss her, Gabe," she whispered. "I miss her so damn much. And yes, I would very much like a hug, please." The last words were muffled, because his arms had already enveloped her. Zelia's face burrowed into his shoulder, dampening the fabric of his sweatshirt.

When her tears finally subsided, the room was quiet, with just the sound of their breath. "Do you have a tissue?" she asked, her voice subdued.

"No." *Should have thought to bring some.* "Sorry."

"No worries." She gave his chest a gentle pat, as if he were the one needing comfort. Then she exhaled slowly and stepped away. "I'll be right back." Her elegant spine was ruler straight as she exited the room.

When she returned, her face was dry and her expression calm. She shoved a fistful of what appeared to be toilet paper and a paper towel into her purse. *Clever girl. Thinking ahead. Not wanting to leave DNA behind.*

"Probably best if we change out your gloves," he said.

"Right." She peeled off the old ones and stuffed them in her purse. "Thanks." She took the new nitrile gloves from his outstretched hand and donned them, then glanced around the office. "I'd like to take the laptop," she said. "I know it's stealing, but there might be something on it that will help us in our search."

"I agree," he said. He saw her shoulders soften.

"I also think — as disagreeable as the task

will be — that if the dumpster hasn't been emptied, we should go through it before we leave."

Zelia held the flashlight steady and watched, fascinated, as Gabe held the magnetic wand over the back-door handle. He gently swirled the tiny black particles over the metal. As with the glass coffee table, the sofa, and the doorknob that separated the gallery from the back of the house, black fingerprints began to emerge. A few more swirls and the fingerprints were clear and defined. "There we go," he whispered. He straightened and pressed the button at the top of the wand, causing the remaining magnetic particles to fall into the small container he held beneath it. He screwed the top on, placed the container and wand in his satchel, then removed the wide, clear tape, tore a piece off, and carefully applied it to the handle, smoothing it down. Then he lifted the tape off in one clean stroke, applied it to the three-by-five-inch white card, and quickly jotted down a few notes.

"I think that will do it for the inside," he said as he placed the card in the envelope with the others.

He held out his hand to her as if asking her for a waltz. "Ready to dumpster-dive?"

he asked, an apologetic grin curving his lips. A dimple briefly appeared among the dark stubble that graced his face, then vanished like a shooting star. But the memory of it remained, causing a joyous ache in Zelia's chest.

"Absolutely," she said, placing her hand in his.

TWENTY-THREE

Gabe sat down on his sofa, drink in hand. It was good to be home, even if it was only for an evening. He swirled the crystal tumbler, the ice cubes tinkling. The color of the whiskey reminded him of the amber tones in Zelia's hair, which the sun had called forth as they'd walked through the rental car lot. She'd glanced over, caught him looking at her, and smiled like warmed honey. Her lush lashes at half-mast partially obscured her eyes. *What was she thinking that caused that siren's smile?*

He took a sip of his drink, savoring the heat as it trickled down his throat. He'd always been a staunch Scots whiskey drinker, but a couple of years ago, while on book tour in Japan, that had changed. After dinner, his host had served him Nikka Taketsuru's seventeen-year-old pure malt. Gabe had taken one sip and was hooked.

Sort of like what happened with Zelia, he

thought. *Although, back at Berkeley it was only a look. No chance to taste. And now that he'd had the merest of tastes, he craved her like a high-octane drug.*

He heard a door open and shut down the hall. Footsteps. Gabe found himself holding his breath, watching for her to appear.

Once they'd left the gallery, they had decided it would be best to put some distance between themselves and Feinstein & Co., so they'd hopped into the rental car, gotten on I-95 South, and headed for New York. The traffic was light, and an hour and ten minutes later they'd pulled up in front of his Tribeca apartment.

Washing up was a priority, as dumpster-diving had proved to be messy, smelly work.

"Thank goodness," Zelia said as she stepped into his living room. "I feel *so* much better." Her wet hair was slicked back from her face, accentuating her high cheek-bones and making her eyes appear even larger. A riot of wet curls cascaded down, rendering the upper back of the white T-shirt she'd borrowed from him translucent as it clung to her skin.

He wanted to move her hair aside, peel the T-shirt off, scrape his teeth along the nape of her neck, taste her with his tongue. Her hair appeared darker, the blond and honey tones temporarily disappearing from the moisture captured in the strands.

"Are you sure the restaurant will let me in wearing these?" she asked, gesturing to his sweatpants. "They're a little too tight in the ass, and the legs are too long."

Too tight? Zelia's curvy, rounded ass and womanly thighs poured into his sweatpants was one of the sexiest sights he had ever seen. He cleared his throat. "They'll let you in," he said, moving to the hall closet. "You'll need a coat. A hat, too." He removed one from the closet, helped her into it, then pulled a knit hat over her wet hair.

"I can't wear this," she said. "On Solace Island perhaps I could get away with it, but New York City is stuffed to the gills with gorgeous women."

"You look adorable," he said, slipping on his own coat.

"Men." She shook her head. "Well . . ." There was laughter in her voice as she tucked her hand in the crook of his arm. "At least I no longer stink. Lead the way. I'm ravenous."

TWENTY-FOUR

"It's time to strap in, sir," he heard the steward say. The flight was a last-minute decision. His secretary had been unable to make contact with his usual steward. Hence the idiotic instructions.

He glanced at his fingernails and sighed. It was so hard to keep them in pristine condition. An impossible task, really, with the life he led.

"Sir . . ."

He snapped his gaze up and watched with satisfaction as the color drained from the substitute steward's face, his jaw working to formulate words. None came out.

He turned back to watch out the window as his Gulfstream jet began its descent. Could hear the steward scurry to the front of the plane, the *click* as the steward's safety belt snapped into place. *Pussy.*

The glittering lights of Seattle shimmered and danced against the dark night sky, beckoning, and beguiling like a lustful belly dancer on the ground below.

The new plan, he thought with satisfaction, *though hastily arranged, is a good one. So fascinating how an accidental interaction might very well be the thing to transform the mundane into something brilliant.* He'd never combined the fluids of two people in one art piece before. One person. One painting. That was how he worked. However, the Alexus painting wouldn't leave him alone. It was like a pit bull that had locked its jaws around his heart and wouldn't let go. The painting was demanding, insisting on completion. Unfortunately, the little time-loss episode two nights prior had decimated an already meager supply of his most necessary ingredient.

He'd toyed with the idea of expediency. Hire some hooker, knock her out, withdraw a couple pints of blood, and then send her on her merry way none the wiser. But it didn't feel right in his gut. Art was like that. It was a demanding mistress. Wouldn't let him slather any old shit on the canvas. It needed to be connected in some way, a brother, a mother, a sister, a niece — and that's when he'd thought of Alexus's little gallery-owner friend.

He tapped his fingertips on the pale

leather-clad armrest.

Tap . . . tap . . . tap . . .

"Zelia," he murmured. "Zelia Thompson." Her name shone before him as if it had been stenciled on the air. "It's perfect really. They're friends. Close friends, and the bitch *did* refuse to show my work."

He heard the whir and then the *clunk* of the wheels descending from the belly of the plane as the ground rushed toward them.

He smiled. "It's payback time," he whispered as a shiver of anticipation coursed through him.

TWENTY-FIVE

"How did you learn to do all that stuff?" Zelia asked.

"What stuff?" Gabe asked, but he had a feeling he knew what she was talking about. She'd been shimmering with excitement ever since they'd left Greenwich. He could feel the residual adrenaline rush buzzing like a million honeybees circling the air around her.

Hell, he was feeling it as well. Had managed to hold it together, do what needed to be done, but once they'd left the gallery the aftereffects had hit hard. It had caused him to feel light-headed, shaky; his knees suddenly had the consistency of Jell-O. He'd been grateful for the solid feel of the seat of the rental car under his butt. Forced himself to focus on steering and the traffic around them to help take his mind away from what they'd just done and how bloody stupid and risky it was. How scared shitless he had

179

been. How he would do it again if she asked him to.

That was when he realized just how deeply invested he was in her and in a possible "them."

"You know . . ." Zelia circled her fork in the air, a green bean stuck in its prongs. She glanced surreptitiously around, making sure the other diners and the waitstaff weren't close enough to overhear, then leaned in. "Disengaging the burglar alarm," she whispered, her eyes glowing. "Picking the lock, lifting fingerprints . . ." Her face was so expressive, literally radiating excitement and satisfaction at a job well done. He could almost see her walking through their visit to the gallery step by step and could tell the instant she arrived at being waist deep in the dumpster. Her nose had scrunched. "And the methodical way you had us sort through the garbage in that dumpster?" She grimaced and sat back in her chair, a shudder running through her. A cat doused with a bucket of water, shaking off the unpleasant evidence and memory.

Gabe didn't blame her. That particular dumpster had been particularly foul smelling.

"It was disgusting," she added. "But we did find the needle."

"*A* needle, a bit of tubing, and a port. Not a syringe. Which is what would've been used to inject heroin," he said. "We don't know if it's connected. If the needle is, it just brings up more questions, not answers."

"Whatever." She waved his comment off, too pumped up for his caution to dampen her parade. "Yes, we'll wait for your brother to run his fancy tests, but we both *know* it's important. I got tingles when we found it. You did, too. I could see it on your face. We are *so* going to prove the truth about Alexus's death." She smiled brightly at him as if she thought he was spectacularly clever. "Totally made it worth rummaging around in that stinky dumpster." She popped the green bean in her mouth and chewed contemplatively. "We were so damned smelly, one could almost chew the air around us. I have *never* been so happy to step into a shower. Didn't want to get out —"

Gabe shifted discreetly in his seat. His writer's imagination was not being his friend.

"Lathered up twice." She shook her head. "Washed my hair three times. *Three* times, just to make sure I got rid of the stink."

Oh Jesus. Now visions of her soaping up her luscious, curvaceous body were embedded in his mind. Zelia moving in slow mo-

181

tion, hot, steaming water pounding down, her lovely rounded arms over her head as she washed her hair. Her head tilted back, long throat exposed as if begging for a kiss, a love bite, right there. Her back arched. Her raised arms thrusting her glorious breasts upward.

It took all of Gabe's willpower not to groan aloud.

"Are you all right?" Her voice broke through his daydream.

"Yeah. I'm fine," he said, failing totally in his effort to sound nonchalant. What emitted had been a cracked growl.

"You sure? You had a rather intense look on your face."

"I was thinking . . ." He paused. *Great. Way to paint yourself into a corner. Don't want to lie, but can't tell her the truth.* "That . . ." *What had they been discussing? The dumpster.* "That I was grateful for a shower, too."

She laughed and finished the last swallow of her Syrah.

"More?" he asked, tipping the bottle toward her.

"Abso-fuckin-lootly." She grinned, scooting her wineglass a couple of inches in his direction.

He topped off their glasses.

"So?" She propped her head on her

clasped hands, elbows bent on the table as if settling in for a cozy bedtime story. "I'm waiting. It's not every guy who has your mad skills at breaking and entering, finger-print lifting, et cetera."

His mind flashed to the sort of mad skills he'd like to show her. Naked. In bed. *Partially clothed would work as well. Hell, we don't even need a bed. I can demonstrate a few of those skills right here on this table.*

Get your mind out of the gutter.

He cleared his throat. "Well, it helps that my little brother's a cop. If there's something he doesn't know, he can generally put me in touch with someone who does."

"And they'll talk with you?"

He shrugged. "For the most part. When you write crime fiction, you get a wide spectrum of readers. Some of those readers happen to be in law enforcement, forensics, FBI. People like to see their jobs and what their lives are like portrayed accurately. I reach out to them, and sometimes they reach out to me. Not sure how to classify the relationships. Not really friends, not quite colleagues. Generally it starts with a chat over e-mail or the phone, and then we go out for drinks. It progresses from there . . ."

"Kind of like dating," she said, beaming at him.

Nothing like dating, his internal horndog caveman wanted to growl. *There is a big difference between hanging out with my brother and his law enforcement buddies and what I'd like to do with you.*

"I guess," he managed to say in a relatively civilized manner. "Soon I was learning how to handle various types of guns, how it felt to load them, hold them, shoot them, clean them. I got to ride along, visit crime scenes, the morgue." He shrugged. She was gazing at him starry-eyed, but in truth, there were things he had seen that he wished he hadn't. Heartbreaking images that would never leave him and shaped his view of the world in a detrimental way. Sometimes he wished he could go back to the innocent that he was before he started writing, diving into research. Believing that at the core of everyone was goodness. That wasn't true. There was evil in the world and it came from the most unexpected places and in all sorts of guises. God only knew what kind of damage it was doing to his brother's psyche being exposed to the monsters, day in and day out.

Zelia took another sip of her wine, looking at him from under her long eyelashes.

She had a small beauty mark high on her right cheekbone that he wanted to kiss. "Gabriel Conaghan." She shook a teasing finger at him. "I can see how you might have learned how to dust and lift prints riding shotgun with your brother and your FBI pals. However, I seriously doubt that the excellent men and women who make their livelihoods by upholding the law would teach you how to (a) disengage an alarm system and (b) pick a lock." She smirked at him, then took another sip of her wine, tipping her head back, exposing her throat.

The woman was so damned erotic without even trying. God help the world if she ever decided to stand in her sensuous power. He exhaled slowly, trying to get a grip on himself. He was seriously hard beneath the table.

"Correct," he said, amazed at how normal his voice sounded. "When I was a teenager I got a job working in a bike shop on the weekends. I had been saving my money to do something special for my godmother. She was turning fifty and had been a little blue about it. Never been married. No children."

"Did she want children?" Zelia asked, sorrow for his godmother reflected in her eyes.

"For sure. She loved us kids and was like

185

a second mother to us. She'd never met the right guy. I hadn't thought about it, just took all that love, kindness, and attention she showered on us kids for granted. Then, one night, I'd come home late from a party. Snuck in the back door. I was being quiet because I'd had a few beers and knew my mom would give me hell for it.

"As I started to climb the stairs, I heard my mom and Nora talking in the kitchen. I was surprised she was still there, that they were both still awake. Nora was crying about turning fifty, saying life had passed her by, no husband, no children, nothing to show for her forty-nine years of life, and in a couple months she was going to be half a century old. She kept saying that phrase over and over, and I could hear my mom's soft murmur as she tried to console her.

"I got a job the very next day, saved every penny. On her birthday I treated her to a fancy dinner and the musical *Wicked* on Broadway. She was so happy, loved the musical. I felt so damned proud. We had a wonderful time. Returned to her cottage and found a kicked-in door. The place ransacked. Nora was devastated. One of the things the thieves had stolen was a locket from her grandmother. It wasn't worth a great deal of money, but it meant the world to her." Still, after all these years, what had happened weighed heavily on him. "I felt responsible."

Her hand covered his. He wanted to lean into the sensation, forget about the burglary, the feelings of guilt. "*You* didn't steal her locket," she said. "The break-in wasn't your fault. If you hadn't taken your godmother out that night, she might have been injured or worse."

"My godmother said the same thing, but . . ." He shrugged. "Anyway, I became obsessed with home security. It's amazing what one can pick up online. The more I researched, the more concerned I became. I figured if I could break into her home, burglars could as well. People always ask, 'What did you purchase when your first novel hit it big?' I pretend I forgot. Don't want my godmother to be embarrassed. But the truth is I know exactly what I purchased. Solid wood outer doors for her cottage, dead bolts with deeper box strikes, reinforced doorjambs with galvanized steel, locks I couldn't pick, and an alarm I couldn't disengage. Still I worry, but she won't move. She's stubborn like my mom."

"And you never know . . . perhaps the act of diving into a thief's mindset to protect your godmother is what piqued your interest in the criminal world, was the catalyst for the successful career you enjoy today."

"Huh," Gabe said, feeling as if he had just been smacked across the head with a two-by-four. "I never thought about it that way."

Zelia smiled, but there seemed to be a trace of sadness lingering just under the skin. "Think of it as an unexpected gift your godmother graced you with."

TWENTY-SIX

Stepping out of the warm restaurant into the cold night air was like a slap to the face. The waiter locked the door behind them, was probably hoping like hell that the couple snuggling in the booth in the corner would take the hint and leave, too.

Zelia tucked her chin into the warmth of her borrowed overcoat and shoved her hands into the pockets. It felt so intimate wearing his coat, breathing in the faint clean scent of him embedded in the fabric. It was almost midnight. The road was relatively quiet, a few pedestrians, an occasional car zipping past, its headlight beams bouncing over the uneven road. Two blocks over there was the thrum of a steady stream of cars on Hudson Street, the occasional bleat of a horn.

Zelia walked alongside Gabe, unable to shake the heartbreaking image of his godmother crying in his mom's kitchen.

"You're quiet." Gabe's voice broke through the fog of her thoughts.

"Yeah. I'm thinking about your godmother wanting kids, never meeting the right guy." She pressed her fist to her chest. "Hurts my heart."

"I think she's probably at peace with it now."

Zelia shook her head. "No. I'd put money on it still causing her sorrow. I know it would me."

Gabe's steps slowed to a halt. "You want children?" he asked.

"Desperately," she said, looking back over her shoulder to where he was standing. His face was in the shadows so she couldn't see his expression, but she could just imagine the stunned, horrified look on his face. "A mood buster, huh?" She laughed, suddenly feeling rather carefree at having broken the unspoken cardinal rule of early dating. "I know. Not supposed to admit it, but it's true. I've always wanted a big family, tons of children running in and out of the house, the mess, the noise, the sleepless nights and burping babies. I want it all. And yet . . ." The laughter had vanished as quickly as it had come and bone-deep sadness had taken up residence. "It's clear . . ." She was having difficulty getting words out. "That a houseful of children is not going to happen for me."

"Why do you say that?" He sounded almost indignant.

"Look at me," she said, anger rising at herself, at him for asking the question, making her say it out loud. "I'm overweight. I'm old, and I grieved way too long after Ned died." And just like that the anger dissipated, leaving an empty hole in the place it had been dwelling.

"That's a ridiculous thing to say. You're gorgeous. Christ, woman, it's all I can do to keep my hands to myself. You are a woman in your prime, with your whole life stretching out before you. And finally, there is *not* an expiration date for grief. It takes as long as it takes for one to find their feet again."

"There is, however, an expiration date for women," she said, dashing away the unexpected moisture from her eyes. "And I, my friend, am right up against the childbearing clock." He started to speak, but she cut him off. "I don't want you to feel sorry for me. Seriously. I can't believe I'm even telling you this. I'm not crying because I'm sad. I'm frustrated is all."

She turned and started walking briskly down the sidewalk in an attempt to step away from the vulnerability she was feeling.

"Anyway, I've got it all sorted out." She could hear his footsteps catching up. "I don't have the cash reserves to raise a gaggle of children by myself. However, I've done the math, and I'd be able to swing one rosy-cheeked, dimple-fingered baby." He was beside her now. He didn't say anything, but she could feel his solid presence, feel the intensity of his gaze. She lifted her chin. She was not going to feel embarrassed or let him feel sorry for her. She was a woman taking control of her future instead of waiting passively for some man to make her dreams come true. "I've done some research. There's actually a good sperm bank in Seattle, which isn't that far away." For some reason, the surprised expression on Gabe's face, as if he'd just swallowed a live goldfish whole, cheered her up immensely. "It's the perfect solution really. No strings attached. No man telling me what to do, how to raise my child. I checked out their site," she said breezily, as if she did this sort of thing on a daily basis. "It's quite amazing. You can literally plug in eye color, hair color, ethnicity, height, and *bingo!* Up comes a bunch of matches, along with personality descriptions that read like dating profiles that any sane woman would swipe right on. These guys are college educated, athletic, supposedly funny and charming —"

"I'm college educated."

"Well, of course you are. You're a world-famous author."

"Not all authors —"

She batted his arm with the cuff on her borrowed overcoat. "This isn't about you, you goofball. Unless you're planning to race over to Seattle and make some money on the side." She laughed at the ridiculousness of the image. Gabe Conaghan jacking off in a little plastic test tube. "In that case, yes. You'd make a wonderful donor. You're highly intelligent, handsome, got a body to die for, and a sense of humor to boot. Your sperm would go flying out the door like homemade hotcakes."

"I'd do it," he said.

She turned and looked at him. Nope. He wasn't joking. *Oh dear. Way to put your foot in it, Zelia.* "Not that there is anything wrong with being a sperm donor," she added hastily. "No judgment here. I mean you had to pay for your Berkeley degree somehow, and God knows it wasn't cheap."

"I haven't donated at a sperm bank. But I would for you. No strings attached if that's what you wanted."

Zelia stopped in her tracks. "Would what?"

193

she asked carefully, grateful that they were near a streetlight now and she could see his face clearly, her heart banging like a drummer going wild in her chest.

"Make love with the intention of impregnating you."

TWENTY-SEVEN

They walked back to his apartment hands clasped, the feelings coursing between them too big for words. There was a sacredness to the silence surrounding them that shimmered with possibilities and hope.

He unlocked the door and pushed it open. She hesitated for a second and then crossed the threshold. "It's so weird," she said, pretending to casually glance around his living room, but seeing nothing. "I suddenly feel shy. Awkward. It's like I'm scared or something, which is ridiculous because it's just you."

"Uh . . . Thanks?" he said dryly, an eyebrow cocked.

"I didn't mean 'just you' like you aren't enough, because you are. More than enough." She shook her head. "I should probably shut up now."

"No. It's important to talk things out, to know how you're feeling. If you've changed

195

your mind —"

"God no. I want this more than anything. I just don't know how to go about it. Never done anything like this before. Do we just march into your bedroom, I strip naked, and you go at it?"

He smiled like she'd said something funny, tenderness in his eyes. "Hopefully, I'll have a little more finesse than that." He smoothed a strand of hair behind her ear and then dropped a gentle kiss on her forehead. "We'll take it slow," he said, tilting her chin up so her eyes met his and she could see that behind the lightness he was dead serious. "If at any time you change your mind, just let me know. My body might complain, but I will honor your wishes. Okay?"

She nodded, the knot in her stomach easing slightly.

"Good. Now, for the record, I have a clean bill of health. No STDs. Haven't been sexually involved with anyone since my physical last fall."

"Me, too. Clean bill of health. No worries on this end."

His hands felt so good, running gently up and down her back as if she were a skittish horse he was calming. "Would you like some coffee?" he asked. "Or another after-dinner drink?"

"No. God no. If it's okay with you, I want to do this with you before I lose my nerve."

As they entered his bedroom, he flicked the light switch on, both of them blinking, pupils trying to adjust. "Stay here," he said, flipping the light off again, plunging her into darkness. "I'll be right back."

She heard him leave the room. A light turned on down the hall, then soft music came on in the living room, the sound carrying to where she was. Lovely gentle music that reminded her of spring and new beginnings, and the sweetness of his thoughtfulness made her heart ache. She heard him rummaging around. Then the light down the hall switched off, but the darkness wasn't absolute. A bobbing orb of warm amber candlelight was heading her way, illuminating the harsh angles and slashing cheekbones of Gabe's beautiful, smiling face.

When he got closer, she saw he had used a candle that looked like it was from an emergency preparedness kit. He'd stuck it on a saucer with a bit of melted wax. That he didn't have a stash of make-out paraphernalia at the ready but wanted this to be nice for her somehow made that plain little candle the most romantic thing she'd ever seen.

He placed the candle on the dresser. She could now see his bed. The gray textured fabric on the headboard and box base had slight hints of bluish-green. The colors reminded her of a stormy winter sea. Behind the bed the entire wall was covered with dark, old shiplap that had been stripped and stained. Black metal pendant lights hung from the ceiling on either side of the bed, the flickering candlelight revealing that the interior of the shell shape was brushed metal. Beneath the hanging pendants were minimalist dark wood tables, their brushed-metal legs gleaming softly.

If she got lucky, this would be the bed in which she would conceive her child.

She felt Gabe step toward her, which brought her focus back to him.

"You okay?" he asked, raising his hands and cupping her face gently between them. "Still want to do this?"

Beautiful. He's so damned beautiful. Inside and out. "Absolutely," she said. "Do you?" Giving him a way out, even though she wanted this more than anything she'd ever wanted in her life. Just the thought of creating a baby was making her uterus thrum.

She could literally feel her vaginal walls and her labia growing slick, her clitoris swelling, pulsating, as every cell in her body seemed to be throbbing with need.

His eyes darkened. "One hundred percent," he murmured. She felt his fingers glide along the side of her head, close into a fist at the base of her skull, capturing the silky strands of her hair. He tugged gently, tilting her face upward as his mouth descended to stake his claim on her.

Yes, she thought. *God yes.* And then his lips made contact with hers and the need thrumming inside her erupted into a raging forest fire, incinerating all conscious thought.

He was trying to keep a tight rein on his rampaging lust. Tonight wasn't about fucking. This was too important. Could be life changing. He wanted to take it slow, make it special. He brushed his lips across hers again, memorizing the shape and the texture of her mouth, tasting the warm sweetness of her breath, which carried the faintest hint of their after-dinner brandy.

She was moaning softly. "More. I need more." Her body arched to meet his, her luxuriously abundant breasts pressed against his chest, soft and pillowy, begging to be touched. Her hands skimmed up his sides, leaving trails of heat marking their paths, up over his shoulders, rising to cup his face, pulling it down to make full contact.

He smiled, causing a little growl to escape from her lips.

She pulled back, and he could see the hunger in her eyes. "I know," she said fiercely, the lower half of her body undulating against his erection as if she were a cat in heat, "that you're trying to go slow, be sweet and kind." She tipped her head forward, inhaling him in. He felt her teeth scraping against his trapezius through his shirt. Then she bit down with another growl, as if she were considering devouring him whole. He had to pull his hips back for a second, away from the friction of her body. He'd known he wanted her, but he'd had no idea that at his age he could go from zero to full throttle so fast. Less than two minutes of minimal contact and he was ready to shoot off in his pants. "But it's been almost *eight years* —" She moaned.

Eight years since what? He was still processing that one when she stepped forward, closing the gap between their bodies "Since I've had a stiff, hard cock buried deep inside me." *Holy shit!* "And I am dying here." Her hands had rid him of his belt and were undoing the buttons of his Levi's, her knuckles bumping against his erection. "Can't take slow. We'll do slow later. I promise." She slipped her hands inside his briefs and clasped them around his engorged cock. "Oh my God." Zelia's voice was husky, hungry. "You're huge." She pulled the elastic band of his briefs away from his abdomen and tugged down his briefs and jeans until they rested low on his hips, the stiff length of him freed and jutting upward. "Wow," she whispered. Her thumb glided over the tip of him, gathering the droplet that had emerged, spreading it until the head of his cock was glistening. Then she wrapped her fingers around him. Her eyes flickered shut for a second as she paused, seeming to take a mental imprint of the feel of him, his shape, width, and length. Then she slid her hand down his hot shaft, her wrist doing a slow rotation on the journey down, as if not wanting to miss even a millimeter of skin.

"Oh God." The words coming out of his mouth were more breaths than sounds. His hips thrust forward, and his balls contracted, ready to blow.

"I need you now," she said, her hand swooping up his cock, over the swollen head, and then back down again.

"You aren't going to get any argument from me." He yanked down her sweatpants and panties, his ass clenched tight so he wouldn't shoot off. The scent of her skin, of her feminine arousal, had consigned his lingering intentions of taking it slow to hell.

Her first shoe came off easily, but the second got tangled in the leg of her sweats. "I can't get it off," she panted.

"Fuck the shoe," he growled, hoisting her up. She wrapped her long legs around him as her wet cunt undulated against the hard length of him. "Give it to me," she demanded, beating her fists on his shoulder.

He gripped his thick cock in his fist, shifted her a little bit higher so he could rub the swollen, sensitive head along the slippery wet petals of her labia.

"Oh God, Gabe, please! I need it now. Can't wait any longer," she cried.

He plunged inside her tight, wet channel, her back slamming against the wall.

"Yes. Just like that. Hard and fast. You're fucking me so goddamned deep. Oh, Gabe, you feel so good . . ." She was glorious in her passion, her head thrown back, hair tumbling down, teeth bared, her beautiful breasts bouncing from the intensity of his thrusts. So damn sexy.

You slay me, he thought. Or maybe he whispered. Didn't know for sure. Didn't matter. All that mattered was that she was in his arms, her warm, wet pussy gripping him tight. She moaned, dropped her head forward. Her mouth latched onto his shoulder, marking him as hers, the ache from her sucking sending him higher. His heart pounded like a locomotive, vision blurring as her nails dragged down his back. Her mouth released his shoulder and traveled up his neck. He could feel her teeth closing around his earlobe, tugging.

"Oh God. Please don't make me come yet."

She added more pressure to her teeth. "Give it to me . . . Give it to me . . ." A growling chant through her clenched teeth as he thrust into her, deep and hard, over and over, the dark picture frame of the sailor's wooly clattering against the wall.

He could feel her pussy gripping around his cock, tighter and tighter. "I'm . . . I'm . . ." She moaned. Suddenly she released his ear, her face thrust skyward, the cords in her arched neck strained further, body undulating as her pussy started pulsating around him, sucking him even deeper. "Oh God, Gabe. I'm coming," she cried, decimating the last vestiges of his control. A powerful climax surged through him as he flung himself, like a drunken Bacchus reveler, over the precipice. Her name burst from his lips as he thrust into her for a final time, buried to the hilt as he shot hot streams of come into her welcoming womb.

Zelia awoke in an unfamiliar bed, the clatter and thrum of New York City waking up audible from the streets below. She could hear the *beep* of a large truck backing up, cars heading out to work or coming home from a night shift, a man's voice calling out, the words indistinguishable. Perhaps he was helping the truck back up.

There was a *thump* and a *flutter* outside the window. She turned her head slightly, still nestled comfortably on Gabe's warm chest. A pigeon was trying to find purchase on the windowsill, wings flapping against the glass, until finally it gave up and flew away.

She inhaled, long and slow, loving the smell of him. Storing up memories for the long, cold winter. Savoring the weight of his arm over her shoulder and the tactile feeling of her smooth legs entangled with his hair-roughened ones. *If only there were a way to hit the pause button.* She'd wanted time to absorb the miracle that she was lying in a bed with this man, possibly the sexiest man alive. And they had made hot, passionate, monkey love up against the wall and then indulged in another round of lovemaking that was slow and sweet before drifting off to sleep.

I'm the luckiest woman in the world, she thought, her hand making slow, hope-filled circles on the swell of her belly.

TWENTY-EIGHT

The next time Zelia woke there was bright sunshine streaming across the bed and she could hear the sounds of the city in full throttle. She found herself alone in the bedroom. She slid her hand over the indentation on the pillow beside her. The linen pillowcase was cold.

"Gabe?" she called. She couldn't hear any noise from him moving around in the apartment, but perhaps he was reading in the living room. She turned to get out of bed and that's when she saw the note, propped against the saucer with the stubby, melted remains of the candle from the night before.

Am meeting with Rick. You were sleeping so peacefully, I didn't want to wake you. Help yourself to food in the kitchen. Will be back soon. xo

A beautiful long-stemmed Belle Epoque

rose lay on the bedside table in front of the note. *My favorite,* she thought, gently running her fingertips along the dark nectarine outer petals. The Belle Epoque had been her mom's favorite as well. *How did he know?* Of course, he didn't *know.* She knew it was foolishness to think it was a sign from her mom, a blessing of good luck, and yet she couldn't stop the goofy smile that spread across her face. She lifted the rose to her nose, the outer petals falling open to reveal the gorgeous golden bronze color on the inner side. She inhaled deeply. It was a stunningly beautiful flower, but the thing about the Belle Epoque that she loved most was its rich fragrance. It spoke to her of summer, of iced cocktails in the garden and love. She inhaled again, shutting her eyes so she could smell more deeply. She slid the silky petals across her lips, making them tingle as she thought of Gabe and his kisses. And just the act of thinking about him had her body humming, readying itself for entry.

"Up you get," she told herself, pushing back the covers and swinging her legs to the side of the bed. She looked at her cell phone. *It's 11:28? Good Lord. Talk about sleeping the day away.* She took the phone off do not disturb and called Mary.

It rang a few times. Zelia could hear a lot

of static in the connection. She was just about to hang up when there was a *clatter,* a faint "damn," and then Mary's breathless voice came across louder. "Hello? Hello? You still there?"

"Mary. Hey, where are you?"

"In the car on my way to the gallery. Had to pull over to answer. The police are on a rampage about driving while using mobile devices, and I do *not* want to get stopped. What's going on?"

Zelia had called to let Mary know that she would be on her own at Art Expressions for another day. *Instead,* what came out of her mouth was, "You're *never* going to guess what I did." Zelia grinned, imagining what Mary's reaction was going to be. "I asked Mr. Tall, Dark, and Mysterious to impregnate me and he said yes!" she said. She held her breath, waiting for Mary's squeal.

Long pause. No squeal.

"You're kidding me, right?" Mary finally replied. She didn't sound excited. She sounded worried.

"No." Zelia was suddenly feeling a little defensive.

"Oh, Zelia." Mary was using that voice she sometimes dropped into that sounded way too old and weary for her age. "Please tell me you haven't already started on your baby-making mission."

"What if I have?"

Mary sighed in exasperation. "Zelia. This is important. You need to think it through. Your friend just died and you are grieving. Now is not the time to be leaping into helter-skelter schemes like this. Did you get him to sign a contract?"

"A contract? What for? It's not like he's going to be involved. He's coming back to New York. It's perfect really. No messiness, no running into each other at the super-market. I know he's super smart. He's gorgeous. I've met his parents and they are lovely. I couldn't get a better gene pool."

"I'm talking about a quit claim contract, so that if he does indeed impregnate you, he gives up any legal rights to the baby."

"Seriously, I don't see why you're making such a big deal, Mary. Besides, I wouldn't mind if he wanted to visit with the child once in a while. It might be nice for my baby to know who her father was."

"So, that means no. You didn't protect yourself legally. You have no idea, do you?" Zelia didn't need to see Mary to know that she was shaking her head. "A girlfriend of mine was an 'accident' baby. Her mom's boyfriend at the time had agreed to be there, help out. However, two months after she was born he took off.

"Unfortunately, her mom had put the father's name on the birth certificate. It was a nightmare. Her mom wasn't able to make medical decisions without his approval. Couldn't get her a passport or travel across the border to visit her mom's family in Ontario without a notarized letter of permission from the deadbeat ex-boyfriend. A notarized letter, which was only valid for one year! Every single year until my friend reached legal age, her mom had to write a new letter, chase this asshole down, physically drag him to the notary, and pay for the service."

"Okay," said Zelia, feeling slightly overwhelmed. "No big deal. I won't put his name on the birth certificate."

"Zelia," Mary said firmly. "You said you met his mother and father, that they're nice people. Are you sure they'd be willing not to have a relationship with their own grandchild? What if they felt you were an unfit mother? They could petition a judge to assign them guardianship."

"I won't tell them. If they don't know about the baby, how could it hurt them?" But even as the words left Zelia's mouth, she knew that her conscience was going to be yammering at her day and night.

Mary didn't answer. She didn't need to.

"I'm so damned tired of putting everyone else's feelings first," Zelia finally said.

"Don't be mad."

"I'm not." And she wasn't. Was her heart suddenly heavy? Absolutely. But how could she be mad at Mary for looking out for her and loving her enough to make her face some uncomfortable truths?

"Why not take it slow, Zee? See where this relationship leads you. Who knows? If you're patient, maybe you'll end up with the man, the baby, and your happily-ever-after."

The idea was so ludicrous it made Zelia laugh. "Come on, Mary, get real. The only reason he offered to help me was out of the kindness of his heart."

"You don't know that."

"Pu*leaze*. The man is a world-famous author, has a great family, is financially secure and fabulous in the sack. He'd *never* settle for someone like me." She was acting jaunty even though her heart felt as if an iron fist were wrapped around it and squeezing tight. "No. The best I can hope for is to enjoy the hell out of his hot bod and hopefully walk away with a baby to boot."

"Let me reiterate, I don't think it's wise."

"Fine. Point taken. Look, I called to let you know I'm still in New York. I can't make

211

it in to the gallery today."

"Think about what I said, Zee."

"I will. See you Monday." Zelia hung up and went into the bathroom to take a long, hot shower. And if she needed to weep a little, no one was the wiser.

TWENTY-NINE

"Have you *lost* your mind?" Rick bellowed as he slammed his coffee mug down. The dark liquid sloshed out and formed small quivering puddles on the Formica tabletop. The middle-aged woman ensconced two booths down glanced over, her mouth twisted in disapproval. Her husband didn't look up from his scrambled eggs and toast.

"Do you know how many fucking laws you just broke?" Rick hissed through clenched teeth, leaning forward, palms flat on the table as if he were considering vaulting over it to wrap his hands around Gabe's neck.

His brother had just gotten off a stakeout and didn't look good. Clearly hadn't slept, hadn't shaven, his eyes bloodshot and red-rimmed. Probably not the best time to ask a favor, but he and Zelia had a plane to catch that afternoon.

Best to try to lighten the mood. Rick's

always better when he's laughing. "I didn't know they had laws about fucking —" Gabe said.

"Don't even think," Rick spit out, "about pulling that erudite, intellectual bullshit wordplay with me, you smug bastard."

Well, that worked well.

Gabe sighed. "It was a *joke,* Rick. When'd you lose your sense of humor?" Gabe was glad he'd asked for a booth at the back of the diner. His brother seemed to be having difficulty keeping his voice down and looked ready to blow a gasket.

"Around the time you told me you'd blacked out several security cameras, disabled an alarm system —"

"And did a damned good job of it, too," Gabe said, feeling oddly proud, which was messed up and would require further thought.

"You committed a ten twenty-one, a ten twenty-two . . ." Two of Rick's fingers were now thrust in Gabe's face.

"Stop with the numbers," Gabe said, leaning back against the burgundy vinyl booth seat and taking a slurp of coffee. "Yes, I'll cop to the B&E, but as for the larceny? We can return the laptop once we've gone through it."

"Don't. Just don't." At least Rick wasn't

shouting anymore. Sounded weary instead. "There's all sorts of ways they can trace it to you. Electronic fingerprints, mail tracking, DNA —"

"We'd wear gloves —"

"The woman is dead. She doesn't need the damn thing, and returning the computer could draw attention to you, complicate things."

"Okay, no biggie. We won't return the laptop."

"You know how to do computer forensics?"

"My guy does."

"Your guy?"

"Yeah. Mitch Clarke. I dropped the laptop off this morning. He helped me on numerous books. Met him way back in the early days, when I was researching *Deadly Kindness.*"

"And you trust him to keep his mouth shut?"

"Absolutely."

Neither of them spoke for a moment. Rick slipped his hand under his glasses and pinched the bridge of his nose, a habit of his when he was stressed.

"I know breaking into the Feinstein gallery wasn't my finest moment —"

"You *think*?" Rick said. He exhaled heavily.

The waitress arrived at their table and dropped a honking platter of greasy breakfast food in front of Rick. "Sure you're good with just coffee, love?" she asked Gabe.

"Yep. Thanks," Gabe replied, watching Rick slice into his eggs, yellow yolks spilling over the whites, mopping up the goo with a triangle of toast. "Were you able to dig up anything on the Richard Rye and Winnie Efford deaths?"

"I'm waiting to hear back from the Portland precinct. I pulled the Richard Rye file. Haven't had a chance to look through it yet."

"Appreciate it." Eggs, sausage, crispy bacon, and home fries were flying off his brother's plate and disappearing into his bottomless stomach, the whole concoction washed down with an exorbitant amount of coffee.

"Damn, I was hungry," Rick said after five minutes of concentrated eating. He leaned back, stretched his arms, and locked them behind his head. He looked in much better spirits. "How are Mom and Dad?" He smirked.

"You dickhead." Gabe launched a packet of sugar at his brother. "You knew they were flying to Solace Island, didn't you?"

Rick caught the packet midair and plopped it back into the sugar bowl. "Who do you think drove them to the airport?" He grinned. "Besides, didn't want you to dissuade them from making the trip. They've been on the warpath. Want me married with a gaggle of kids."

An image of Zelia round with his baby popped into Gabe's mind, and a feeling of fierce longing swept through him. "Wouldn't be so bad."

"It would be a nightmare. Anyway. I'm glad to have the parents out of New York for a while. It's been hell since Dad retired. He's become such a busybody with his matchmaking schemes, poking his nose into everybody's business. Hopefully, micromanaging you and the renovation of the hotel will keep him occupied for a while."

"Yeah. Thanks a lot, little brother. You always were a pest," Gabe said. They both laughed. "So, you'll run the fingerprints through the Integrated Automated Fingerprints Identification System for me?"

Rick sighed, held out his hand. "All right," he said. "Give them to me. If they are readable, I'll run them."

Gabe removed the sealed envelopes containing the latent fingerprints from his bag and slid them over to his brother along with two paper bags.

Rick scowled. "What are these?" he said, jerking his chin toward the bags.

"I also need you to see if you can get anything off this needle, port, and tubing. I couldn't lift any fingerprints, which seems odd."

"It might not be connected."

"I know. But why are there no prints? There should be trace blood on the needle. And I'm wondering if the DNA matches with this lipstick Zelia found under the leather love seat in the deceased's office."

"Even if your hunch is correct and the woman was murdered, this" — he gestured to the pile of sealed envelopes and paper bags on the table between them — "might not be admissible in court. Both you and Zelia would need to attend a hearing with the judge on the case outside the presence of the jury. The judge would then determine whether or not the evidence had been correctly gathered or if it had been compromised by —"

"Give me a break. The scene was already compromised when the Greenwich Police Department, in their infinite wisdom, ruled Alexus's death an overdose."

"Be that as it may —"

"Zelia needs answers."

His brother tried the death stare on him. It didn't work.

Rick sighed. Ran his hands wearily through his hair. "Fine." He looked haggard. "I'll see what I can get. But, Gabe . . ."

"Yeah?"

"I know you meant well, helping this chick out, but seriously, dude. You're a *writer,* for Christ's sake. You've got to trust me when I tell you, you are *not* cut out for this. Leave the sleuth work to the professionals."

THIRTY

A heavy rain had been thundering down, keeping the Saturday art browsers at home, snug under their down comforters or nestled in front of wood-burning fires with mugs of warm beverages and a slew of good books.

Not a single person had entered the gallery all day, and if the deluge continued, Mary didn't imagine anyone would. She'd kept herself busy trying not to worry about Zelia. She updated the computer, deleted old files, and sorted through the constant barrage of artist queries that arrived daily. She answered the majority, inserting the artist's name in their standard form letter rejection. A few garnered a personal response. Every once in a while she would come across true talent, and those she'd place in a file for Zelia to look over.

When she heard the front door swing open, she was more than happy to exit the office and stretch her legs a little.

A slender man in his early thirties was entering the gallery. He shook the rain off his large black umbrella and onto the floor, then shut and secured it.

Really? Would it have killed you to shake it off under the awning outside? She smiled. *Probably. Entitlement seemed to be bred into the man. Ah well,* she thought wryly. *That's what mops are for.* She couldn't really fault him. That could have been her not so long ago. Marching along her merry little life, believing in happily-ever-afters, taking all the privileges life had gifted her for granted.

She sighed. *No sense crying over spilled milk,* she told herself sternly, and tugged her focus back to the present.

The man's umbrella was quite unique. *Perhaps it was custom made?* Seemed more solid than the regular run-of-the-mill. The engraved knob handle seemed Victorian inspired and was made with a high-quality gold. *Looks quite dramatic, but gold isn't light. It must be heavy as hell.*

The man obviously wasn't from Solace Island. Not because of the umbrella. She could think of at least half a dozen local residents who would seriously lust after that umbrella. It was everything else about him that screamed old money and city chic. He was wearing a double-breasted, slim-cut

221

gray suit that looked to be cashmere, a crisp white shirt, a knotted striped tie, and dark-framed glasses.

Mary was tempted to say, *Rabid fan of the Kingsmen movies, much?*

She didn't.

She smiled politely. "Hello," she said. "Welcome to Art Expressions."

He swiveled to look at her. His motions were graceful, and yet there was something odd about them. *It's almost as if he were an extremely refined robotic clone of a human,* she thought, smothering a smile.

He wasn't tall — five eight max. His excessively perfect eyebrows were raised, as if the sound of her voice had surprised him. Shocked him even.

"Sorry. I didn't mean to startle you. Feel free to take a look around."

He didn't answer. Just looked at her with his head tilted slightly to the side. His slim, elegant fingers were moving restlessly, tracing the floral pattern on the golden knob of his umbrella.

There was something in his gaze that made Mary feel off-balance, uncomfortable. She took a step back, then another, but he closed the gap. He was staring at her intently. His eyes had an unfocused look, almost as if he were sleepwalking. Mary wasn't sure what to do. This guy was circling her now, as if she were up on an auction block. "Tatiana?" he whispered. He almost looked teary-eyed.

"Pardon?"

"You colored your hair."

Mary tried to smother a sudden flash of fear. "Right. Well, if you have any questions," she said, retreating a step farther, "please let me know."

He blinked once, twice.

"Oh . . ." he said, shaking his head as if she'd somehow let him down. "We're playing that game, are we?"

The guy was clearly unhinged. Mary didn't bother replying, just smiled politely.

He rapped the point of his umbrella on the floor, the crack of sound making her jump. "Fine. Hello there, whoever you are," he said, breezily gesturing to the side as if encompassing her and a crowd of twenty. His mouth was a mocking moue, as if to say, *Happy now?* "I've come for my Michael Lowdon painting, *Below the Surface.*" His voice was smooth, melodious. "I fear I've arrived earlier than expected. Unforeseen circumstances . . ." The end of his sentence was an elegant shrug, as the outer edges of his lips lifted in a smile.

There was an echo of something familiar

in that smile. Flashed her back to a memory she had worked hard to suppress for the last three years. It took a second to regain her equilibrium. *Now is not the time to freak out. Kevin is on the other side of the country. Thinks you are dead. You are safe. No one knows who you really are.* She forced her mind back to the present. *What did this gentleman just say? The Michael Lowdon painting,* Below the Surface. *Who was the purchaser? Focus, woman.*

"Mr. Guillory?" she said, plucking a name from the recesses of her brain, hoping it was the correct one.

He nodded. "Yes. Guillory."

Relief washed through her. He was a customer, an art collector, in which case weirdness was often par for the course.

"But we both know you can do better than that," he said, a gentle correction, as if she were remiss in not remembering his given name as well.

Pompous prick. "It's a pleasure to meet you in person," she replied with a gracious smile. "I don't blame you for deciding to come early. Solace Island is so lovely and not too crowded at this time of year. Is this your first visit?"

"Yes. I'd been meaning to come for some time. Your boss and I have some unfinished business, but alas, work got in the way." He sighed bemusedly. "Ah well. I'm here now."

"I'll wrap your purchase. Will be right back." Listening must not be his strong suit because she could hear him following her through the gallery to the office. The sound of his footsteps was accompanied by the staccato of the tip of his umbrella striking the floor.

She stopped. She didn't want to be rude, but the idea of being trapped in the small confines of the office with him made her uneasy.

"If you'd like to wander through the town, have a coffee and a delicious slice of pie at the Intrepid Café, or browse through the shops, I can hold the painting for pickup later in the day."

"In the rain?" He arched an eyebrow. "Oh no, my dear, you should know better than that. I am not a waterfowl. Nor am I the sort of person who walks around town carrying parcels. No. I would like you to deliver my painting within the hour." He stepped past her into the office and pulled a Mont Blanc fountain pen from his pocket. "Some paper, please," he said, looking at her expectantly. "I'm staying at the marina, which is remarkably dreary with all this rain. Ah well. Needs must. I will write the boat slip number and the yacht's name down for you so you'll know where to bring it."

"Fine," she said, shoulders set as she stepped into the office. There was no way in hell she was going to deliver that painting. "We have a wonderful local delivery service, very reliable." She rounded the desk, bent down, and pulled open the drawer. "I'll call and have Scott send someone over." She reached for a sheet of paper.

"Oh no," she heard him say, his voice languid, almost dreamlike. "Tati, that will never do. We have much to discuss."

There was something about his tone that jerked her gaze upward to lock with his — the glittery intensity she saw in his eyes froze and trapped her. *Move. Run. Take flight!* Her internal voice screamed at her, but it was too late. As she lunged for the door, a flash of gold arced downward, the golden knob smashing into the back of her head. Pain. Blinding pain. She managed to stagger one more step before she was swallowed by the darkness, the sound of his soft laugh echoing around her.

THIRTY-ONE

Gabe pulled to a stop in front of Zelia's darkened cottage and shifted into park. "Thanks for the ride," Zelia said, and then winced. *Hopefully he knows I'm talking about the ride from the airport and not the ride where he'd been buried deep inside me,* she thought as she hastily exited the SUV.

Damn. He'd gotten out as well. *Don't want him to think you're inviting him in for another round of baby-making pleasure.*

She could see him in her peripheral vision rounding the vehicle as she yanked open the rear passenger door and grabbed her bag.

Too late. He was beside her now.

"You want to tell me what's going on?" Gabe asked.

"Nothing."

He huffed out a laugh. Did not look amused.

"Nothing. Is. Going on," she said, feeling

grouchy at him, which wasn't fair. It wasn't his fault that she hadn't thought things through.

"Bullshit. You've barely spoken two words to me the whole trip back. If you're pissed off that I left this morning, I already explained to you —"

"I'm *not* pissed off," Zelia cut in. "I'm grateful your brother's running the fingerprints and stuff. Thank you for doing that." She could feel a wet trickle of rain making its way down the nape of her neck, her bag heavy in her hand. "I'm just tired. It's been a long trip." She forced herself to look him in the eyes.

"So, I take it you don't want me to come in?"

"No." She recoiled backward a step. If she let Gabe into her house there was no way she'd allow him to leave the premises before he fucked her brains out. "God no." She regretted the harshness of her tone, her choice of words the instant they left her lips. Had to close her eyes briefly to shut out the flicker of hurt she saw flash across his face.

When she reopened her eyes, the vulnerability was gone. His face looked as if it had been carved from a block of granite.

"Got it," he said. Steel shutters had dropped over his eyes as he stepped away.

"Gabe," she said softly, reaching out for him, wanting to soothe, make things better. But she was talking to air, because he'd already rounded the SUV and was getting inside.

She made herself turn and walk up her front steps, could hear him start the engine, the gravel spitting as his vehicle peeled out. She inserted her key in the lock on her front door, thinking of Gabe and how he'd refitted his godmother's house. Couldn't help glancing over her shoulder as she turned the key to watch the red taillights of his vehicle turn out of her drive and disappear into the night.

Thirty-Two

He paced beside her inert body, his hands fluttering anxiously. Once his two burly crew members had deposited his "new carpet purchase" on the floor of the master bedroom, they'd departed. He'd hastily scampered to the door and locked it behind them. Pulled down the blinds in case another boat was passing and the occupants happened to gaze in. Then he quickly unrolled his present. He didn't want her to suffocate. Didn't want her fragile lungs to have to breathe musty carpet air a second longer than necessary. It might aggravate her asthma.

She'd been breathing normally, which was a relief. There had been none of the discoloration around the nose and mouth that sometimes occurred during her bad asthma bouts. However, she'd appeared to be sleeping. *Maybe her brain had to shut down to accommodate the shock of seeing me after all these years,* he'd thought. *Let her rest. We can talk later.*

But here it was several hours later, and still she wouldn't wake up.

"I'd only meant to disable you briefly," he said as he knelt beside her. The purloined carpet under his knees was a jarring note of color that clashed with the serene decor in the master suite of his yacht. "If only you had agreed to deliver the painting, I wouldn't have had to take such drastic measures," he explained softly as he gently placed two fingers against her carotid artery.

Her pulse was still steady and strong. He smoothed her hair back from her face. It was Tati. He *knew* it. She might have been hiding, but he had seen past her disguise. Had clocked the tilt of her nose the second he'd caught sight of her standing in the gallery like a long-lost dream. And then, when she'd approached him, looking cautious and wary — and rightfully so, because she didn't know the whole story — when she approached, he could see the familiar cornflower-blue eyes of their ancestors hiding behind the dark frames of her glasses. Once she was standing before him, he could see with his keen artist's eye that the mousy brown color that covered the bulk of her hair was due to cheap hair dye. The beginning roots of natural blond were just starting to show. That was when he *knew* for sure. No woman would voluntarily cover glorious Scandinavian blond for mousy brown unless she was on the run.

He squeezed his eyes shut, overcome with emotion. *She didn't die in the fire. Thank God.* He felt like the weight he'd been carrying for the last fifteen years had been lifted, but another sorrow had quickly taken its place. A pain had lodged itself in his chest with the knowledge that his beloved sister, Tati, had been running from him for all these years. Only one explanation for that: she must think him a monster. Hadn't heard his side of the story. Didn't know how their mother had mocked and belittled him when she'd discovered the portrait of her he'd spent months refining. She'd flipped into crazy mode. "Ugly!" "Disgusting!" Screaming like a banshee. "You're a no-talent hack!" Slashing the canvas of his precious painting into ribbons with a butcher knife while he'd wept. Then the bitch had gathered the tattered remains and marched down the wide circular staircase, past the library where his father was ensconced, reading the *Wall Street Journal* and sipping his martini. Father hadn't even looked up as they had flown past, his son trying to explain that his art wasn't *supposed* to be realistically rendered, that its very ugliness *made* it beautiful.

But there was no talking with her. Never had been. Mother had made a bonfire out of his painstaking work in the hand-carved marble fireplace.

In hindsight, that's where she had made her fatal miscalculation. She should have listened. Discussed the portrait like a reasonable human being. But no, to her he was a helpless child to be tortured and tormented by whatever whim took her fancy.

No more. At sixteen years old, he might have been "a scrawny underdeveloped runt," but under the skin he was a man full grown. Mother had been stupid to drop the knife on the hearth while she knelt to light the fire, stupider still to leave it there while she cavorted around the flames like a fucking witch. Laughing hard. Her mouth opened wide as if she were an anaconda hoping to swallow him whole, derogatory laughter spewing out like toxic waste, wounding deeper than any beating ever had. And then he noticed through blurred eyes — almost as if hypnotized — that past the gold fillings in her molars, past her bobbing uvula, the perfect target was waiting. Right there at the back of her throat.

How surprised she had been.

He smiled. *Who's laughing now?* The shock in Mother's eyes, and dare he say it, respect, too, in that final moment before she breathed her last.

He'd manned up. Done what needed to be done. Didn't have a choice. If one finds a cockroach in one's kitchen, it needs to be squashed. Father had been an unfortunate casualty. Perhaps he'd deserved what he got, for never choosing his children's emotional health and physical well-being over placating his bitch of a wife.

However, Tati? He shook his head. For years he'd had no one to blame but himself for Tati's passing. But now he had discovered that by some miracle Tati had escaped the fire and was *alive* and well, and he was inordinately grateful.

There was a light rap on the door, startling him slightly. "Sir." Fredrick's discreet voice came through the African cherry door with the amboyna burl accent panels. "Chef informed me that whenever you are ready, dinner would be served."

He pressed his hands together, the sides of his forefingers against his lips, his mind spinning. *What to do?* He couldn't leave Tati lying on the floor, curled on her side in that

234

loose fetal position. She was too heavy for him to manage alone. *If only she had woken up.*

Another rap. A little louder this time. "Sir?"

His butler had been with the family as far back as he could remember. A constant ballast in an ever-changing world. After the house fire, many members of the staff had chosen to take employment in other households. Frightened perhaps by the unsubstantiated rumors. But not Fredrick. He had stayed, loyal and true.

"Fredrick?"

"Yes, sir." Fredrick's mournful baritone reminded him of a distant foghorn at sea. Comforting.

"Are you alone?"

"Yes, sir."

He unlocked the door and opened it a crack. There was no one visible over Fredrick's dark-suit-clad shoulder. "I need your help," he whispered. "And a vow of absolute secrecy."

"Sir." There was an odd hitch to Fredrick's voice, as if he were wounded. "Have I ever shown you less-than-unwavering fidelity?"

"Right." He took another quick glance down the hall, then opened the door a hair more and stepped aside so Fredrick could enter. "Come in," he said. Once Fredrick was inside, he reshut the door and locked it. When he turned back to the room, he could see Fredrick standing stock-still, the color draining from his face as he stared down at Tati's inert body, the gash on her head, scarlet against her mousy brown hair and pale skin.

"What have you done?" Fredrick's voice sounded lower than normal, as if roughened by sorrow. Fredrick dragged his hound-dog eyes away from Tati to look into his. Only for a second and then Fredrick's gaze lowered, his eyelids drooping to half-mast, his hands clasping before him as if he were a monk ready to participate in a walking meditation.

"It's Tatiana," he said, even though an explanation was redundant. Clearly anyone who had known Tati would *know* that this was her, all grown-up.

"Are you sure, sir?" Fredrick asked gently, his voice neutral.

"Of course I'm sure," he replied impatiently. "You can't see her eyes because they are closed, but they are the exact same color."

"Blue is not an uncommon color —"

"Look here." He dropped to his knees and

pushed her hair back from her forehead. "What do you see?"

"An unconscious woman who needs help."

"That's not what I'm talking about," he said, batting Fredrick's reply aside. "Yes, I *know* she's unconscious. That's why you're here. I'm unable to move her to the bed on my own."

Fredrick took a step back. "Sir," he said, shaking his head. "I'm sorry, but I —"

"Not for *that.*" He had to laugh. Even with the grimness of the situation, the horrified expression on Fredrick's face was quite comical. "God, Fredrick. What kind of animal do you think I am? She's my sister, for Christ's sake. I'm not planning on ravishing her. I need you to help me lift her to the bed so she'll be more comfortable," he explained, the epitome of patience. He gestured for Fredrick to come closer. "But look here. See her hair? See these blond roots coming in? Why would she do that? Who else do we know who had hair this color?"

Fredrick sighed heavily. "Miss Tatiana?"

"Yes, my good man!" He clapped Fredrick on the shoulder. "Miss Tatiana! Now, help me, will you? You take her shoulders and I'll take her feet. Ready? One . . . two . . . three . . . lift!"

237

With the two of them it was an easy thing to get her situated on the bed. She looked much more relaxed lying there.

"And this wound on her head, sir?" he heard Fredrick ask as the good man dabbed a wet washcloth on Tati's pale brow, attempting to remove dried trickles of blood. "How did that happen?"

"Ah. Well," he said, avoiding Fredrick's eyes, moving into his dressing room to change into a clean shirt. "I ran into Tati in town. What a reunion! She wanted to see the boat. Unfortunately, she tripped and fell while she was looking around. Hit her head on the corner of the bedframe." He could see Fredrick's reflection in the mirror, bent over Tati and looking quite distraught. "Don't worry. She'll be fine. Her pulse is strong. Tati will wake up soon and tell you herself. She's going to be so very pleased to see you, Fredrick. You wait and see."

He exited the dressing room, straightening his cuffs. "By the way, I've decided I don't want to be moored at the dock. I need a break from the hustle and bustle of the marina. The noise coming from the other boats might disturb Tati." He walked to the bed where his sister was resting, placed a kiss on his fingertips, and then gently touched her forehead. "Tell the captain I'd like him to anchor in a nice quiet cove. Nearby, so the town of Comfort is easily accessible by tender."

THIRTY-THREE

Zelia stared out her kitchen window, mug
of tea in one hand and the remains of her
buttery cinnamon-sugar toast in the other.
The rain had continued throughout Sunday
and into the night, which had suited her
mood. Zelia had used the foul weather to
catch up on her housework. Did the laun-
dry, ironing, unloaded the dishwasher,
dusted, vacuumed, and mopped, all the
while turning the Gabe conundrum over
and over in her mind. Evening fell. Her cottage was spotless and still clarity had not
arrived like a chorus of angels.

She had hoped the clouds would have
blown out, but Monday morning had arrived and rain was still thundering down.
She hadn't slept well. The high winds and
heavy rain had sent small broken branches
and loosened pine cones plummeting onto
her roof. The thumps, bumps, and howling
wind kept her on edge, ensuring her sleep

was fractured. With each thump came the worry that one of the larger branches might snap off the tall Douglas firs that stood like sentinels on either side of her cottage. It didn't help matters that in the dark hours of the night her mind continued to veer back to the situation with Gabe, unable to settle on a solution. Yes, the desire for a child was still there, even with the complications Mary had mentioned. More troubling was that her body, having tasted him, was gluttonously hungry for more. Even getting into bed, the feel of her practical cotton sheets gliding against her body reminded Zelia of his touch. Making her legs restless, her body hot, needy, and wanting.

Zelia pushed her hip away from the counter, popped the last bite of toast in her mouth, enjoying the crunch and the buttery, cinnamon goodness. She downed the last of her tea and placed her mug in the sink. *If you were wise,* she thought, *you'd take the car, to give you some protection from the storm.* But with her brain swirling around the baby-making issue, she felt the need to burn off some energy. She donned her long raincoat, rain boots, and hat and headed out the door. She gave Old Faithful her daily pat on the hood before heading down the driveway, all the while thinking about Gabe and how much she longed for his touch.

Nicolò was leaning against the doorway of his pasta shop, tucked under the dripping awning, taking a puff on his vape cigarette pen, his latest attempt to wean himself off the tar ones. *"Ciao, Zelia,"* Nicolò called as she sloshed past. "*Sei pazzo.* Why you walk in such dreary weather?"

"Exercise," she replied.

"If it's exercise you want, *bella,* I am free tonight. I could make you dinner, turn on some music, and dance?" he said, throwing in a few free-form dance steps as a way to entice.

"Thanks, Nicolò," she said, his antics pulling forth a laugh. "But I already have plans." Suddenly she had an image of Gabe's naked, hard body poised over her as he thrust his cock inside her, stretching her, filling her . . . She felt her face flush and her body heat, despite the cold and rain.

"Oh! What's on the agenda? My evenings are so boring, it makes me want to weep. Maybe you take pity, make room for one more?"

Eww . . . "No. I really don't think that would work," Zelia said hastily, putting her legs in motion. "Sorry, Nicolò. See you around."

"Wait," Nicolò called. "Before you leave, I wanted to ask what carpet cleaning service you use."

Zelia paused midstep. "Pardon?"

"Carpet cleaning service," he repeated, like he was making any sense at all.

"Ah. Yes," Zelia said, nodding. *Must be a language miscommunication.* "Don't have one," she said politely, and continued on her way.

The back door of the gallery wasn't shut properly or locked, which was weird, because Mary was the one who insisted it always be locked. Before Mary started working for her, Zelia would leave the back door unlatched. When her arms were full of packing material it made runs to the dumpster easier, deliveries, too.

Maybe living on Solace Island has finally softened Mary's vigilant need to batten down the hatches. Wouldn't that be something?

"Hey, Mary," Zelia called as she stepped over the threshold. She slipped out of her raincoat, held the garment outside the door, and shook the droplets off. "I'm back from the big bad city." She repeated the process with her rain hat, then shut and locked the door, stepped out of her rubber boots, and tucked them in the closet. "I've been giving

243

our conversation a lot of thought," she called over her shoulder as she removed her beloved pair of sling-back leather pumps from her bag and slipped them on. She liked the whimsy of the dark blue shoe with its cream kitten heel and tan piping. Was especially fond of the unexpected choice of the pale tangerine strap, sole, and interior that topped it off. "At the time I found myself resisting what you had to say, but it was important for me to hear. I know it wasn't easy, and I appreciate your honesty."

No answer.

"Mary?"

Silence.

The bathroom door was cracked open. No one was in there. The blinds were pulled up in the office. Zelia could see through the window that it was unoccupied.

"Mary?" Zelia moved through the main portion of the gallery to the loft staircase. She took the stairs two at a time, hoping to see Mary's smiling face, earbuds in, bebopping to music while assembling a new piece.

The feeling of tension in her belly was building, but she wasn't sure why. *It's probably the aftereffects of the last few days.*

She arrived at the top of the stairs.

No Mary.

You didn't check the storage room. She

went down the stairs, through the back room, down another set of stairs into the basement. The door to the storage room was locked, the padlock in place. If Mary were in there, the lock would be open and sitting on the file cabinet.

Zelia stared at the door. A shiver ran through her. *Oh my God. I hope she's okay. She hasn't come to some harm, has she?* The taste of fear was coating her throat, making it hard to breathe. *Nonsense,* she told herself sternly. *Buck up, Zee. You're jumping at shadows. This is not the first time you've found the gallery unoccupied. Mary is a good worker, but sometimes she's a flake.* She looked down at her hands. *So why am I shaking? You are* shivering *because you're wet. It was the height of stupidity to get soaked to the bone because you fancied a walk.*

Zelia forced herself to take the stairs back to the main gallery one at a time at a sedate pace. The place felt cold. She checked the temperature. It was normal at seventy degrees.

Maybe Mary had to leave, locked the front door and forgot she'd left the back open.

Zelia checked the front door of the gallery.

It was unlocked, too.

She pushed the door open, stood in the doorway, and scanned the parking lot. Her stomach had constricted into a hard knot. *All right, Zee. You've got two choices. You can either allow yourself to be engulfed by this irrational fear, or you can look at the facts. Mary has done this before. Why are you searching for some kind of cockamamie explanation for her behavior?* Zelia shook her head, suddenly pissed. It was one thing for Mary to go on a bender, or whatever the hell it was that Mary got up to when she would drop off the map. But to check out when Zelia *wasn't* in town and *she'd* been left in charge? *That's pushing the bounds of friendship just a little too far.*

The minute Zelia had the uncharitable thought, she felt guilty and backtracked. *Maybe there's a good reason. Maybe Mary got in early and went on a quick coffee run?*

Zelia rubbed her hands over her face, suddenly weary. Even so, to leave the gallery unattended and the doors unlocked was inexcusable. Someone could have waltzed in and cleared the place out, bankrupting Zelia in the process. *I can't run a business like this.*

THIRTY-FOUR

Gabe had spent Sunday slogging through the slew of data Mitch was e-mailing him. Mitch was a little OCD, which was one of the things that made him so excellent at his job. However, the never-ending barrage of information landing in his in-box was rather like an undertow had grabbed Gabe by the ankle and yanked him out to sea.

Every now and then Gabe would take stretch breaks. Occasionally he'd mix things up and wander to the front window and gaze out. A luxury yacht had dropped anchor in the cove. The interior lights had gone out a little after midnight, but he could still see its dark silhouette bobbing on the water, every once in a while capturing a strand of moonlight when there was a break in the clouds.

Mostly, however, he would find himself staring out the back window at the moonlit sculptures, wondering where he'd gone wrong. What was the misstep? Why had Zelia recoiled from his offer to stay? He'd spent hours racking his brain to no avail. Then he'd dive back into the rabbit hole of data on Alexus, while consuming the offerings of the minibar. At one point Gabe had attempted to work on his manuscript, but everything that came out was crap and had to be deleted. That was the problem with taking a couple days off from writing. It took that long again to wiggle his way back into the story. It wasn't until the night sky started to lighten that his brain was sufficiently anesthetized to allow him to collapse in exhaustion.

When he awoke, he felt like shit. He needed to eat something to help combat the ravages of last night's excesses. Splitting headache, sandpaper eyes, and his mouth feeling as if he'd slept with a gym sock stuffed in it. He fumbled for the hotel phone on the bedside table. Dialed the dining room.

"Hello," he croaked. "This is Gabe Conaghan in the Hampstead Cottage. I'd like to order some breakfast."

"I'm sorry, sir," the voice on the phone replied. "Breakfast service ended several hours ago." The person didn't sound sorry at all. Sounded bloody cheerful about the fact.

"What time is it?"

"One thirty, give or take a minute or two."

"Fine. I'll order something from the lunch menu. I'll have some toast, ginger tea, and . . . Do you have chicken noodle soup?"

"We don't serve lunch in the winter months, sir. Just a shortened breakfast service and dinner of course. Would you like to make a reservation for tonight?"

Gabe stifled an oath. "No thanks," he said in a reasonably civilized tone and managed to hang up the phone without slamming the receiver down. That was another thing he would recommend his father rectify during the Mansfield Manor overhaul, the lousy room-service hours.

By the time he'd brushed his teeth, showered, downed a Nespresso and a bag of potato chips from the minibar, he felt a little more human.

The front porch of his room was in clear view of his parents' cottage and, as much as he loved them, he needed time to get his bearings. He stuck his notes and computer in his satchel and slung it over his shoulder. He would go to the Intrepid Café, park himself in a corner table, get some food, and perhaps fit in a few hours of writing.

He scanned his room and chose a window on the far side, out of view of his parents' cottage. He opened the window and stuck his head out, took a quick glance around. The coast was clear. He swung one leg over the windowsill, then the other, and dropped to the ground, his satchel hugged to his chest to protect the computer. He was feeling pretty good, despite the headache. Couldn't help grinning. *I'm no longer watching life through my window. I'm jumping out of it. An odd thing to feel proud of,* he mused. *Basically, you're a thirty-six-year-old man who just leapt out a hotel window to avoid the possibility of running into your parents.* Chastising himself only made the ludicrous feeling of joy expand.

Once he was safely in the shelter of the trees and heading down the stairs, laughter escaped. He almost felt as if he were channeling Troy Masters. Granted, the man was a figment of his imagination, a character in his book. *However, a spur-of-the-moment trip with a beautiful woman, disabling an alarm system, breaking into a building, the hottest lovemaking session of your life, sneaking out of your own hotel room . . .* He shook his head. *Good God, Gabe, what's next?*

The image of Zelia's shuttered face from Saturday dropped into his mind. She'd

looked so unhappy.
Right. What would Masters do?

THIRTY-FIVE

"I can't," Zelia moaned, her fingers flying on her keyboard. "I'm swamped." Her hair had loosened from its clasp, and tendrils were tumbling around her face.

Gabe leaned against the doorframe of her office, enjoying the view. "How long has it been since you've eaten?"

"I had a piece of toast this morning."

"That's it?"

She slapped her hands down on the desk. "Gabe," she said, clearly trying to keep a rein on her temper. "I know you mean well, but I can't just waltz out the door in the middle of my workday."

"You don't eat lunch?"

"Not today."

"Are you on a diet?"

She hit send with more force than was warranted, then pushed back from the desk and scowled at him, her eyes narrowed. "Are you calling me fat?"

He took a half step back. "No. God no. I love your body."

Zelia's gaze dropped, and her shoulders slumped. "Sorry. It's been a lousy morning and I'm taking it out on you. I know I need to lose a good forty pounds —"

"Are you nuts?" Gabe broke in. "You're perfection just the way you are. I love your luscious curves, your silky-soft skin, the glorious texture and the creamy color that's brushed with a hint of peach. If you lost forty pounds you'd be skin and bones."

"Don't be ridiculous. I'd be the weight I was in college."

"Well, you were too skinny then."

"Didn't seem to bother you. If I recall, you mentioned something about falling for me back then."

"I fell for you in *spite* of you being too skinny. It was your *joie de vivre* that pole-axed me, the glow in your eyes, the curve of your lip —"

"Anyway." Zelia blew out a breath, her cheeks puffing up and then deflating. "As much as I'm enjoying this pointless argument, lunch is out of the question. I have work to do."

Gabe turned and headed for the closet by the back door. "I'm not going to let you blow me off," he called over his shoulder as he opened the closet and removed her raincoat. "Mary can watch the shop for an hour while you grab a bite to eat."

Zelia had risen from the desk and was standing in the office doorway, her eyes weary. "She's not here."

Zelia's raincoat was soaked through. She'd probably get a chill donning it. "When's she getting back?"

"I don't know."

Gabe felt his eyebrows rise. "You don't know?"

Zelia rolled her shoulders as if trying to dispel unwanted tension. "It's the cost of running a business on Solace." Her teeth worried her lower lip. "Sometimes employees" — she exhaled shakily — "even the good ones, occasionally flake out." She shrugged, feigning a nonchalance she didn't feel. "So, it's up to me to hold down the fort solo." Gabe opened his mouth, probably to protest, but Zelia cut him off at the pass. "Believe me," she said, keeping her voice and her hand steady. "When Mary shows up tomorrow — or whenever the hell it is that she decides to waltz through that door — we are going to have a serious conversation. I am well aware that it is not okay for her to leave me in the lurch like this."

THIRTY-SIX

"Tati. Come on, Tati. Time to wake up . . ."

Mary could feel someone patting her cheeks, his voice tugging her upward out of the darkness.

"That's right." It was a man's voice, smooth and melodious. She had heard that voice before. *Where?* "That's a good girl. Come on now. Open your eyes."

Her head was throbbing. She turned her face into the pillow. *Pillow. I must be in bed. But why is a man in my bedroom?* Her eyes flew open. A slender blond-haired, blue-eyed man was bent over her. He appeared to be in his thirties. He was smiling at her. "Tati," he said, his long, cool fingers stroking her face. *Who the hell is he?* He looked relieved. Happy. Shy. *Why?* Her gaze darted past him, taking in the room over his shoulder. None of it familiar. The sound of rain was loud on the roof.

"Where am I?" She frowned, confused.

255

Her voice sounded croaky from disuse.

"On my boat," the blond man said.

A boat. That's why the room was rocking.

"*Our* boat." He smiled again. There was something about his smile that reminded her of a little lost boy. "I'm so glad I found you."

"Oh," she said, and then the memory assailed her. He'd been in the gallery. The unease she'd felt. Seeing the flash of gold out of the corner of her eye before the heavy knob of his umbrella made contact with her head. "Oh Jesus," she murmured. "In trouble. Big trouble." Then the pain wrapped its arms around her and pulled her under again.

THIRTY-SEVEN

"This is the problem with going to the Intrepid Café when ravenously hungry," Gabe said as he pulled a veritable feast from a large brown paper bag and placed it on the small table in the back room of the gallery. "I overbought." He shook his head in bemusement, dislodging some of the raindrops that had gathered from his tramp through the rain. He never went overboard like this. "So, take what you like. Don't be shy. We've got" — he pulled some more cardboard containers from the bag and flipped the lids open — "piping-hot turkey mushroom pie with a flaky crust. A delectable ham and cheddar croissant with some kind of chutney, or an albacore smoked tuna salad with vinaigrette, if one is in the mood for something lighter." As he removed the round containers from the bottom of the bag and took off the lids, the delicious smells were making his mouth water. "Two

257

creamy tomato soups." He unwrapped the little white pouch, revealing crackers. "With Parmesan crisps, and if that isn't impressive enough" — he grinned at Zelia, rattling the second bag at her — "I also purchased several desserts."

"You're crazy, you know that?" She was pretending to be disapproving of his excesses, but he could see the corners of her mouth reluctantly quirked upward as she turned and walked to the drinks station, the sway of her gorgeous hips singing their siren's song. "I'll get us some cutlery and plates. Do you want something to drink? Tea? Coffee? Espresso?"

You, he thought. *I want you.* "Coffee would be great, thanks. Black."

She must have heard something in his voice because she glanced over her shoulder at him. Her gaze slid down to his crotch, taking in the swollen state of him, and her cheeks flushed.

Her lips parted slightly, as if catching her breath, the tip of her tongue moistened her lips, and he went from swollen to rock hard.

She swallowed, her gaze rising to meet his, caught. He could see her pupils dilating, making the stormy ocean-blue gray of her irises a thin band around the black. Primal-hot need was arcing between them like an electrical current.

He wasn't sure who moved first, or if they had moved toward each other in unison, beginning to rip clothes off themselves and each other. Her hot mouth latched onto his, her fingers running through his rain-slickened hair, tongues tangling. Her blouse half unbuttoned, shoved down to her waist, the front-hook bra was easily managed, her abundant breasts spilling into his hands, her skin silky smooth, her nipples taut.

"My God, Zelia, you're so fucking gorgeous." Her hands had somehow freed him and were wrapped around his hot, hard length, stroking up and over in a twisting move that was about to make his head explode. He started to tug her skirt up, but she dropped to her knees and wrapped her warm, wet mouth around him, her hand continuing to glide and twist, up and over, her lips making room for her hand and then diving back down, sucking him deep into her throat. He watched, mesmerized as his thick, hard cock glistened slick and wet as it drove into her welcoming mouth, her lashes fanning across her cheeks, a slight humming noise arising as if nothing made her happier than the taste of him.

"Jesus, woman," he moaned, gathering her hair in his fist, tilting her head back slightly so he could get a better view of her face, of his ruddy stiff cock disappearing between her ruby-red lips. The movement of her head was causing her glorious breasts to undulate, the upturned peach nipples ruched and wanting his touch. Keeping his cock thrust forward into the embrace of her mouth, he reached his free hand down and cradled one of her breasts, playing with the nipple, squeezing it slightly, which caused her to squirm and moan.

The front door of the gallery chimed.

He froze. "Shit," he whispered. "Zelia. Someone's here."

She lifted her mouth from his throbbing cock. "Then you'd better be quick and quiet," she whispered, a dare in her eyes and a naughty curve to her lips. Then she engulfed him in her hot mouth, deep down into her throat. Her enclosed hand twisted down to the base of his shaft, her other hand cupping his balls. Then her fingers traveled even farther, to stroke the spot between his balls and his asshole.

"Hello," a woman's voice called, just as Gabe's head jerked back and an explosive, knee-weakening orgasm started to slam through him. He tried to pull out, not wanting to drown her, but her greedy mouth followed him, drinking up every last drop while his cock emptied its load down her throat.

When the pulsing in his cock stopped, she rocked back on her heels and grinned up at him, her lips, her chin slick with his come.

You slay me, he mouthed, undone by how goddamned beautiful she was, her face glowing at him, luminescent as the moon.

He heard another voice. Lower. A man. Footsteps. "Anyone here?"

Zelia, still grinning, obviously quite pleased with herself, dragged her forearm across her mouth, removing the gleam of his come, her eyes dancing with merriment. "Be with you in a minute," she called as she rose to her feet. It took her only a couple of seconds to straighten her clothes, and then she sailed through the doorway into the front of the gallery, back straight, head high, regal, like a queen.

The food was cold by the time her customers had left, but she had sold one of Kendrick's sculptures so all was well with the world. Having indulged in impromptu oral sex with a handsome hunk? Well, that was an added bonus that made her slick and wanting when her mind alighted on the memory.

She scraped the last crumbs of the lemon

drizzle cake off her plate with the side of her fork. "So good." The perfect balance of tart and sweet. "Thanks for lunch. That was lovely."

"My pleasure," Gabe drawled, a slight smile on his lips, his eyelids at half-mast. "Am happy to oblige, anytime, day or night."

"Okay, okay." It was remarkable how seeing him had lifted her spirits. "Away you go. I've work to do."

"I can help."

"Thanks for the offer, but not necessary. I can manage and you've got a book to write."

He got to his feet, poetry in motion. "Want to grab dinner after work?"

She hesitated. Mary's cautioning started traipsing through her mind, and on the heels of that came anger. "I'd love to," she said defiantly.

THIRTY-EIGHT

Mary kept her lashes lowered, her body still. She knew how to do that. Make herself small, invisible. The blond man was talking to a tall, gloomy-faced man through a crack in the door. He seemed agitated. *What was his name?*

"No, Fredrick. I told you. A doctor is not necessary."

Guillory. Mr. Guillory. And he called her Tati. *Why? Who is Tati?*

"Send him away," Guillory hissed, then shut the door and latched it.

She could hear the sound of two male voices murmuring softly in the hall, the words indistinct, not penetrating through the glossy burled-wood door. Their voices were further muffled by the sound of the blond man pacing back and forth and muttering. "Idiot. What an imbecile." Beyond that she thought she could hear the sound of footsteps retreating.

There was another rap on the door, which caused her to flinch. Luckily, Guillory had spun toward the door and hadn't noticed. She could see him though, and the violent expression on his face caused a tremor of terror to ripple through her. Her husband, Kevin, had looked like that right before his fists would crash down, or that final time, when he'd drawn back his steel-toed boot and launched it like a baby-seeking missile into her belly, over and over.

"Sir." The voice came through the door again. "A moment please. I need to clarify."

Guillory didn't answer. Just stared at the door, eyes intense, unblinking, lips in a feral snarl.

"I'm alone, sir," the voice pleaded. "I sent the physician to the aft deck to enjoy a light meal and a glass of wine. You see, sir, he's not local. I had the helicopter pick him up from Seattle."

She saw the blond man's posture soften.

"No one knows he is here," the voice through the door continued. "*He* doesn't even know where he is, sir. I was very discreet. However, the woman" — she could hear him pause, clear his throat — "Tati, she is still unconscious, and I was worried, sir. Very worried."

"Oh, Fredrick" — the blond man moved

forward and unlocked the door — "I'm so sorry. I never should have doubted you. Come in. Come in."

The gloomy-faced gentleman entered the room. Mary couldn't risk him noticing she was awake, so she gently lowered her eyelids the rest of the way, keeping her breathing slow and even.

"I didn't realize you were so worried," she heard the blond man say. "I would have told you immediately. Around fifty minutes ago Tati woke up."

"She did?"

"Only for a brief moment. But she opened her eyes. We spoke."

"What did she say?"

"She wanted to know where she was. She seemed surprised to see me, but happy, too. She's going to be okay, Fredrick. I know it. It's such a relief to have my baby sister back in my life. Like a dream come true."

"Yes, sir. I'm very happy for you. What a blessing." But there was some other emotion in Fredrick's voice. Mary could hear the subtle notes of it. Something hidden.

One thing she was certain of. Until she found a way to escape, she must play along. Above all else, she must be extremely careful not to arouse the deadly violence that seethed just beneath his skin.

THIRTY-NINE

It wasn't until the wee hours of the morning — after they had made love two more times, slow and sweet, skin against skin, without any protection, and had collapsed in a sweaty tangle of limbs — that Zelia was wrenched from her sleep, fear thick in her mouth. An image of her bare office floor kept appearing, over and over again, like one of those old record players when a vinyl had a scratch. She'd tug her mind away only to have it return to the image. "Why?"

"Why what?" Gabe murmured, a warm voice in the dark, lulling her away from the image, back to her bedroom.

She lay back down, snuggling into the comfort of his arms, inhaling the clean male smell of him. He felt so right. As if she'd found a box containing the missing pieces to a puzzle that she had given up on a long time ago. "I had a bad dream."

"What about?" he asked, pushing to his

elbow, moonlight on his face, eyes tender.

"I don't remember. It has mostly faded." His fingers were trailing through her hair, gliding gently over her scalp, calming her mind. "Just an image remains. My office. The floor bare." A small puff of a partial laugh escaped. "I know it doesn't sound like much, but I woke really scared."

His fingers continued their peaceful caress, pulling her toward sleep again. "Maybe your subconscious is trying to tell you something."

She smiled in the darkness. "Or maybe it was only a dream."

"Either way, I'll go with you to work tomorrow morning. We can sit in your office and see if anything arises."

They were standing in Zelia's office. Her arms were crossed over her chest, her hands resting on her shoulders, which were slightly hunched, as if she were cold. She'd been subdued ever since they'd arrived at the gallery and it had become clear that Mary hadn't returned to work yet. Zelia's teeth were worrying her lower lip again.

"Anything jump out at you?" Gabe asked.

She took a glance around. "Not really."

"Walk me through yesterday morning."

Zelia blew out a breath, long and slow, as

if centering herself. She dropped her hands so they were tucked into the crooks of her elbows, arms still wrapped around her chest. "When I arrived at the gallery, I noticed the back door was unlocked and slightly ajar. I walked through the building. She wasn't here. Fine. 'Went for coffee,' I thought. Then I came into the office," she said, gesturing toward the room. Her voice seemed pretty calm, but he could see a slight quiver in her hand. "The first thing that struck me was that the desk chair was against the far wall instead of in front of the desk. 'That's odd,' I thought. Then I looked down and noticed the rug was missing."

"The rug?"

She nodded.

"You didn't tell me that yesterday."

He could see her mouth tighten as if try-ing to hold words back.

He waited.

"I didn't want you to think badly of her. I was hoping she would come back, that my rug would be in place, and she'd have a reasonable explanation as to why she was gone."

"And she still might."

"I just . . . I don't want to cause trouble for her. I decided a missing rug isn't that important."

"Maybe it isn't." He shrugged, keeping his manner casual, but alarm bells were ringing. "But maybe it is. You dreamed about it. Sometimes when I'm working on a book, characters show up in my dreams and lead me to unexpected places. Have you gone through the gallery? Is anything else missing?"

"No. Not that I'm aware of. Just the rug."

"How big was it?"

"I don't know the exact proportions, eight by ten maybe. It covered most of the floor."

"Was it expensive?" he asked.

Zelia shook her head, her expression adamant. "I know what you're thinking. Mary is no thief."

"Was it expensive?" he repeated gently.

"Not in the grand scheme of things. It wasn't a flawless diamond and ruby necklace passed down through generations."

"So, the rug was expensive."

Zelia's gaze dropped from his, her eyes troubled. She nodded. "The rug was a splurge." She reminded Gabe of a helium balloon the morning after a party, ribbon dragging on the floor, ebullience gone. "But she wouldn't . . ." She trailed off, her lip caught between her teeth. Then she straightened her shoulders, lifted her chin. "Some of my previous employees, yes, I wouldn't be shocked to discover they had absconded with goods, but Mary?" She seemed to be struggling with an internal debate. "I . . . I liked her." Sad. Disappointed.

"We should call the cops."

"No." Her head jerked up, eyes blazing. The word had shot out of her mouth like a bullet. "We leave the cops out of it."

"Zelia. Your employee has gone missing, along with an expensive rug. The police should be informed."

"I don't care about the rug. Mary will come back. She always does."

"She's disappeared before?"

Zelia gave a short nod. "It's only happened a few times and —"

"A few times?" Gabe couldn't believe his ears. "And you kept her on your books?"

Zelia thrust her chin out. "She's my friend and a damned good worker. Besides, I'm not convinced she stole my rug. Someone could have come in while the place was unlocked, knew rugs, and helped themselves to it. If Mary were going to steal something, why not grab the artwork? She knew what they were worth, could have easily walked away with a few select pieces and pocketed several hundred thousand dollars."

"Stolen art is difficult to unload —"

"She *didn't* take it." Zelia seemed to be

trying to convince herself, but he could see the traces of doubt in her eyes.

"So, where is she? And why is your rug missing?"

"I don't know."

FORTY

Even with her eyes shut Mary knew exactly where he was in the room. Didn't matter if he was in motion or absolutely still, it was as if her sixth sense had kicked into high gear. Right now he was lounging in the armchair, just sitting there, watching her. It was creepy.

If she could have, she would've stayed there on the bed pretending to sleep, but she had to pee something fierce. She pushed to a seated position and swung her legs around, her feet on the floor. Her shoes had been removed, and her feet were bare.

She kept her gaze averted, but still, she felt him lean forward in his chair.

"You're awake." He sounded joyful. She felt him start to rise to his feet.

Head still tilted away, she thrust her palm out, stopping his upward momentum. "I need to use . . . the bathroom," she rasped.

"Right." He sat down again.

She stood. Her legs felt shaky. Her head hurt. "Where is it?" She swayed slightly. He was up in a shot, his hand at her elbow, steadying her. Her instinct was to jerk her arm away, but she didn't. "Thank you. I can manage."

"You sure?"

"Yes."

Reluctantly, he released her. "The bathroom is through that door. If you'd like to shower there's a clean robe on the hook that you are welcome to use. I've ordered some clothes. They should arrive later today. Hope I got the sizes right." He smiled anxiously. "I had to guess, but as you probably remember, I'm pretty good at studying bodies."

What the hell does that mean? Panic flared, but she stuffed it down. He'd been looking at her while she was unconscious, estimating her weight, her size. Had removed her shoes. Had he touched her, too? Mary repressed a shudder. *No. He thinks you are his beloved sister. You need to keep it that way.* She was convinced her survival depended on it. "I'm sure the clothes will be fine." She headed toward the bathroom door, wanting to run, but keeping her movements calm and measured. She knew from experience that running showed weakness, labeled one as prey. "Thank you. That was very thoughtful of you." She stepped over the threshold, onto a white marble floor that was cold under her bare feet. She closed the door behind her, then leaned against the glossy, burled-wood surface, her heart beating hard. Slowly, she turned the lock until it had silently slipped into place. *His name. What was his given name? She'd need to find out in order to maintain the deception.*

"You'll need some sustenance," she heard him say. He'd moved and was standing on the other side of the door. "Any dietary restrictions?"

She straightened and stepped away, staring at it, staring at the lock, willing it to hold. But the door handle didn't budge. She listened, heart beating way too loud in the silence that had fallen.

"No. I eat everything." Her mouth was so dry, sticking her words to the roof of her mouth. "Thank you," she said.

"Very good. I'll have Chef whip something up." He rapped a pattern on the door. *Tap. Tap. Tap-tap-tap. Tappity-tap.* There was an expectant pause. "Remember that?" he asked.

Panic rising. *What the hell am I supposed to say?*

"Tati?"

"I . . . I really have to go."

He laughed, a carefree sound. "Right. Silly me! There will be plenty of time to reminisce later." She heard the sound of his footsteps crossing the bedroom, another door opening and then shutting solidly behind him.

Mary raced to the toilet. No sense trying to make a break for freedom when one's bladder was bursting. She did her business, quickly washed her hands, unlocked the bathroom door, and sprinted across the room. She listened at the door leading to the hall.

Silence.

She pulled the door handle downward and tugged.

Shit.

The door was locked.

She ran to the window and yanked back the curtains. The windows were sealed tight, but even if they had been the kind that opened, it was clear she could not escape through them. The Pacific Ocean was cold in February; hypothermia would set in long before she managed to reach the shore.

FORTY-ONE

Zelia was attempting to work on the layout of the new catalog but was having difficulty focusing. It might have had something to do with the large, powerful male who'd ensconced himself at the small table by the coffee station and was pounding away on his computer. Or it could have been that her unease over the events of the last week seemed to be intensifying.

She lifted the office phone receiver and dialed Mary's number again, hoping that this time she would pick up.

Ring . . . ring . . . ring . . . ring . . . ring . . . ring . . . ring . . . ring . . . ring . . . ring . . .

Frustrated, Zelia hung up. It was getting rather embarrassing, the amount of times she had called. She was like a bloody stalker. If she didn't fire Mary, the woman would probably quit once she got a look at her missed-call feed.

"No luck?"

Zelia's gaze jerked to the door. Gabe was leaning against the doorframe, rather like a large predatory animal waking from a nap. He tipped his head toward the phone. "I assume that was Mary you were calling?"

There was no need to answer. Apparently the damn man could read her mind. She turned to her computer screen and started fiddling with various fonts. Pointless really. She always used the same one. Totentanz. Branding and all.

"You're obviously stressed about her. Why don't we lock up and swing by her place?"

"I'm trying to run a business here." She didn't look away from her screen even though she wasn't actually seeing any of the images before her.

"We'll drive by. You can knock on her door. Make sure she's okay."

"Oh God." Zelia rose from her desk, hand on her mouth. "You're right. Mary might be sick." She raced past him to the coat closet. "Need help. Her phone battery's dead because she's been too ill and unable to get out of bed to charge it." Zelia yanked on her raincoat, kicked off her pumps, and shoved her feet into her boots. She ran back into the office and scribbled a message on a yellow Post-it, to place on the front door. She glanced over her shoulder at Gabe, who was watching her with an amused smile. "Well? What are you waiting for?" she demanded as she peeled the note off the pad. "Grab your coat. Pack up your stuff. We gotta go!"

FORTY-TWO

Zelia knocked harder on the door. She could hear the cat yowling inside even over the noise of the vacuum that the greasy-haired man was wielding at the opposite end of the narrow hall. "I don't understand," she said to Gabe, who was standing beside her, "why Mary chose to rent in this depressing apartment complex. There are so many cute cottages on the island that were available. Or at least she should've taken one of the units on the ground floor. She could've had a sliding glass door that led out to a little garden patio space. Sure, most of them looked scrappy, but with a little bit of care . . ."

The vacuum at the end of the hall switched off. The man yanked the plug from the outlet. The cord whipped into the body of the vacuum with a *thwack.* He grabbed the handle of the vacuum and stomped down the hall toward them, jowls and beer belly jiggling.

"Excuse me," Zelia said politely. "Are you the building manager?"

The man didn't even glance in their direction.

"Excuse me?" she said a little louder. "We're friends of Mary and we were —"
The man shuffled past.

"Sir?" Gabe reached out and clapped a hand on the man's shoulder.

"Huh?" The man jumped, clearly startled, and turned with a scowl. "Hands off. Hands off, young man. Or I'll give you what for." His gray caterpillar eyebrows were waggling in a threatening fashion.

"We don't mean any harm," Zelia said in a conciliatory manner. "We were hoping you could help us. I'm a friend of Mary's —"

His scowl left Gabe and was now focused solely on her. "What?" he barked, his head jutted forward like a snapping turtle. "Speak up!"

"I'm a friend of Mary's," Zelia said loudly. "She didn't show up for work and she's not answering her phone. We're concerned."

"For Pete's sake, why must the world mumble so?" He held up a stumpy finger. "Hold on a second." He stuffed his finger in the pocket of his shirt, fished out a gross-looking ancient hearing aid, and jammed it in his ear. The device emitted a few high-pitched squeals before settling down. "All right. Tell me what you're yammering about."

"I'm a friend of Mary's," Zelia said. "I'm also her employer. She didn't show up for work and she's not answering her phone. We're concerned."

"You're not the only one." The building manager cleared his nasal passages indignantly. "Rent was due two days ago and I haven't seen hide nor hair of Ms. Browning. Been getting an earful from the wife, who hadn't wanted to rent to her in the first place on account of her having no references. And now that damned cat of hers has been yowling up a storm and I've been getting complaints."

"I want to check on her. Make sure she's okay. Would you happen to have a master key —"

"Hey now," he interjected as his rheumy gaze traveled down Zelia's body. "I see what's happening here. Nice try. Wasn't born yesterday, you know. Get a motel."

"Why, *you* —" Zelia sucked in a lungful of air, preparing to give the old geezer a piece of her mind, but suddenly there was an unyielding solid wall of hard male between her and the source of her irritation.

"Fifteen minutes, sir," she heard Gabe say, his hand keeping her securely behind him. "Just need to take a quick look around to make sure Ms. Browning is still alive and breathing. If you are getting complaints about the cat, just think what sort of complaints you would get in a few days if things aren't on the up-and-up."

"What are you getting at?"

She could hear the suspicion in the old guy's voice.

"Have you ever smelled a decomposing body?" Gabe said politely. "I have. It's not something that's easy to forget."

"I'll have you know," the guy sputtered, "this is a high-class establishment. We don't allow dead bodies in our complex."

"I'm sure you don't," Gabe said soothingly. "And that's why it would be best if you let us check to make sure Ms. Browning is okay. That she hasn't fallen and is in need of medical attention. Here's a little something for your trouble."

Zelia peeked around Gabe, saw the old guy's hand close around a folded bill and slide it into his pocket. "Money?" Her voice squeaked a little. "You're *bribing* him to do what he should be doing out of common decency?"

"I'm thanking him," Gabe said, clear

warning in his voice. "For helping us."

"Out of the goodness of my heart," the old coot muttered as he thumbed through a plethora of keys on a large round key ring affixed to his belt loop with braided elastic cord.

Zelia snorted derisively, but she managed to keep her mouth shut.

"Here we go." The building manager inserted a key into the lock, opened the door. "I'll be back in fifteen minutes," he said to Gabe. "So you'd better be zipped up and ready to vacate."

"Go to h—" Suddenly the world tilted on its axis and Zelia found herself slung over Gabe's shoulder.

"Thanks," Gabe said, striding into the apartment. He kicked the door closed behind them and then placed her on her feet.

"That disgusting little worm." Zelia tugged her raincoat and skirt back into place and smoothed her hair out of her face. She huffed out a breath and set her chin. "Mary?" she called, just in case Mary was in the bathroom and hadn't been able to answer when they knocked on her door. "It's me, Zelia. I wanted to make sure you're okay."

There was no answer. She hadn't expected

one. The air felt still, like the apartment was waiting for Mary to return.

She started to step forward, when she heard a soft *thud* in Mary's bedroom. She froze in midstep. Her hand flew to the side and landed on Gabe's abdomen as if it were a seat belt holding him back from the windshield. It had been instinct, but now it rested there, plastered against the rock-hard warmth of his washboard abs. The muscular solidity of him was comforting. Made her feel safer.

"I heard something," she whispered.

An ancient, gray male tabby cat appeared around the corner and bolted toward them.

"Oh. It's the cat," Zelia said, her body relaxing.

"Mrrrouw . . ." the cat complained. Then he wove around Zelia's wet boots, leaving a smattering of gray hair in his wake.

"It's her cat, Charlie. She talks about him all the time." Zelia bent to pet him, but he dodged out of the way.

"Mrrrouw . . ." He padded a few steps back the way he came, tail erect, then looked over his shoulder at them. "Mrr-rouw . . ."

He seemed to be trying to tell her something. "What's he want?" she murmured. Charlie returned and nudged her with his

284

nose and then walked away again, pausing to look over his shoulder with his unblinking blue eyes.

"Mrrrouw . . ."

Zelia stepped toward the cat, who then turned and walked briskly into the kitchen area. Zelia followed apprehensively, not sure if the cat would lead her to Mary's inert body lying on the floor behind the island.

The floor was clear, which was a relief. She glanced at Gabe. "How much time do we have left?"

"Eleven minutes."

"I'll take a quick look around in her bedroom and bathroom."

She returned to Gabe's side a few minutes later. "She wasn't there," Zelia said. "Everything looks normal. No sign of struggle or disarray."

"You didn't see your rug anywhere?"

Zelia shook her head.

Gabe glanced around the room. "She didn't take her belongings, which means she wasn't planning to skip town."

"I know," Zelia said, a lump of worry in her belly. "So where the hell is she?"

"Mrrrouw . . ." Charlie wailed. He bumped his head rather forcefully against her leg and then padded back into the kitchen and leapt onto the counter.

"Charlie, get down from there." She followed him into the kitchen, scooped him up, and plopped him back on the floor. "I'm pretty sure that's not allowed." She turned back to Gabe. "Would you take a look through her bedroom as well? You might notice something that I missed."

"Sure." Gabe strode across the cramped living quarters and disappeared down the hall.

"Mrrrouw . . ." complained the cat as he leapt back onto the counter, his tail in the air.

"Charlie." Zelia reached for him, but he dodged out of the way and then rose onto his hind legs and batted the cupboard door with his paw. "Maybe you're hungry?" She opened the cupboard, and sure enough there were some stacked cans of cat food. Charlie launched into serious purring action that was vibrating his entire body as he rubbed against her.

"Okay, I get the hint." Zelia opened a can of cat food and dumped the contents into the empty cat dish on the floor by the fridge. It smelled very fishy. She grabbed the empty water bowl and was refilling it when Gabe reappeared.

"I checked the bedroom, bathroom, closets. There is no residual water in the shower, and the bar of soap is dry. Her toothbrush is as well. Of course, she might have decided not to shower or brush her teeth this morning."

Zelia shook her head. Charlie was practically doing a face-plant in his food. "I don't think she's been home for a while. There was no water in Charlie's dish. She jokes that he's a bit of a glutton, but I've never seen a cat gobble food this fast." She felt Gabe's hand alight on her shoulder.

"You okay?"

"No," she said, turning to him, stepping into the comfort of his arms. "I'm not. I'm scared shitless. Where is she? This is not normal for her. She loves Charlie. She would never skip town and leave him behind. Never." His hand was making soothing circles on her back. She leaned her head against his chest, grateful she wasn't alone.

"All right, you two," the building manager barked as the front door of the apartment crashed against the wall, startling the both of them. "Time's up!" the guy crowed gleefully. "Out you get. If you need another fifteen minutes, it'll cost another fifty."

"*Another* fifty?" Zelia sputtered.

The old guy leered. "Not my fault if the man has a slow trigger. You play. You pay."

"You gave this loathsome little toad fifty

dollars?" Zelia demanded.

"Aaand unless we want to give him fifty more," Gabe replied, scooping up the cat, "I suggest we vacate the premises."

"Hey now! What do you think you're doing with Ms. Browning's cat?"

"We are taking care of your noise problem," Gabe informed him.

"Cats don't come cheap," the guy said. "And that cat there looks like some kind of fancy purebred."

"You idiot," Zelia said, stalking to the kitchen cupboard and grabbing the cans of cat food. "She got this cat at the SPCA. It was a rescue that was going to be *put down* because *no one* wanted it."

He moved to block their exit, a mulish expression on his face. "Well, it seems your gentleman friend wants it. And me, bein' a man of business . . ."

Gabe removed a bill from his wallet. "Let's go," he said, ushering Zelia before him, Charlie yowling under his arm. Gabe looked at the building manager and raised an eyebrow. The old coot hitched up his trousers, wiped off his mouth with the back of his hand, and then stepped aside.

"A pleasure doing business with you, Gov," the building manager said when Gabe handed him the bill as they stepped past.

"You should be ashamed of yourself!" Zelia would have liked to give him a proper lecture, but she couldn't escape the firm grip Gabe had on her arm.

They were almost at the front door when Zelia heard the old guy call down the stairway, "You forgot to pay me for the cat food."

"Screw you, you *asshole*!" she bellowed, trying to jerk her arm free. "Gabe. Let. Go," she said through gritted teeth. Gabe did not oblige. He tugged her through the entry door, down the steps, and along the walkway. And once again, the two of them were at the mercy of the torrential downpour that had blanketed the island.

The icy rain was like a slap to the face, draining the rage out of her.

Zelia exhaled, trying to steady her breath. Adrenaline was still coursing through her, embarrassment, too. "Wow," she finally said, shaking her head. "I don't know what the hell came over me. I wanted to beat the crap outta that man. Don't laugh. I'm serious. I wanted to charge up those stairs and box his ears." She huffed out another breath. "Sorry about that." Zelia avoided Gabe's gaze as she reached for the yowling cat wedged under his arm like a football. "I don't normally flip out."

"Totally understandable. It's been a stressful time."

"And the guy was a dickhead," she said, opening her rain jacket and gently tucking Mary's cat inside.

"Yes." Gabe nodded solemnly, but his twinkling eyes gave him away. "The guy was a dickhead. But even dickheads don't deserve the fury you were about to unleash on him."

"Mm . . ." Zelia tilted her face forward to nuzzle the top of Charlie's furry head. The cat quieted, but his body was still shaking. "It's okay," she whispered. "Don't worry. We're gonna find her." It was comforting to have Charlie's warm body snuggled next to hers as they sloshed their way to Gabe's vehicle. Strapping in required a bit of maneuvering so she didn't squash the cat. Gabe started the engine. "What now?" she asked.

"I wish I had some answers for you, but we just seem to be accumulating more questions. Let's go back to the gallery and take a more thorough look around."

FORTY-THREE

The man he'd called Fredrick entered the bedroom carrying a tray. He had table linens tucked under his arm. The aromas drifting toward her made her mouth water. Mary wasn't sure how long she had been incapacitated, but from the hungry rumbles her stomach was making, it must have been a while.

"Ma'am." He shot a troubled look in her direction. "Where would you like to be served?"

"You don't have to serve me," Mary said, trying to put him at ease. "Just plop it on the dresser. I can help myself."

"I'm sorry. I . . . can't do that. This is a . . . quality household. There are standards that we, the staff, are expected to maintain."

"Oh. Sorry. Didn't want to make extra work for you is all."

The butler was standing stiffly by the door, waiting for her instructions.

"How about over there?" Mary gestured to a round side table by the armchair.

"Very well." Fredrick walked to the table, placed the tray down, and then moved the square squat vase of tightly packed white roses to the dresser.

"Thank you," she said. The butler seemed upset. She watched him lay a white linen place mat on the glossy wooden table, then set out a crisply folded napkin. "I was hoping you would help me?" she ventured, keeping her eyes downcast, her voice demure. She could see out of the corner of her eye the butler's body stiffen. "I appear to have bumped my head and my memory is off."

He didn't look over. Didn't reply. Just doggedly continued placing the silverware in their appropriate places.

"I don't seem to remember who I am." She shrugged as if embarrassed and managed a soft, wistful laugh. "Or who you all are for that matter. It's quite confusing. I was hoping you could give me a hint or two to jog my memory. Or maybe if you helped me get back to Solace Island, I'd be among familiar things and surroundings and my amnesia would lift?"

She waited, breathing shallowly, hoping. Praying.

His hands were shaking as he poured ice water into a crystal glass.

"Please . . ."

His gaze darted to the door; then he tipped his head slightly upward toward where the ceiling met the far wall.

Mary's gaze followed his. How had she missed that faint red dot of light? A camera. Recording her.

The butler shifted, bending his body so his back was to the camera as he picked the silver domed plate from the tray and set it in the center of the place mat. "I can't," he said in a hoarse whisper, using the clatter to camouflage his words. "You have no idea what you're dealing with here. You must be careful. Play along. Your very survival depends on it. Do you understand me?" Fear was emanating from his pores like a bitter perfume, making it difficult for Mary to breathe.

She gave a minuscule nod, keeping her face blank, like she wasn't freaking out, was just idly watching the dining preparations.

Good, he mouthed. Then he straightened abruptly, gave a slight tug to his waistcoat, adjusted his cuffs, his dispassionate butler's mask back in place. The only thing that gave him away was the barely visible, agitated rise and fall of his chest.

The butler lifted the silver dome. "Your meal is served," he intoned. He picked up the serving tray, inclining his head slightly, and glided toward the doorway. "Please ring if I can be of any further service."

He disappeared into the hall, closing the door firmly behind him.

She rose to her feet, her gaze fixed on the door handle, once again hoping, praying. *Please . . . please . . . please . . .* She took a quiet step forward, and then another, before she heard the scrape of the key locking her in.

FORTY-FOUR

"I need to grab a few things. I will be right back." Gabe switched off the SUV's engine, removed the key from his jeans pocket, and placed it in the cup holder. "In case you need to crack open a window or something."

Zelia nodded. She had a death grip on the jacket that was wrapped around Charlie. Gabe didn't blame her. The cat clearly was not a fan of riding in cars. The instant Gabe had started up the engine, the cat yowled and tried to claw his way up Zelia as if she were a telephone pole with a snapping German shepherd at her feet. Gabe had ripped open her raincoat and yanked the crazed cat out before it could do any more damage. Holding the spitting, clawing cat at arm's length, he'd peeled off his leather jacket and wrapped it tightly about the frightened bristle-furred cat. Zelia had laid her purse flat on her lap for added padding before she took the leather-bound cat back in her arms. Charlie had squirmed and yowled pitifully the entire drive to the Mansfield Manor. Judging from the quantity of gray cat hair that clung to Zelia's wet raincoat, it looked to Gabe as though stress had caused Charlie to lose his winter coat early.

When Gabe jogged down the wooden steps that led from the parking lot to the Mansfield Manor resort below, the cold cut through the thin fabric of his shirt. Fortunately, the rain was not as intense under the canopy of the tall evergreen trees that flanked the stairs. His mind was in overdrive as he sprinted down the pea-gravel path to his cottage, turning over the events of the last couple of days.

Once inside his room he crossed to the closet, pulled on a sweater, and grabbed the tool satchel he had purchased for their Feinstein & Co. foray. Probably too late to pick up any helpful fingerprints — too much time had passed and people had been entering and exiting the gallery — but it was worth a try.

"You're back."

He whirled around. His mom was standing in the doorway, beaming at him.

"I told you he was," Fergus said, huffing up the porch steps behind her. "I saw the lights were on in his room when I got up to pee."

"Yes, but that could have been the house-keeper." His mom crossed the room and wrapped him in a hug, his dad on her heels. Her blouse was damp from the rain.

"Ma," Gabe said. "You can't go running out in the rain. Where's your coat?" His dad wasn't wearing a jacket either. "Dad, you just got over a terrible cold. What on earth —"

"How was your trip, son?" Fergus thumped Gabe on the back, bumping into the satchel, causing the contents to rattle. "What do you have in here?" His dad poked the satchel with his gnarled forefinger.

"Fergus," his mother said, giving her husband a stern look and slapping his finger away from the bag. "Gabe is a grown man and is entitled to some privacy. Why you always have to poke your nose in everyone's business is beyond me."

"Don't you fall for her blarney, boy." Fergus chuckled. "The second your mother saw you run into your room, she yanked me out of my comfortable armchair. I was enjoying a nice hot toddy, minding my own business, reading peacefully by the fire."

"Reading? Ha! You were fast asleep, Fergus Alroy Conaghan." Alma turned to

Gabe. "Of course a mother would want to see her firstborn child after he's been away. There's no shame in that." She grabbed Gabe's hand. "My goodness. What happened here? You're bleeding."

Gabe glanced down. Shrugged. "Cat scratch."

"Oh dear. It could get infected. I've got alcohol wipes back in my room."

"Mom. Thanks, but it's really not necessary." Gabe gave her a kiss on the head. "Will catch up later. I gotta go."

"Why?" Fergus demanded. "We just arrived, and now you're running out the door. What's wrong with you? You want to break your mother's heart?"

"Seriously?" Gabe stared at his father incredulously. "You're going to pull that? It's been only three days. *Three* days!"

"At our age . . ." Fergus lifted his shoulders in a mournful shrug. "Those three days could have turned out to be all the time we had left before we shuffled off this mortal coil."

The interior of the car had gotten cold. The windshield had fogged. Zelia pulled her cell phone out and checked the time. Gabe said he was going to be right back, but almost twenty minutes had passed. *I'll give him five more minutes and then go down to see what's taking him so long.* She swiped open her phone screen. *Oh jeez.* A hundred and sixty-four e-mails were now waiting for a response on the artexpressionsgallery@gmail.com e-mail.

She clicked on the most recent one.

Hi there, Art Gallery owner,

"You gotta be kidding me," Zelia muttered as she switched her phone off and shoved it back into the depths of her purse. "This is the kind of thing that drives me nuts, Charlie. The idiot couldn't even be bothered to do a minuscule amount of research and insert my name in their stupid form letter." Charlie didn't answer. He was a cat, unversed in the finer points of the English language. "I miss Mary. You, too, I bet, huh? She feeds and cuddles you, but I think I win the who-misses-Mary-more contest. She's not only my friend, but she also heroically slogs through all these bloody e-mails for me, day in and day out. Oh God, where is she? I hope she's okay."

Zelia was grateful for the added warmth emanating from Charlie, who had finally settled and seemed to be sleeping. She flipped down the car's visor to check in the mirror the scratch damage Charlie's claws had caused, as her hand gently stroked his fur, as much to comfort herself as him.

A noise snapped her head up. Gabe opened the back door for his mom, the sound rousing Charlie from his nap.

Sorry, Gabe mouthed over Alma's head. He tipped his head toward his father, who was rounding the SUV, and rolled his eyes.

"Well, this is exciting," Alma chirped as she strapped herself in, excitement adding extra sparkle to her deep brown eyes. She reached forward and patted Zelia on the shoulder. "It's such a pleasure to see you again. I'm sorry about the circumstances, though. Hopefully nothing has gone awry and we'll arrive at your workplace, where your colleague will be waiting."

Zelia cast a questioning glance at Gabe, who shrugged wearily. "I wasn't able to shake them. Didn't want to leave you sitting in a cold car." He shut the door behind his mother.

"And right he was, too," Alma said approvingly as her son walked around the front of the car, got inside, and started up the engine. "Don't let the tough-guy exterior fool you, Zelia. Gabe is one of the sweetest men you'll ever meet."

Fergus leaned forward. "That's right," he

said, using the front-seat headrests to brace himself against the momentum of the SUV backing up. "Our boy is excellent marrying material."

"Mrrrouw!" Charlie wailed. His fur started rising, claws extending. Zelia quickly flattened her purse, hoisted the cat up, and plopped him on it, crooking her elbow so her arm was out of striking range.

"Makes a bloody fortune on those books and even better —"

Gabe shifted gears and their vehicle headed down the drive.

Charlie started making choking noises, as if he had swallowed a hairball, his body undulating.

"Oh dear," Zelia cried. "Something's wrong with the cat!" And then the entire contents of Charlie's stomach erupted out of his mouth. "Oh no." Zelia was torn between using her free hand to unroll the window, plug her nose, or try in any way possible to remove the warm vomit that was oozing down the side of her purse and into her raincoat-clad lap. The fishy smell of partially digested Salmon Delite was noxious.

She hit the window button, stuck her head out, and gasped in gulps of clean air. Scooped up what she could of the slimy goo with her hand and flung it out of the window. *Oh God.* Her hand was now covered in the disgusting stuff. *Best to leave my hand out the window until we arrive at the gallery and I can wash it off.* She sighed. *Maybe the rain will remove some.*

Alma leaned forward and tapped Zelia on the shoulder. "Here you go, dear," she said, handing Zelia a delicate lily-scented handkerchief with an embroidered sprig of flowers in one corner. A nice sentiment, but there was no way Zelia was going to use that small bit of feminine perfection to mop cat vomit.

"See, Gabe here has triple-A Conaghan blood running through his veins," Fergus continued, clapping Gabe on the shoulder, apparently unperturbed by the recent events or the smell of cat vomit that had filled the car. "Great genes and very powerful sperm —"

What the hell?! Zelia swung around and glared at Gabe. "Did you —"

"Dad," Gabe said warningly.

"That was private," she growled through clenched teeth, which made things more difficult because she was trying not to take in air through her nose.

"What's private?" Alma chirped.

As Gabe turned left onto the main road,

he glanced at Zelia. The look in his eyes was dead serious. He gave an imperceptible shake of his head, and then his expression smoothed over. "Zelia is quite right, Dad," he said, his tone casual, conversational. "It's not appropriate to talk about bodily functions, sperm, and whatnot. I do apologize, Zelia, for my father's lack of manners."

"What did I say?" Fergus said, looking slightly chagrined.

"For crying out loud, Fergus, sit back and curb your tongue," Alma said sternly.

"I'm just trying to help the boyo," Fergus muttered. "He's too shy. Won't brag about his merits."

"What you're doing is scaring her off," Zelia heard Alma whisper softly.

"But you want him married and a passel of grandbabies, darling," Fergus whispered loudly. "And I'm trying to get your dearest wish for you. If I don't meddle, we'll be dead and buried before the blessed event happens."

"Oh, Fergus . . ."

In the visor mirror Zelia saw Alma's hand rise and tenderly stroke Fergus's cheek. There was a lifetime of love in the gesture. Zelia needed to shut her eyes, block it out. She took a centering breath, then exhaled slowly. *Clearly Gabe didn't tell them about my crazy scheme. Thank goodness.* On the heels of relief came guilt. She could feel heat building behind her eyelids, because in that moment she knew her decision had been made. She would no longer be indulging in sweet, heartbreakingly tender baby-making sessions with their son.

FORTY-FIVE

Zelia washed the cat vomit from her rain-coat, cleaned her purse, and scrubbed her hands in hot water, allowing the scent of the lavender rosemary soap to fill and soothe her nostrils. Charlie had seemed overwhelmed, so she used a couple of hand towels to make him a cozy nest and set up the litter box that Alma had had the fore-sight to suggest they purchase. She put food and water out. But Charlie just looked at her blearily and twitched his tail as if to say, *Are you f— in' kidding me?*

Once the cat was settled, Zelia went into her office and sat down. She was going to systematically work her way through the room, starting with the desk, hoping to find a note or a clue as to where Mary had gone and why.

The office felt bare without the warmth of the rug. *Colder, too,* she thought as a shiver ran through her. She tapped on the keyboard, rousing the computer from sleep. Rather than entering her own password, she typed Mary's. The screen lit up and a partially finished e-mail to Otto appeared on Mary's desktop. *Was Mary interrupted midtask — a phone call, perhaps, or a customer? Was the person she was writing to at the time of any significance?*

She could hear Gabe, Fergus, and Alma walking through the gallery, the occasional sound of their voices. She was glad she wasn't alone.

We are searching for the proverbial needle in a haystack, she thought. *Best if I write down anything that seems different. Who knows what dots will connect?*

She reached down, pulled open the middle desk drawer to take a sheet of paper out. Instead of a smooth sheet of paper, her fingers landed on a crumpled one. *That's odd.* She glanced into the open drawer. *Oh shit.*

She bolted to her feet, the back of her knees bumping the seat of the chair. She could hear the sound of her heart banging in her ears, the chair's wheels behind her as it spun across the floor. "Gabe," she yelled, unable to wrench her eyes from the desk drawer. "Gabe!"

She heard the thunder of feet.

Gabe appeared in the doorway, his mother and father bringing up the rear. "What is it?"

"There." She pointed at the drawer. Her chest felt constricted. She couldn't seem to control the shaking of her finger. "There was a crumpled paper and there are brownish flecks . . ."

He was beside her now, his arm around her shoulders, steadying her.

"See those? I think they might be dried blood."

"I think you're right. You okay? You look pale."

"Mm-hm . . ." She wasn't okay. She might never be okay.

"Do you need some fresh air?"

"No. I can keep going."

"This was a very good find, Zelia." His hand was making soothing circles on her back. "But I think now it would be best if we called in the police."

307

FORTY-SIX

"I don't think we can," Zelia said, her eyes troubled.

Gabe was aware of his parents in the doorway watching avidly, his mother's hands clasped to her chest. She wore a similar expression when watching — for the millionth time — the make-out scene between her movie-star crush, Jack Nicholson, and Diane Keaton in *Something's Gotta Give.* He was going to need to talk to his mom. Didn't want her to get her hopes up.

"Mary was hiding something," Zelia continued. "She was always very distrustful of the police."

"Many people get nervous around the police, but that doesn't mean she wouldn't want you to call them," his mom piped in. "If you are right and those *are* blood splatters, foul play might have occurred."

"What if she'd just had a bloody nose?" Zelia said, clearly grasping at straws.

"It's possible," Alma conceded. "However, she could be in grave danger."

"I know. Calling the police would be my first instinct as well. But Mary's situation was complicated." She bit her lip, clearly wrestling with how much she should say. "She was in trouble. She covered it well, but I could feel her desperation shimmering below the skin . . ."

"Zee," Gabe said. "While I appreciate your loyalty to your friend, it is important to share as much information as possible if we are to have a fighting chance to figure out what happened to Mary."

Zelia's fingertips were pressed against her mouth, as if that would keep words from spilling out. He could see her waging an internal struggle. Finally, she blew out a breath, long and slow, and met his eyes dead-on. "Mary didn't have a social security number," she finally said in a monotone, her face grim. "Needed to be paid in cash. She hesitated before writing down her name on the application form. Hesitated again at her date of birth. I'm not even sure if Mary is her real name."

"And you decided it would be a good idea to *hire* her?"

"Don't bellow, son," his mother cut in. "Zelia has had a traumatic day —" Alma broke off, bent over slightly, her eyes narrowing. "Did you know there was some sort of lumpy thing under your desk?"

Both he and Zelia bent down and looked under the desk at the dark gray object that was tucked way back in the shadows.

"Oh no," Zelia said softly. "Mary's purse. She always carried it with her." She turned and looked at him. He could see the devastation in her eyes. "We had a running joke that that purse was her third arm." She crossed her arms, hunching over slightly. Her eyes squeezed shut as if that would keep the conflicting emotions contained.

The office was silent, just the sound of Zelia's shuddering breath. Then she straightened, threw her shoulders back, picked up the phone, and dialed 911.

FORTY-SEVEN

The food was stone cold by the time Mary ate it. She had held off as long as she could. When the butler had warned her to "be careful," she'd thought he was talking about his employer's rage issues. But as she was cutting into the steak, fear suddenly engulfed her. What if the food was drugged? Was that the warning? The butler had been placing the food on the table. She'd dropped her knife and fork and backed away from the table.

Eventually, hunger forced her to return. *If the food is drugged, so be it.* She was actually trembling as she scarfed the meal down. Great gulps of cold water, ice cubes clinking, bumping against her lips as she drained the glass, wanting more. There was a pot of tea. She drank that, too. Was eating the last of the fresh raspberry trifle when abdominal pain doubled her over.

"You're an idiot," she murmured as she

gingerly made her way to the bed and curled into a fetal position. *Was the food poisoned? Or did I just eat too quickly after breaking a fast?* Her eyes fluttered shut as she attempted to push back a wave of nausea. *It's possible. How long has it been since my last meal? Don't know. How long have I been here?*

Tears squeezed past her lashes as she wrapped her arms around her distended abdomen and tried to force her breath to deepen. Cold sweat coated her body and her face.

FORTY-EIGHT

Zelia watched as the older police officer placed Mary's purse into a brown paper bag, labeled it, and then plopped it in the box. It felt wrong to let them take her things, but they needed all the information they could find.

Brring . . . The phone on the desk rang, causing a jolt of adrenaline to shoot through her. She recentered herself before picking up the receiver. "Hello, Art Expressions Gallery. This is Zelia Thompson. How may I help you?"

There was a slight pause on the other end of the line. "Uh . . . Yes. My name is Eve Harris. We had an appointment today?"

"An appointment," Zelia repeated, trying to focus on what the woman on the other end of the line was saying. Her brain felt mushy, like it was on overload.

"Yes. At one p.m."

Oh. Damn.

"It's possible I wrote down the wrong day?"

"No. No, you didn't." She'd just stood up Eve Harris, the spectacularly gifted artist at the Intrepid Café. "I am *so* sorry!" She could feel a hot flush working its way up her neck toward her face. It didn't help matters that Zelia could feel the policemen's eyes on her. Her palms felt damp. Were they considering her as a possible suspect in Mary's disappearance? Her stomach lurched, and the heat in her cheeks and along her ears intensified. *You had better clarify why you are acting so guilty.* "So *very* sorry, Eve," she repeated, making sure her voice carried to the listening ears in the room, "that I missed my appointment to view your paintings."

"I'm still here if you'd like to come by," Eve said.

Double damn. "Unfortunately, I'm a little tied up right now." She was doing her best to pretend her office wasn't crawling with police. "Would it be possible to rebook for tomorrow?"

Another hesitation before Eve replied. "Sure. What time were you thinking?"

"Does nine a.m. work for you?"

"I'll make it work."

Zelia apologized once more and hung up

the phone, embarrassment lingering at having stood up Ms. Harris. This was *not* the way she liked to run her business.

There was another flash from the younger policeman's camera. The sudden harsh flare of intense light caused a slight panicky feeling in Zelia's chest.

There had been blood splatters on the floor beside the desk where the rug hadn't been, a couple more on the baseboard along the wall that needed to be documented. *How could I have missed blood splatters?* The taste of fear in her mouth was making it hard to breathe.

They need to know Mary was in hiding. It might be relevant to the case. She clasped her hands to stop their shaking. *I've been paying her under the table. If she's done something bad and is running from the law, that might make me an accomplice. Will they arrest me?*

Zelia cleared her throat, braced herself. "I need to tell you something." The older cop's faded blue eyes locked on hers. Her mouth was void of moisture, but somehow she managed to move her lips and get the words out. "I think Mary was in trouble. That she was on the run. She was scared and was very wary of law enforcement. She didn't have a social security number. I'm not sure

315

if Mary Browning is her real name." Zelia puffed up her cheeks and exhaled. "I was paying her under the table. I know that it's illegal, but she needed help and I didn't know what else to do."

The cop nodded. Didn't seem too perturbed. Didn't haul out his handcuffs and slap them on her. Picked up his pad and scribbled a few notes. "Okay. Notice anything else that might pertain to this case?"

"Her office rug is missing."

Zelia's gaze jerked up to Gabe, who was now lounging in the doorway. "Mary didn't," she enunciated, glaring at him. "Take. It."

"It's relevant," he said softly. "It vanished when she did."

"Can you describe the missing rug, please, ma'am?" the older cop said, his ink-stained thumb flipping to a fresh page.

She didn't answer.

The cop waited.

"She didn't steal it," she finally said.

"Duly noted. Can you give us a description?"

Zelia shut her eyes. She felt so torn.

"If we find the rug, we might find her." The cop's voice was matter-of-fact, but she thought she could hear compassion underneath the words.

"It was an eight-by-ten" — the words were slow to travel past her lips — "terra cotta and gold."

"Make?"

She sighed heavily. "It was an antique Serapi rug, but I would put money on the fact that she didn't . . . Wait a minute!" She whirled to face Gabe. "Nicolò! That morning when I walked past his shop, he asked me what rug cleaning service I used. I didn't know what the heck he was talking about. Thought it was a language thing. Oh my God. I *knew* she didn't steal it." She turned to the policemen. "Nicolò said to me, 'What rug cleaning service do you use?' Not, 'I saw Mary loading your rug into a van.'"

"Nicolò?" the older cop said, looking from Gabe to Zelia.

"He has the pasta shop across the square," she replied. "Do you want me to ask him to come over?"

"We'll swing by his shop when we finish here."

FORTY-NINE

"How could I have forgotten Nicolò saying that about the carpet cleaning service?" Zelia scraped the minced shallots and garlic into the butter that was sizzling in a large pot. "What is wrong with my brain?"

"Could I venture a guess?" Gabe raised an eyebrow as he handed her a cold glass of pinot grigio. "You might have had a trifle on your mind, what with your friend being murdered, flying across the country, breaking into her office, starting a torrid affair, your assistant going —"

"We *aren't* having a torrid affair." She was stirring the garlic and shallots with more intensity than they deserved, her jaw set.

"Right," Gabe said carefully. "I stand corrected. Not a torrid affair. We are, however . . ." He paused, trying to figure out what the correct word would be. *Fucking? No. Bonking our brains out? Seriously? Okay, fine. Copulating? Are you kidding me? "Copu-*

lating" *sounds like we're a couple of chimpanzees on a National Geographic show.* "Having intimate relations on a frequent basis." He stifled a groan. *Christ. He sounded like he belonged in a bloody historical novel. "Intimate relations." Who the hell says that? Move on, Mr. Wordsmith.* "Anyway . . ." He clinked his wineglass against hers in an attempt to regain his footing. "Here's to whatever *it* is we are involved in, which hopefully will result in a beautiful, healthy baby."

Zelia flinched, as if a glug of ice-cold water had aggravated a new filling. "Um . . ." she said, and then poured her wine into the pot. Steam rose upward, infusing the air with the mingled smell of garlic, shallots, butter, and wine.

Right. He exhaled. *Alcohol and babies don't mix. What the hell were you thinking, handing her a glass of wine?*

Zelia still hadn't looked directly at him. She strode to the fridge and removed the bag of mussels they'd purchased on the way home. She returned to the stove, cut the bag open, dumped the mussels into the pot, and brought the lid down with a *clang.*

Even in profile, it was clear the joy that had infused Zelia's face every time they'd talked about a baby was missing.

"You're having second thoughts?"

She nodded.

"Ah . . ." He should be feeling relief. He hadn't planned on having children until after he was married. Had gotten swept up in the moment. In hindsight, he realized the conversation he'd overheard between his mom and his godmother might have influenced his decision-making process. He could also blame his rash offer on the alcohol that had been consumed that night. But if he were being truthful, it was the sheer pleasure of being in Zelia's company, combined with the sorrow he could see in her eyes, that had caused the words to drop out of his mouth.

Even more surprising was that he hadn't backed down. Hadn't wanted to.

He, who was famous for mapping everything out, for thoughtful contemplation of all sides of a situation before moving forward, had offered to impregnate a woman he barely knew. Not only that, but with no strings attached.

If anyone who knew him had overheard that evening's conversation with Zelia they would have been dumbfounded. He'd been rather shocked himself when his brain had managed to compute what he had just said.

And yet he'd moved forward, made love

with her several times. For that's what it had been. Making love. Not fucking, or clinically depositing sperm into a woman who needed it. *He* had been making love. Deep, true, and committed to the core. He hadn't realized the depth of his feelings, had miscalculated how powerfully those feelings had been reawakened after a decade of lying dormant. Hadn't counted on the desire that gradually, over the last week, had wrapped its silken strands around him, drawing him ever and ever closer. He hadn't realized that in spite of the linear, mathematical exterior he had fortified to dazzle the world with, underneath beat the heart of a romantic fool who believed in love at first sight and happily-ever-after. *Jesus.*

He tipped his head back and drained his wineglass.

"You okay?" he heard her ask.

He couldn't look at her yet. Too much would show in his eyes. "Yeah, sure," he said, busying himself with refilling his glass, disappointment weakening his knees.

He'd convinced himself he was doing her a random act of kindness. But once he'd had her up against the wall, his cock buried deep inside her, the realization had struck him like a bolt of lightning. There was nothing evolved or enlightened about what he

321

was doing. All his years of university, intellectual pursuits, and cerebral conversations with like-minded people were nothing but a front. A cheaply made suit that would tear at the slightest provocation and reveal the primitive roots of his cavemen ancestors lurking beneath. She was his mate. The other half he had been searching for. If she wanted a baby, he wanted to be the man to impregnate her. But more than that, he wanted to be at her side, to watch her belly swell with their offspring. He wanted to help feed and take care of them, to love them and watch them grow.

"Don't get me wrong." She placed her hand on his forearm.

He knew he had it bad when even an innocuous contact like that — especially given that she was blowing him off — sent heat straight to his groin.

"I think it was very generous of you to offer to . . . assist me."

"I did more than offer," he growled.

"Yes, well." She flushed a deep rose and waved her hand in front of herself as if shooing away a wasp. "I . . ." She cleared her throat as she donned potholders and gave the covered pot a shake. "I appreciate your efforts."

"My efforts?" he repeated, feeling quite

grim. Good God. Was that why she was slamming the door in his face? He sucked in bed? Jesus. He'd always thought of himself as a good lover. Never had any complaints. Clearly, he'd been delusional. The two nights they had spent together had been mind-blowing experiences for him. He'd assumed that they had been for her as well.

He watched her remove two bowls from the cupboard and place them by the stovetop. It took him a moment to recenter himself after that body blow. He tried to think through the problem rationally. Was he willing to walk away from Zelia without trying to change her mind?

No.

She lifted the lid of the pot and peeked inside, fragrant steam wafting out. "It's ready." She removed the potholders and ladled the steaming-hot mussels into the bowls, then sprinkled some fresh parsley over the top.

Well, then, you need to fix this. The tips of his ears and the back of his neck felt hot. "Perhaps with shared conversation and experimentation, where you let me know your preferences, what feels good, what doesn't, what kind of pressure you like, I can improve my . . . 'efforts.'"

"No, no, no." Now both of her hands were flying about as if the wasp had morphed into a swarm, tiny bits of parsley scattering. Her face couldn't get any redder. "It's not *that*! Good grief, man. You're the best fuck I've ever had. Seriously. No disrespect to Ned, because I loved him. But . . ." She trailed off, bit her lip, then plucked the two bowls off the counter and carried them to the table.

Okay, so maybe it was fucking for her, but at least her reticence isn't because I sucked in the sack. He felt the knot in his chest loosen slightly. He removed two forks from the silverware drawer, tucked the fresh baguette under his arm, and then sat down opposite her. She avoided his gaze as she slid the bowl of mussels over. "Thanks," he said, his mind turning over various reasons why she might have decided on a change of plan.

"I just . . ." She lifted her chin, meeting his eyes. "As I got to know you better, I realized it might be impossible for you to walk away from responsibility. Even though I'd given you carte blanche to do so." Her gray-blue eyes had darkened like the sea when a storm was overhead. "If I had a baby . . ." She looked so sad. "It would be a child of your blood. The baby might have your smile, your wavy dark hair, your methodical way of going about things, your mother's stubborn sweetness, and your father's twinkling eyes. And your parents, how do you think they'd feel to know there was a grandchild of theirs out in the world and they weren't involved in its life?"

It would devastate them. But he couldn't say that. Not if it would mean walking away from Zelia. "This isn't about them. It's our decision."

"Gabe." Her eyes were shiny with emotion. "Be honest. Even taking your parents out of the equation, would you really be able to impregnate me, walk away, and not look back?"

He jabbed his fork into a mussel, stuck it in his mouth, and chewed.

He wasn't talking. Neither was she. The room was quiet, as if it were holding its breath waiting for someone to break the silence. There was the sound of their forks scraping against shells, food being chewed, and the ticktock of her mother's clock sitting on the mantel.

Zelia poked at her food, feeling slightly ill.

When his bowl had been emptied, he pushed it to the side before shifting forward, resting his elbows on the table, his hands loosely clasped, tapping against his lips. "How would you feel . . . ?" His voice was casual. Nonchalant. His gaze was shuttered, eyelids at half-mast, a lock of hair tumbling forward onto his brow. She clenched her hands into fists to stop them from reaching out to smooth it.

He tipped his head slightly, as if by listening to her breathe he would know her answer to the question he hadn't finished forming yet. "About changing the initial plan?" He paused as if searching for a better word. "Refining it?"

"I'm not sure what you mean," she said, her heart pounding as if she were blindfolded and perched at the edge of a precipice.

FIFTY

Mary woke to someone stroking her head. She opened her eyes and there he was, lying on the bed next to her. The room was dark, but she could see him, propped up on his elbow, backlit by soft light spilling through the cracked-open bathroom door.

"You're awake," he said, smiling that little-boy smile at her again.

She shut her eyes, relief filling her. She wasn't dead. Hadn't been poisoned. She almost laughed at the extent of her paranoia. Yes. She was being held hostage. Why? She didn't know, but at least the food was elegantly prepared and apparently unlaced with poison.

"Yes," she said, attempting to smile. She needed to gain his trust, to be allowed a modicum of freedom if she was to have a chance at making an escape. "I'm awake."

He wasn't his usual impeccable self. There was a dab of paint on his cheek and he smelled of turpentine. Turpentine, paint, and something else she couldn't identify.

"How do you feel?"

She did a quick internal scan. "All right. All things considered."

"I wanted to show you something," he said, almost shyly. "You okay to walk?" He swung his legs off the bed, stood up, and held out his hand. There were paint splatters and smears on his hand as well.

She froze. Didn't want to touch him. He made her skin crawl. *A sister would accept assistance from her brother. Take his hand. Take it, you idiot!*

"I think so," she replied, her eyes cast down to hide her revulsion as she took his proffered hand and let him draw her to her feet.

FIFTY-ONE

"Marriage?" Zelia stared at him, clearly in shock. "Gabe," she finally said, carefully placing her fork on the table. "You aren't thinking rationally. You barely know me, for crying out loud." She kept her hand pressing into the handle as if the fork and the table beneath it were tethering her to the earth. "You have *years* to find the right person and fall in love. It would be crazy to commit to something like this." She shook her head, then compressed her lips as if steeling herself for a difficult task. "No. I can't let you do it. Guys don't have a ticking biological clock. Can have babies in their frikkin' eighties, for crying out loud. It's not fair."

"Interestingly," Gabe said, "there's a clock ticking for me as well. I just wasn't aware that it was." She shot him a skeptical look. "Seriously. I don't want to be an old father. I want to have the energy to run around with my kids, to teach them how to throw a baseball, shoot hoops, ice hockey, whatever."

"Hate to break it to you, Mr. Macho Man, but when you *do* decide to have a baby, the odds are fifty percent on having a girl."

"And?" He looked at her and arched an eyebrow. "My sisters played sports with relish. Went head-to-head with Rick and me." The image of a miniature Zelia flashed through his mind, with her tumbling, spun-amber curls, the hidden dimples that peeked out only when her smile had reached full force, her strong nose, her intelligent gaze. "I'd love to have a daughter, and hopefully she'd look like you."

"Like me?"

"Don't make that face. Any girl would be blessed to take after you. You see, Zelia." He leaned across the table, took her hands in his, and it felt so right. "Once we embarked on your madcap scheme, I realized that I wanted to start a family, too. Not just with anyone. I think you'd be a marvelous mother. Now, I know you've made it clear you weren't looking for a partner. That your heart is still tied up with Ned, but" — he pressed his fist to his chest to ease the ache that had arrived with the words — "I was thinking that since he's no longer an option . . ." His voice trailed off at the stricken look on her face.

"Gabe . . . I just —" She was shaking her head. Looked sad, weary.

"It's okay," he said. Jumping in before she felt the need to name the million ways in which Ned had been everything Gabe wasn't. "I understand. But I want you to know that I'd like to make this a real relationship. Both feet in."

She pulled her hands away, crossed her arms, her jaw set as if steeling herself for bad news. "This is not the type of decision you can make with a snap of the fingers. It would have long-reaching implications that require careful consideration."

"I've never been more sure of anything in my life," he said, and the rightness of that statement calmed the turmoil in him. It was strange how his universe had shifted on its axis. He'd been moving through life, almost as if he were a hovercraft, never quite making contact with the ground. He wanted more now. He craved connection. "This isn't just about a baby anymore. I'm crazy for *you,* Zee. We're good together. You want to get married? Okay. No marriage? That's fine, too. Whatever form this" — he circled his hand between the two of them — "takes on. I'm telling you, I'd be there one hundred percent, solidly committed to you, and as a father to our child."

"Whatever may come?" she said, looking at him skeptically. "Poop, vomit, sleepless nights, hormonal swings, the terrible twos? Being called into the principal's office when you're in the middle of writing? Teenagers sneaking off to a drunken beach party?"

"Zelia. Whatever may come."

She studied his face, eyes narrowed as if by looking long enough she would discover hidden clues. Then she jerked her gaze away. "No." She ripped off a bite-sized piece of baguette. "I can't . . . It's very generous, but . . . I can't."

He opened his mouth to speak, but her hand cut the space in the air between them.

"Uh-uh." She shook her head emphatically. "I don't want to hear it." She swirled the bread into the juice at the bottom of her bowl, then stuck it in her mouth, chewed, and swallowed. She ripped off another piece, her face tense. "You'll thank me for this later."

FIFTY-TWO

"What do you think?" He nudged his sister playfully in the ribs. Tati had been struck speechless at the sight of his beautiful half-finished masterpiece drying on the easel. "Say something," he prompted, because she was just standing there in his studio as if the magnificence of what she was beholding had turned her legs to stone. Her hand was clasped to her mouth in an attempt to smother her exclamations of astonishment and joy.

She blinked slowly, as if trying to awaken from a dream. "It's you," she whispered.

He hadn't realized that was what he was waiting for until he heard the words. "Yes!" he cried out, sweeping her into an enormous hug, spinning around so her feet left the ground like he used to do when they were young. "You get it! My art *is* me. It is *so* me! You understand, Tati. You always have, like no one else in this godforsaken world."

He pulled back, thumped his fist against his chest, blinking away the unexpected dampness from his eyes. "And I think *this* painting especially — once it's complete — will represent the essence that resides at the very core of my being. That's why I came to Solace Island, to get the necessary supplies to complete this painting. And lo and behold, miracle of miracles, I also found you." He laughed, feeling almost giddy. What a pleasure to share this with his beloved sister, to share himself, his growth as an artist. "Lord knows, it took me a while to find my style, to find my own unique artist's voice. Mother didn't think I could." Pacing now. Couldn't help it, so much energy boiling inside. "She said I was a 'no-talent hack' and that my work was 'ugly' and 'disgusting' and I'd never amount to anything! Do you remember how she refused to let me take art classes? Remember that? Didn't matter how often I begged. Said it would be 'a waste of time and money,' but that night . . . ? When you were at your sleepover with Zoe-Ann, Mother went too far. Slashed my painting to ribbons. Burned the remains. Told me they were shipping me to a military boarding school! *Me.* I would've died there. A place like that would've destroyed my soul. Fucking bitch!" He could feel the rage rising, feel himself teetering on the edge of control. He needed to rein it in. Tati was still a tad skittish. Who could blame her, being on the run for so many years? She needed to know she was safe with him. He pulled himself back from the brink. Ran his hands through his hair, smoothing the strands into place. "Well," he said, placing a benign smile on his face. "I've shown her, haven't I?" He returned to his sister's side. "So, you like it, Tati? You really do?"

Her mouth worked, unable to find words. Finally she nodded. His masterpiece had drawn her gaze back to it like a lodestone. "Your art is unlike any I have ever seen." Her voice was barely audible.

"I know. It has an intensity, doesn't it? A real depth of feeling. One can almost taste the life-and-death struggle embedded in the paint." He slid a sly glance at her to see if she had picked up the cue. When they were younger they could sometimes finish each other's sentences. He would just look at her across the dinner table, not saying a word, and make her bust out laughing. But Tati wasn't looking at him. She was still enraptured in his half-finished painting. "I was going to call it *Champagne Time,* but now, with the new direction I'm going to be taking, I thought *Bosom Buddies* was a more apt title. I'll be going into town tomorrow morning to pick up the supplies I need to complete the piece."

She turned to him, her face pale. "Dattg. That's you?"

"It's us," he corrected. "It's both of us combined." He let his finger hover over the signature at the bottom. "See? Death. Art. And then I slipped in this 'T' here to represent you. There is my initial, of course, and then the 'G' for Guillory to top it off. I wanted to honor you, Tati. I thought you were dead." Tears came now. There was no stopping them. "You have no idea the anguish I suffered when the fire chief told me you had perished in the flames. You were supposed to be sleeping at your best friend's house. But Zoe-Ann's mother said you had woken up agitated a little after eleven o'clock and insisted on being driven home. That you didn't want to wake the household so you used your key and went in through the back." He swiped his forearm across his face. "But she was lying. I know that now because here you are. I'll deal with the woman's duplicity later.

"Yes. I've been giving it some thought since I found you and realized what happened. One of the housemaids must have known about your sleepover and crept into your bed, pretending to be the fine daughter for a night." He laughed. "Well, she got her just deserts, didn't she?" He whirled in a happy circle and then hugged Tati again. Hugged her because he could, because she was alive and he wasn't alone anymore. All was well with the world.

FIFTY-THREE

Zelia turned on the hot water and added some dish soap. She should be glad a decision had been made, but instead she was weary and sad. Felt heavy, as if she were pushing her way through invisible sludge. Gabe standing beside her — tea towel at the ready — was not helping matters. His presence, the masculine pheromones he was emanating, were making every cell in her body feel as if she were hooked up to a defibrillator. "Seriously, Gabe," she said, scrubbing the chopping board in the soapy water. "You don't have to help with the cleanup. It's been a long day."

"I'm not going anywhere," he said, his expression unyielding.

She turned to him, exasperated. She was not going to let him throw away his life on her because of some sort of misguided idea of chivalry. He deserved better. "Gabe, I meant it. We aren't going forward with —"

His cell phone lying on the kitchen counter buzzed.

"I understand," Gabe said calmly. "I'm not planning on sharing your bed."

The phone buzzed again.

He ignored it. "Unless" — he tossed her a wolfish grin as he plucked the clean chopping board from the dish rack and started to dry it — "you decide to invite me there."

Buzz . . . buzz . . .

"Not going to happen."

"Look, Zelia." His grin had vanished, his eyes dead serious. "Alexus was one thing. She lived on the other side of the country. But Mary disappearing?" He shook his head. "I'll be damned if I'm going to let you stay here alone."

Buzz . . . buzz . . .

"I'm not going to argue about this. I'll be commandeering your sofa until we figure out what the hell's going on."

She knew he was right, but it didn't make the realization any easier.

Buzz . . . buzz . . .

"Look," she snapped, rinsing off the pot and banging it onto the rack. "Either pick up your damn phone or switch it to do not disturb." She glared at the offending object.

His brother's name was on the screen. "Oh my goodness. Gabe, it's Rick! He must have some information for us." She plucked the buzzing phone off the counter and shoved it at him. "Answer it!"

He crossed his arms, unperturbed. "Do we have a deal?"

Buzz . . . buzz . . .

"Yes. Damn you! Now answer the bloody phone."

Gabe tossed the tea towel over his shoulder, picked up his phone, and swiped. "Hey, bro. What's up? Uh-huh . . . yeah . . . Hang on a minute. I'm with Zelia. Gonna put you on speakerphone so she can hear. Okay. We're here. Zelia, Rick, Rick, Zelia."

"Hi, Rick."

"Nice to meet you remotely. So, what I was telling Gabe is, I got the results back from IAFIS — good job, Gabe, by the way. Interestingly, they were able to match several of the fingerprints you lifted from the doorknob leading into the upstairs office. One matched with Alexus Feinstein, the deceased."

Zelia winced. Gabe must have noticed because she felt his free arm settle around her shoulders.

"How did they know it was hers?" Zelia asked.

"She had a DUI a few years back and was in the system. The DNA we picked up from the lipstick matched the blood left in the needle. There were traces of heroin in the needle, tubing, and port, which was odd. Sixteen-gauge needles are generally used for blood donation, not injections. The second set of prints came up with a hit as well. Apparently, Kenneth Oakley, aka Mr. Makeout-interruptus, had a PL 221.10 a few years back. Since it was his second MJ offense, the conviction stuck and he spent three months in jail. I dug a little further, to see if maybe he was Ms. Feinstein's dealer, but since the conviction, he's been clean. It was just a case of being in the wrong place at the wrong time." Rick sounded tired. His voice was more gravelly than Gabe's, as if he'd spent a lot of time out in the elements, or yelling. Or maybe he was a smoker.

"Didn't know you guys were still arresting people for smoking weed." Gabe grinned. "Lucky thing your adult self couldn't travel back in time to your senior year of high school."

"Drop it," Rick said over the speaker-phone.

"Jeez," Zelia added. "They'd have to toss half the population of Solace Island in the slammer."

"This was a while ago. The MJ landscape has lightened up considerably. On a more interesting note, one of the prints you lifted was a direct match to one found at the office of Richard Rye."

Zelia felt Gabe's body tense slightly, could feel her own eyes widen. "The Chelsea gallery owner" — her throat felt tight — "who was murdered?" She whirled to face Gabe. "You were right. They were connected." Her mind was reeling. "This confirms that Alexus *didn't* overdose. She was murdered, too."

"It confirms," Gabe said to her gently, "that they found a print at a crime scene that matches. Nothing is certain until it is proven so." He turned back to the phone in his hand. "Which print was that?"

"The one from the knob on the back door of the Feinstein gallery leading from the alley into the back of the house. There was a partial print on one of the dead bolts, but it was too smeared to make a positive identification. However, the print on the outside doorknob did not match any of the prints you picked up inside Alexus's office or on the knobs of either side of her office door."

"That doesn't make sense," Zelia said.

"What it means is there's a possibility that whoever killed Richard Rye tried to open the back door of the Feinstein gallery," Rick replied. "Whether or not the killer entered the building through the alley, or any other way, is unknown. Since there are no matching prints at the site where Alexus died, either Richard Rye's killer had nothing to do with Alexus's death —"

"Or," Gabe added, "he or she was wearing gloves, as we did."

"Unfortunately, the identity of the person to whom the print belongs isn't yet in the Integrated Automated Fingerprint Identification System," Rick clarified.

"That sucks." Zelia exhaled. The remnants of adrenaline were still coursing through her. "So, we're really no closer to discovering and apprehending whoever the killer is."

"Unfortunately," Rick said, "that's true. However, each bit helps. It's like pieces of a puzzle, which hopefully someday we'll be able to put together. Given this new information, which I passed on to the chief, the decision was made to reach out to the Greenwich Police Department. They will be taking another, closer look into the circumstances of Alexus Feinstein's death."

Cool, healing relief rushed through her. *The police are going to reopen Alexus's case.* "Thank you, Rick. Truly." Her eyes were hot, and she was having a difficult time keeping her voice from breaking. "I can't even tell you how much this means to me."

"Yeah. Thanks, Rick," Gabe said. "Appreciate it."

"No prob. Give Mom and Dad my love —"

"Wait," Gabe said. "Don't hang up. I need to call in another favor."

"Are you fucking kidding me?" Gabe's brother did not sound pleased.

"Hey now," Gabe said mildly. "There's a lady on the line."

She heard Rick exhale heavily. "Sorry, Zelia," he muttered. He exhaled again. "What is it this time?"

"Zelia's assistant has gone missing. The Solace Island police were here. They picked up a few prints. Would you see if you could get them to share the prints with you? I need you to run them against the prints we have. I know it's a long shot, but I want to make sure there isn't a match."

Zelia whirled to face Gabe. "You think it's a possibility?"

"Anything's a possibility until we rule it out," he replied.

Rick's voice came over the phone. "I'll see what I can do."

"Thanks, Rick," Gabe said.

"No promises."

"Understood."

FIFTY-FOUR

When Gabe had insisted on driving her to her morning appointment, Zelia hadn't protested too vigorously. She was glad now. Dark clouds had closed ranks around the scraps of blue sky, and the rain was thundering down once again. Spontaneous creeks draped themselves across the lower portions of the road. Much better to be plowing through all that excess water in Gabe's SUV with its all-wheel drive than trying to navigate through the storm in Old Faithful. Zelia was very fond of her parents' twenty-six-year-old Volvo. She had served Zelia well over the years, but lately Zelia was using the car less and less. Wanting to not wear her out. She walked voraciously in an attempt to extend Old Faithful's life.

"What are you thinking about so intently?" Gabe's voice pulled her back.

"My parents. I was thinking about their car." The SUV windshield wipers were going full blast, and still it was hard to see out the window. "I don't know if you noticed it sitting in my driveway?"

"The 1992 Volvo Turbo sedan? Sure. Didn't know it was your parents'. Hm . . . Babysitting. Dog sitting. You must be car sitting for them." He smiled, his dimple appearing briefly and then vanishing again.

She opened her mouth to make a lighthearted quip back, but words didn't get past the sudden lump in her throat. Weird how after all these years, the missing them would sometimes sneak up and bite her in the butt.

"What is it, Zee?" She could hear the concern in his voice.

She shook her head, waving his question away. "Nothing. Really."

He eased the vehicle to the side of the road. "Bull," he said gently. He switched the engine off and turned to face her, taking her cold hands in his warm ones. "Tell me."

There was something incredibly soothing about sitting in that SUV with him, safe and warm, while the rain pounded down on the roof. "My parents passed away ages ago, my freshman year at Berkeley, so I'm not sure why I'm suddenly feeling emotional about it now."

"Grief is like that. It follows its own

rhythm. Perhaps Alexus passing and the worry about Mary has called memories of your parents to the forefront."

"Yeah. I think you're right."

"So, what is it about the car specifically that is causing this sadness?"

"Well, it was theirs, and my dad was so proud when he bought it. Treated it like it was a second child. Spent the weekends washing it, applying wax until it shone. Yet when it came time for me to get my learner's permit, he didn't bat an eye. He braced his shoulders and marched me over to the driver's seat."

"Sounds like he loved you."

"He did. So much. Mom, too. And yet, that last summer before they died, I was such a brat. I didn't want to spend it on the boat with them. I was bored and longed for home, for familiar friends before I headed to university."

Gabe wrapped his arms around her, laid her head against his shoulder. It must have been a bit uncomfortable for him, given he had to maneuver past the center console and the gearshift, but she was glad for the comfort.

"When they died, I tried to hang on to our house, but it was an impossible task. There were taxes and bills and the remainder of the mortgage. The money I earned working on weekends at a pizza parlor needed to go toward my university expenses. I was sliding deeper and deeper in the red. Had to sell the family home.

"But I kept their car. Drove it to Berkeley. On spring break, I drove to the Grand Canyon, because that was on my mother's bucket list. I hiked down, said a prayer, and scattered my mom's favorite rose petals on the canyon floor. I'd packed down a cold beer and a peanut butter cup and toasted my dad. I needed to make some kind of ritual to say my good-byes. They'd gone down with the boat, no bodies to bury.

"I took a lot of trips with Old Faithful. Drove through the Great Plains, across the Canadian Rockies . . ." Her voice petered out, lost in memories. "But she's old now. The floor is rusted out. I can actually see pavement whizzing past as I drive." She felt Gabe drop a gentle kiss on the top of her head. "Dave, my mechanic, says she's on her last legs, but I don't want her to be. It's a conundrum because I need a reliable vehicle for my work, which Old Faithful, bless her heart, is not."

Zelia sighed and straightened. "I know I have to say good-bye to her, but it's hard. Don't like to think of her squashed flat for scrap metal in some junkyard."

"Because she feels like a tangible link to your past. To your parents."

"Yeah. That's it."

Gabe nodded. "Makes sense."

Zelia tipped her head toward the clock on the dashboard. "We'd better head out. I do not want to be late after yesterday's fiasco." Humor laced her voice. "Thanks, Gabe, for listening. I feel lighter already."

He turned the SUV on and pulled back onto the road. "I was thinking, why don't you turn your folks' car into a driveway sculpture, like you did with that old bike at the end of your drive. Paint it —"

"Plant it! With my mom's favorite flowers. Oh, Gabe, you are a genius."

He grinned. "Far be it from me to try to talk you out of that erroneous misconception."

FIFTY-FIVE

Eve Harris's paintings did not disappoint. They were spectacular. There was a unique energy that radiated from her work. Her passion and colossal talent were evident in every brushstroke, in the way she used her palette knife, in her use and blending of colors. Even with everything that was going on, it had been impossible not to be swept away by Eve's artwork.

"Thanks again for being so understanding about yesterday," Zelia told Eve as she zipped up her raincoat. "Words can't express how excited I am to have the opportunity to represent your artwork. You're *incredibly* talented. I'm going to mull it over, come up with a plan for the best way to launch you. I should have a contract ready later this week. One year to start. Does that work for you?"

"Oh yeah. That works for me," Eve said with a grin.

"Great. We'll see how it goes. We can renegotiate at the end of that time for a longer period if we're both happy."

"I still can't believe you are taking me on. Art Expressions Gallery! Never in my wildest dreams."

"Look, I'm honored to have the opportunity to hang your artwork in my gallery. Speaking of hanging, don't get mad, but I'll need you to remove your paintings from the walls of your café. We are going to try to create a mystique and buzz about your art. Having them hanging in a bustling, steamy café/bakery, where they are viewed more as wallpaper than art, isn't the way to do it."

"How did it go?" Gabe asked when a sopping-wet Zelia landed in his front seat.

"Great," Zelia said. "Her paintings are superb, and the fact she's a lovely person is an added bonus. Just gotta figure out the best way to present her. Thinking I might add a couple of her paintings to the batch I'm taking to Frieze in May." She pushed back the hood of her raincoat and smiled at him. Little droplets of rain were clinging to the mass of curls around her face that hadn't been protected from the elements. Tiny watery diamonds shimmered in her hair. He wanted to lean forward and taste the rain on her lips, the warmth of her mouth. To dive, once more, into experiencing a life lived fully instead of by observation. Lust. Yes, that was there, but the deep internal longing was even greater than the lust. He craved the sweet intimacy that had been building between them as they shared meals, their uncensored thoughts, and their bodies. He wanted her. Needed her like he needed oxygen. The feel of her hands entangling in his hair, the soft mewing noise she made in the back of her throat as she opened her mouth to allow him access.

No. He turned his body to face forward. *You are playing the long game.* Gabe took a deep breath and slowly released it, then started the engine and headed back down the drive. "Where to?" he asked.

Once back at the gallery, Zelia was even more grateful to have Gabe at her side as she approached her office door. It looked odd. Cold. Like she couldn't recognize the place anymore. Not only was the rug missing, but the police had removed a portion of the office baseboard, part of the flooring, and the desk drawer with the blood splatters in it as well. She exhaled shakily. At least the strings the police had put up to map the trajectory of the blood splatters had been removed.

She stood in the doorway, her hands gripped tightly before her. "What am I supposed to do? Am I allowed to wipe things off? Sweep? Mop? Call a contractor to repair the damage?"

"Let me talk to Rick," Gabe said. "My impulse would be to leave it as is for a day or two in case they need to come back."

"But I have to work." She exhaled again, trying to calm her breath, but slow breathing wasn't working. "According to my phone there are now two hundred and thirty-one e-mails waiting to be answered, some important, some not, but all need to be sorted through. That huge shipment that came in yesterday right before we left needs to be unpacked and every single item entered into the computer. Advertising needs to be designed and sent out for the upcoming show . . ." Her voice was rising along with the panic quotient. "The show that I have done diddly-squat on needs to be designed and the artwork hung and labeled."

Gabe was silent for a second, his jaw set. "You're right. You can't work in here." He stepped past her into the office. "I'm going to create a temporary workstation in another part of the gallery for you." He reached for the computer.

"No," she said. She started to step forward but caught herself before the movement hit her feet. She swallowed, trying to rid herself of the nausea that had risen in her throat, her hand flying to her mouth. "Not the computer. I can't. I think she was working on it when . . ." Her words trailed off.

"Okay." Gabe moved away from the desk, his voice calm, reassuring. "Not the computer. How about you borrow mine for the time being?" She felt his hand alight on her elbow and gently steer her through the small hallway to the coffee station. "We can set you up at this table. It will be nice and convenient when you want to refresh your tea. As a matter of fact, I'm going to put the water on to boil now." He pulled out a chair and sat her down, gave her a gentle pat on the shoulder, and then moved to the drinks station and filled up the kettle.

There was something about the calm, competent way he moved that comforted her. "Thanks." She wasn't shaking as badly now. "I don't know what got into me."

"Not me." Gabe held up his hands, palms out. Then a teasing smile chased across his face. "Much as I would have liked to," he added ruefully.

And just like that, her anxiety lightened

and actual laughter bubbled forth.

"That's better," he said, nodding with satisfaction. "The color is returning to your face."

Gabe had honored her wishes the previous night. They hadn't made love, but he had remained, camped on the sofa. They'd talked until the wee hours of the morning, going over the photographer's photo files from the Feinstein & Co. event that Mitch Clarke had hacked into. Clicking through photos of the gallery, the event the night that Alexus had died. Looking closely at the attendees milling about, trying to see if anything unusual stood out. They'd also looked through the PDF of the brochure of the event. It had been emotional work wading through it all. Finally Gabe had shut his laptop and lay back on the makeshift bed on her sofa. "Come here," he'd said, opening his arms.

"I don't think it's wise. We can't —"

"I know. You're looking weary. Like you need a friend. I can be that friend."

"Totally platonic?"

"I give you my word." He'd waited patiently.

She had been tired and heartsore as she'd eased her way down, the two of them precariously balanced on the narrow sofa.

He tucked her under his arm, her head on his chest, her arm and leg draped over him to keep from tipping backward onto the floor. It felt comforting and right lying in his arms. Charlie claimed a spot, nestled on top of them, a warm, purring accent note of coziness. They talked quietly, until finally words got blurred, then started to peter out. "I'd better go to bed," she said, wanting him to convince her to stay, but he'd opened his arms and released her, smiling a sleepy, tender smile.

"Sweet dreams," she'd heard him murmur as she'd forced herself to cross the room, all the while longing to race back into the warm comfort of his arms.

Instead, she'd climbed into her cold bed alone and managed to grab a couple hours of sleep. And now, here they were, in the gallery, and even with all the worry, the wanting hadn't dissipated.

The kettle clicked off. Gabe turned and removed two mugs from their hooks, dropped a tea bag in each, filled them with steaming water, and then brought them to the table and sat down. "So, what I need from you is a list of supplies you'd like to make this a functioning workspace. Can you do that for me?"

She nodded.

"Good." He walked to his satchel, which he'd left leaning against the wall by the back entry. She watched him remove his laptop, a cord, a power strip, a pad of paper and a pen. She liked the way he moved with such absolute competence, no fumbling or knocking things over. She tried to imagine Ned under this kind of pressure, and the image that came to mind made her smile.

Ned was more like a lazy summer afternoon, drifting down a river in an inner tube, going where the water wanted to carry him. His easygoing approach to life was lovely and quite enchanting to a heartsick Zelia, who had just lost both of her parents in the blink of an eye. She'd envied his ability to live in the moment and not sweat the small stuff. However, Ned's style in dealing with the practical matters of life had been a bit more challenging; like coming up with his portion of the rent or forgetting to transfer his share of the electric bill into their joint account. He had been a man-child. Would he have matured, learned how to be a responsible adult? Or would his lackadaisical approach to life ultimately have driven her crazy and them apart?

Unfortunately, neither one of them had had the privilege of finding out.

Gabe flipped to a blank page and placed

the pad, laptop, and accessories on the table before her. He scribbled a series of letters and numbers at the top of the blank page. "This is the password to unlock my computer." She could smell the clean male scent of him. She wanted to lean in, wrap her arms around his neck, and pull him to her. Run her tongue along the strong-corded length of it until her mouth reached his. She wanted, needed to taste the determination and aura of protection that surrounded him like a force field. She knew in her gut that this man would do anything, would walk through fire to protect and defend those that he loved, and that was such a turn-on.

"Gabe," she murmured. She wanted him to take her rough and hard to make her forget her friend was missing. Wanted him to mark her as *his* in the most basic way, longed for the burn marks the dark stubble that now covered his face would cause. Wanted him to bite her like an animal mounting its mate, to suck on her tender skin so intently that purple marks would arise. Wanted him to grip her hard while he fucked her, leaving fingerprint bruises in his wake like flower petals sprinkled on a lake, floating on the surface for a few hours, maybe days, before disappearing into a wispy memory that would one day fade as well.

She didn't have to say anything more, could see he knew.

He stared at her, eyes dark, tortured, and then he stepped away, shoved his hands deep into his pockets. "I can't," he said, his voice strained, hoarse. "I made you a promise and I'm going to keep it." He tipped his head toward the pad on the table before her. "Write down what you need." He took another step back. There were four feet between them now, but she could feel the heat pulsing from his body. Could see the engorged state of things, even with his hands fisted in the pockets of his jeans. He exhaled slowly. Took another step back. "I'm going to" — he set his jaw — "do a sweep of the gallery to make sure it's secure. Once your list is complete, you will lock the door behind me. I will be as quick as humanly possible making the purchases. You won't open the gallery to customers until I return. Agreed?"

She wanted to argue, but about what? Him honoring the promise she'd dragged out of him? The fact that he was unilaterally making decisions, never mind that they were good ones? *It's not like opening the doors a little later is going to affect business. Potential customers rarely wander in before eleven.*

She nodded, took a sip of her tea, and then picked up the pen and started to write.

FIFTY-SIX

Zelia had made pretty good progress on the design for flyers for the March show when she heard the *rattle* of someone trying to open the front door of the gallery.

She froze.

Knock . . . knock . . .

Someone was rapping on the glass door.

"Go away. We aren't open," she murmured.

They knocked again.

Damn. I should have turned the lights out back here. Put a note on the door.

Knock . . . knock . . .

"Zelia?"

Wait a minute. She knew that voice. She got up from the table and rounded the corner. Could see the blurry slim figure of a man through the rain-spattered window, one hand cupped around his eyes as he attempted to see inside, a dark overcoat to keep the damp cold at bay, the other hand holding an umbrella that was still aloft. Zelia couldn't place who he was. With the dark gallery space between them, her eyes were still adjusting from the bright computer screen and the overhead light in the kitchen area.

"Yes?" she said cautiously, taking a couple of steps forward. "Who is it?"

"Zelia?" the man called. "Is that you? It's me, Tristan."

"Tristan . . . Tristan . . . Who the hell is Tristan?" she murmured to herself, combing through her mind, pulling up possibilities and then discarding them. And then a light went on. "Oh my God, Tristan!" She hurried to the door and unlocked it. "What are you doing here? Come in. Come in. Sorry about leaving you out there in the rain. I couldn't see your face. Would you like a cup of coffee? Tea?"

"A hot beverage would be appreciated," he said in that funny formal diction he had. He shut his umbrella and secured it with the strap.

"What are you doing here?"

"I came to see you."

"Me?"

"I felt bad that I wasn't able to let you into the back rooms of Feinstein and Company when you'd flown all the way to

Greenwich. I've been thinking on it and —"

"Oh, that," Zelia said, trying to waft away the sudden guilt with her hand. "No worries. I totally understand." Images of the night she and Gabe had broken in bombarded her. She could feel the heat rising in her face. "Oh my," she said brightly. "What a beautiful umbrella, but then Alexus always said you had an eye for the unique."

He glanced at the umbrella in his hand, his thumb absentmindedly tracing what looked to be a twenty-four-karat gold knob from the Victorian era.

"Well, come this way. I'll put on a pot of tea and we'll have a nice chat." She briskly headed toward the back room, flicked on the lights in the gallery, and then turned back to him.

Tristan had traveled a few steps deeper into the room, as if he'd been following her, but something had stopped him in his tracks. He had the umbrella slung over his shoulder like a batter stepping up to the plate. Both hands were wrapped around it as if he were gunning for a home run. The wet fabric from the umbrella was going to soak the shoulder of his cashmere overcoat.

"There's an umbrella stand by the door. You're welcome to plop it in there to dry. I'm going to be opening the gallery late today, so you won't have to worry about a customer absconding with it."

Tristan didn't respond. He appeared to be frozen in place, staring at something just beyond her line of vision, almost as if he were in a trance.

"Are you okay?"

His mouth worked, but no words came out. He seemed stunned.

"Tristan?" She stepped toward him, concerned. The mere fact that the poor man had traveled across the country to apologize for not letting her have access to Alexus's back rooms spoke volumes about his troubled state. Zelia knew only too well the odd ways in which grief could manifest itself. He probably needed to talk, process what had happened with someone else who had also been close to Alexus.

"How are you holding up?"

"That painting," he asked in a hoarse whisper. "Where did you get it?"

"Which one?" Zelia stepped beside him and turned to see what he was so transfixed by. "Oh." On the wall in the nook hung the Dattg painting, full of rage and despair. Sometimes it seemed to Zelia as if the paint below the surface was seething, undulating like a living, breathing entity. "It's quite powerful, isn't it?"

He whirled to look at her, the expression on his face intent. "You think?"

"Mm . . . Yeah. The artist's work affects me in a very intense, visceral way when I look at it. Obviously Dattg is amazingly talented — I would even say gifted, to get that much feeling and passion onto the canvas. I find it quite scary, to tell you the truth."

"Gifted?" he repeated softly, and then suddenly his shoulders caved inward, and he started to weep, his umbrella dropping to his side as if it had suddenly become too heavy to hold.

"Here, let me." She removed the umbrella from his slack grip and crossed the room, placing it in the umbrella stand, and then returned to his side. "Let's get you out of that wet coat and get a nice warm cup of tea into your belly."

FIFTY-SEVEN

Gabe pulled his SUV up to Art Expressions. The lights in the interior of the gallery were blazing. He jumped out of his vehicle and ran to the front door, leaving his purchases behind. The front door was still locked. He exhaled, trying to recenter himself before entering. When the cashier had been ringing up some of the items Zelia needed, a sudden sense of unease was reaching a crescendo within him. He felt impelled to return to the gallery and check on Zelia before continuing on to the electronics store.

He dug the key she had given him out of the front pocket of his jeans and opened the door. "Zee?"

"In here."

The knot in his belly eased a little at hearing her voice sounding healthy and well. He walked through the gallery to the back room, where he found Zelia ensconced with a pale-haired, slender, narrow-faced man who reminded Gabe of the priest that had presided over his elementary school's morning service. *He looks vaguely familiar, but from where?* The man's eyes were red-rimmed and his lashes clumped, as if he'd been crying.

"Look who came to see me," Zelia said, rising to her feet with a smile. "Tristan."

"Tristan?"

"From Feinstein and Company. You met him, remember?" Zelia was shooting him some kind of meaningful look, but it wasn't clear what she was cautioning him about. And why had she let the fucker in?

"That's right," he said slowly. "I remember now. What brings you to Solace Is —"

"Stop glaring at him, Gabe," Zelia cut in. "The poor man has had a rather hellish time of it, and yet when I told him of our troubles at the gallery, he offered to help."

"What?"

"With paperwork and such, which was incredibly generous of him."

"Can I speak with you for a moment please?" Gabe was looking as if he were about to bust a gasket.

"Certainly." Zelia waved a hand for him to continue.

"In private," he said through gritted teeth.

■ ■ ■ ■

"The man is in pain, Gabe. He's grieving and needs to be around someone who knew Alexus." She pressed her clenched fist to her chest. "I *know* how that feels. Think about it. Not only has he lost a dear friend, but he also lost his employer and his job in one fell swoop. He flew all this way to apologize. I will not turn my back on him."

"*Zelia.*"

She had never seen Gabe look quite so angry. "Yes?" she replied breezily.

"You will *not* hire him."

"I'm not 'hiring' him, per se. That would be crazy. He's got a whole life set up on the other side of the country. However, since he's in town and willing to pitch in for a day or two, until Mary returns, I'd be foolish to turn him down." Zelia placed her hand on his arm, her tone softening. "Gabe, the grief factor aside, I am drowning in work. There is no way I will be able to get the next show ready and keep the gallery running smoothly on my own. There's too much to do."

"I can help you."

"I appreciate the offer, but I remember you mentioning that you have a manuscript due. Besides, you don't know my business. The amount of time it would take to teach you would put me even further behind. Whereas, with Tristan, it will take five minutes max to get him up and running."

"I don't feel comfortable with this decision. There is something odd about him."

Zelia laughed, even though she was feeling off-balance as well. "Darling, welcome to the art world. *Odd* isn't exactly in short supply. That's one of the things I love about what I do. I get to celebrate and nurture that which is unique. Oddness, individuality — these are traits that arise when artists have been kissed by God. The homogenized standard of sameness that the rest of the world requires in order to be accepted is thrown out the window in the art world. Of *course* this business I'm in will attract people like me, like Tristan. Because even though *we* don't have an artistic bone in our body, being in the presence of all this creative vision" — she gestured around her at the beautiful art that was gracing her gallery — "makes 'oddballs' like us not feel so alone."

Gabe didn't answer. His arms were folded across his chest.

She touched his clenched jaw. The dark stubble felt rough against her fingertips.

"Please don't be angry."

"I'm not angry," he said, glaring over her shoulder at the wall as if he had X-ray vision and was attempting to incinerate poor Tristan, who was innocently sitting and sipping his tea. "I'm frustrated." Gabe exhaled, and the tension in his shoulders seemed to soften. "And scared," he added softly. "I don't like this, Zee. I don't know this guy."

"But I *do*. Alexus was constantly singing his praises."

"And look what happened to her," Gabe said, his face grim.

"That's *not* fair. He was devastated. You didn't hear him on the phone when he told me what happened. He was inconsolable. And just now, before you came, he broke down again. He misses her, Gabe. I do, too. We'd been friends for years, and I just can't imagine a world without her. I keep wanting to text her and then realize she's gone." As she was talking, it was clear Gabe didn't understand. His face was totally shut again, implacable, as if it had been carved out of stone. He'd had a fairy-tale life with a brother and sisters and both parents who obviously adored him. He couldn't comprehend the concept of people like Tristan, Mary, and her and how they limped along in their fractured lives, forming their own makeshift families and communities.

"I understand that you miss her," she heard him say. "But, Zelia, we have to be practical. Mary's gone missing and he just *happens* to be in town? Maybe he's the common denominator."

"You're being paranoid. Totally understandable. You write crime fiction. Of course you'd see nefarious connections. However, Tristan arrived on the morning ferry."

"How do you know?"

Her arms were crossed now. "He *told* me."

"I'd like to see proof."

Enough with trying to explain. Gabe would never get it. Besides, who the hell did he think he was with his disapproving look and patriarchal posturing? It pissed her off. She jutted her chin into the air. "I have to say, Gabe, you have a lot of balls thinking you can just march into my life and start ordering me around. Telling me how to run my business. Who I can or cannot hire. And you want to talk marriage?" She shook her head. "Ha! Over my dead body."

"Which is precisely the situation I am trying to avoid, madame," he said grimly.

FIFTY-EIGHT

Mary snapped her head up, listening. Footsteps were approaching. It was him. The man who thought he was her brother. She could differentiate his footsteps from the slower, heavier tread of the butler, Fredrick.

She tried to calm the rising panic coursing through her as she straightened in the armchair, unfolded her legs, and placed her feet solidly on the ground. The book she'd been attempting to read fell to the ground. She left it there. Didn't want to be bent over in a vulnerable position when he entered the room. She heard the key turn in the lock, and then the door flew open, slamming against the wall.

"Why didn't you tell me?" he demanded, the expression on his face causing nausea to arise.

"T-tell you wh-what?" She hated that the stammer she'd developed while married to Kevin had suddenly returned. She could taste violence shimmering in the air around him. It tasted like copper and fear and nowhere to hide.

He thrust his snarling face into hers. "That *she* had my painting. That. She. Had hung it. On. The. Wall." He backhanded her hard across the face. The force of the blow sent her flying out of the armchair and onto the floor. She tried to clamber to her feet, to scramble away, but his Gucci-loafer-clad foot crashed down hard on her neck, slamming her to the floor, knocking the air from her lungs.

"Please . . ." she pleaded.

"Please what?" He grabbed a fistful of hair and yanked her head back hard. "Show you mercy?" His laugh was harsh, bitter. "Why should I when you showed me none!" He spit in her face and then slammed her head down, his foot driving hard into the side of her belly. "Pretending to be my beloved Tati! How could you, *Mary Browning*? That's right. I learned a lot of things at my new job, *including* your *real* name. I bet you were laughing at me, huh? Thinking you were playing me for a fool, but I'm onto you now." He yanked her head back up. "I figured out your game —"

"There's no game. I promise you. Please let me —"

"Silence!" he screamed, shaking her like a rag doll. "I'm speaking!" Another kick. This time to her ribs, and she could feel them snap. A moan escaped.

"Yeah, that's right. Who's crying now?" He let go of her hair, ambled to the door, glanced into the hall, and then shut it. "Sure," he said, leaning against the door, crossing his legs at the ankles as he shifted into idle elegance. He glanced at his manicured nails as if he hadn't a care in the world. "You could have been my sister, given Zelia a fake name. I'll grant you that." He shrugged. "But no. I figured out your con because Tati, my beloved sister, would have told me *immediately.*" His lip curled into a sneer, the thin veneer of civility rapidly disintegrating. "The *second* she saw me, she would have shared the wonderful news."

He pushed away from the door, closing in on her.

Mary didn't make a noise. Just shut her eyes and curled into a protective, fetal position, her arms wrapped tightly around her head.

"She would have told me *Zelia Thompson,* a highly respected purveyor in the art world, owner of the prestigious Art Expressions Gallery, not only *hung* my painting, but *loved* it. Unbidden, Zelia Thompson said to me that the artist Dattg was 'amazingly talented.' She called him 'gifted.' Told me his painting was 'full of passion and emotion.' You worked there! You *knew* she had my painting and had hung it and *you* didn't tell me!"

She could feel him towering over her, droplets of his spittle splattering on her as he raged. "You could have. Last night. You had *every* opportunity, but you didn't. And *that* is how I know you are an imposter. Tati *loved* me. She *never* would have kept something so vitally important to herself."

Mary braced herself, waiting for the blow, but it didn't come. *He seems to be waiting for something, for me to speak?*

"I didn't mean to hurt you," she croaked. She hated that she was cowering on the floor. How quickly the old patterns had reasserted themselves. *Move,* she told herself fiercely. *Get up! Fight back! You are not that woman any longer.* But her body was frozen in fear, trapped in the cellular memory of the past.

"And yet you did." His voice grew quiet suddenly, which was even more terrifying. "Deeply. Causing me to realize I must change my plans." She felt him straighten. Heard his footsteps as he started to pace erratically around the bedroom. "My artistic vision for *Bosom Buddies* has once again shifted. *You* shall provide the resources to complete my painting. Of course, the previous title will no longer work. *Betrayal,* maybe. It has a nice ring." She heard him giggle. "Not only shall you grace one of my paintings, but first I think I shall surgically remove your lying tongue. Very exciting! Now, you hold tight. I'll be back in a jiffy with my tools. This is going to be fun." The giddy excitement in his voice caused her body to break out in a cold sweat.

As soon as Mary heard the door close and lock behind him, she shot to her feet. The searing pain in her left ribs made it difficult to straighten totally. "I will not," she whispered to the empty room, "be a victim any longer." She kept her elbow pressed against her side to minimize movements as she glanced wildly around the cabin.

There wasn't much time. She had to act fast. Mary grabbed the heavy brass floor lamp that was tucked behind the armchair, yanking the cord from the wall. Despite biting down hard on her lip to keep the scream from escaping, dizzying pain made her knees wobble.

She hoisted the lamp over her shoulder, gripping it hard with the heavy base in front of her like a battering ram, and raced toward the bedroom window. The first charge cracked the thick glass, and the second one shattered it, like icicles landing on concrete. For half a heartbeat she couldn't move. "I'm not ready," she whispered, thinking of all the things she'd wanted to do, to experience before she died. "Ah well. Better to die quickly in the freezing waters than endure whatever torture he has planned." She tossed the lamp aside, bracing herself for what was to come. *"Non est ad astra mollis e terris via,"* she murmured. "There is no easy way from the earth to the stars." She ran the words on a continuous loop, in Latin and then in English again. The soft repetition of her litany gave her courage as she pushed the chair to the shattered window, heedless of the broken glass under her feet. She climbed onto the chair — her vision blurred with tears — and then dove out the window into the dark waters of the freezing Pacific Ocean below.

FIFTY-NINE

There was a discreet tap on the door — as there was every morning — and then the sound of footsteps retreating.

"Allow me, my love," Fergus said as he hopped out from under the warm covers of their cozy nest of a bed. Alma watched him cross the room, her heart full of soft, gentle love. For a second, time morphed and she was watching a younger Fergus make the same journey to the door. His stride was longer then, without the slight hitch. His hip must be bothering him. No wonder, given the way he'd carried on last night — she'd rub arnica on him later to help with the soreness.

She pushed herself to a seated position. *I'm a little sore myself,* she thought with a smile as she watched her beloved husband crack open the door and poke his head out, making sure the coast was clear.

"Fergus," she said. "Put on a robe." But

did he listen? No. He never did. He darted out in his birthday suit, snagged the wicker basket loaded with goodies off the front porch, and then sprinted back inside, slamming the door behind him.

"I got it," he said, holding the basket triumphantly over his head as if it were the Stanley Cup trophy, a cocky grin on his face.

"I see that," she replied. "However, for the record, I really do think — especially at our age — that a robe would be a seemly addition."

"Nonsense." He plopped the basket on the round table in the alcove. "It's tradition, my dear. You don't want to mess with that." He drew open the curtains, allowing the early-morning sunshine to stream in. He pounded his chest with his fists, then took a deep breath, threw back his head, and let out a loud coyote howl.

It was impossible not to laugh at his antics, and as she did, a contented happiness surrounded her like a warm bath. "What am I going to do with you?" she said, shaking her head.

She watched her husband unpack the early-morning snack that was to tide them over until the restaurant opened for breakfast. The scent of warm apple muffins and coffee had her rising from the bed and approaching the table.

It wasn't until she sat, her coffee poured, and she was reaching for the sugar tongs that she noticed the change on the horizon. "Look at that, Fergus. The fancy yacht is gone. Must have pulled anchor in the night. Wonder where they're heading to."

"Up the coast, I reckon. Must have gotten tired of the quiet beauty of our little hidden cove." He didn't glance up. He was too intent on gobbling down his buttered muffin. Last night's activities must have worked up an appetite. "Probably going up to Canada, maybe even Alaska — see some glaciers, explore the islands, catch some king crab." He smacked his lips. "I could eat some king crab right now, with garlic and butter." He swiped a lonely crumb from his plate with his forefinger and stuck it into his mouth.

"Would you like the rest of my muffin?"

"Really?" The expression on his face made her laugh.

"Really," she said, sliding the remainder of her muffin over, and watched him eat, her heart overflowing with tenderness and love.

SIXTY

Yesterday had gone well, but today Zelia was having misgivings. Tristan had arrived at work forty-five minutes late. "Are you all right?" she'd asked.

"I lost something quite valuable last night. Circumstances forced me to relocate."

"I'm sorry about that. What a pain in the ass. Hopefully you'll find it soon."

"No. The chances of retrieving my lost parcel in good working order are nil." His face had been grim and determined. "Even if it is recovered, the item will no longer be functioning and therefore wouldn't be of use to me. Finding a replacement is my only option."

"That sounds like a good plan," she'd said soothingly, because seriously, the man looked in dire need of consolation. "Look, Tristan, if helping out here is too much for you, I totally understand. You didn't come to Solace Island expecting to be corralled into work." His mood from yesterday had dramatically shifted. There was a wild, unhinged quality about him, like a volcano ready to erupt.

When she'd asked him to do a quick sweep of the gallery with the dust mop, he'd looked at her as if she'd asked him to polish the floor with his tongue.

Apparently light cleaning was beneath him. Fine. She'd swept the floor and was freshening the bathroom. She'd set Tristan to work wading through the e-mails. Luckily, he'd been unperturbed by the torn-up state of the office and was pecking away at the keyboard quite diligently. However, the dark storm cloud that was hanging over him seemed to be growing at a rapid pace. It made her feel uneasy.

Everyone has a different way of processing grief, she told herself as she rinsed out the sink. *Yesterday it was tears. Today he's like a bear with a sore paw. Give him time and space. Don't take it personally.* She spritzed the mirror and wiped it down with a paper towel, then used the moist towel to polish the chrome. She bent over to pick up the bucket and mop.

"Can I ask you something?" Tristan's voice cut into her thoughts.

Zelia whirled around.

He was standing in the doorway. He had moved so quietly she hadn't heard his approach.

"Sure." She pushed a strand of hair out of her face, suddenly feeling clumsy and awkward standing there holding the cleaning supplies. Almost as if she were a frumpy intern and he the impeccably dressed, hard-to-please boss.

"Why is the Dattg painting titled *Insurance*?"

"I'm not sure." She wished he would take a couple of steps back. It felt weird for the two of them to be sharing such close quarters. "You'd have to ask the artist."

"The artist?"

She nodded.

"I don't think the title suits."

"Well, it's what came with the painting." He showed no inclination of moving of his own volition. "Excuse me," Zelia said, moving forward, then stepping past. It was a tight squeeze. Her hip brushed his thigh, and she had to steel herself to hold back a shudder. She rounded the corner and opened the broom closet, then put the cleaning materials inside, all the while aware of him close behind her.

"Look, Tristan." She turned and faced him. "If you're going to work here, you need to know, I'd prefer to have a little more space."

"Pardon?"

"You stand too close to me. It makes me uncomfortable." Even though she'd said it nicely, she could see she had wounded him before his lashes swept down and shuttered his eyes. "It's not you. It's me. I just like to have . . ." She shrugged and smiled apologetically, even though she was lying. It was definitely him. "Space."

He took an exaggerated step backward, his palms up. "Is this better?" he asked, his nostrils flaring, his face tight.

"Yes. Thank you," she said, knowing that she'd made a gross miscalculation. As desperate as she was for help, Tristan was not the answer. The unease she felt around him seemed to be growing exponentially. She was grateful Gabe had insisted on shadowing her to work again today. It was a relief to know he was down one flight of stairs, unpacking the shipment that had arrived. "Now, if you'll excuse me."

He stepped in her path. "I'm not done."

She settled back on her heels and exhaled, her hands on her hips, striving for patience. "Okay."

"I was wondering how the Dattg painting came into your possession?"

"Alexus sent it."

Surprise flickered across his face, followed by something else she couldn't put her finger on. "She did?"

"Yes. She was a fierce champion of his. Working so closely with her, you must've known that. She hung three of his paintings in her last show."

He nodded slowly. "That's right. I forgot."

"I understand why she was so blown away. Although" — she gestured to the artwork surrounding them — "as you can probably ascertain, Dattg's not really my cup of tea."

"But you hung him. You said he was *gifted*." Tristan's voice had switched into a slightly higher pitch. There was almost a childlike pleading tenor to it. *What an odd little creature.*

"And he *is* gifted. No doubt about it." She turned and gazed at the Dattg painting, her stomach knotting up. "But his artwork's just not for me is all. If Alexus hadn't sent me this painting and then died, I would have returned it."

"Returned it?"

"I find him a bit . . ." She shrugged.

"A bit what?" There was a sudden sharpness to his voice, which snapped her gaze back to him.

"Come on, Tristan," she said, trying to

385

joke her way out of the tension that was ricocheting around the gallery. "Look at it. You gotta confess it's a little bit creepy."

"Cr-creepy . . . ?" His face was rapidly turning puce, his fists clenching and un-clenching.

"Zee?" Zelia had never been so happy to hear Gabe's voice, because Tristan's head and shoulders were thrust forward, almost as if he were about to launch himself at her. Which was weird behavior, even for a pas-sionate art aficionado.

She turned, acting relaxed even though every cell was in fight-or-flight mode. Gabe had come up from the basement and was standing at the top of the stairs, framed by the arched doorway that led downstairs. His posture was casual, but she felt the coiled strength in him, could see the protective intent in his eyes. One wrong move by Tristan and she had no doubt that Gabe would rip Tristan's head from his torso.

Apparently, Tristan felt the threat as well, because he gave her one last glare. "You. Know. Nothing." He spit the words through clenched teeth and then did an abrupt about-face. Stalked into the office and slammed the door behind him.

"You okay?" Gabe asked.

"Yeah," Zelia replied, even though she was

shaking.

"Would you like to step outside for a second? Get a breath of fresh air?"

"Sounds good, but I need to do something first. If you could provide backup, it would be appreciated."

"Absolutely."

How amazing, Zelia thought as she headed toward the office with Gabe bringing up the flank. *I don't need words to tell this man what I want. He seems to intuit it.*

She opened the office door. Tristan's head snapped up, his eyes locking with hers, the feral expression in them stunning in its intensity.

"Tristan, I'm sorry," she said, speaking carefully, politely. "While I appreciate you offering to help at the gallery, it's clearly not working for either of us."

"Are you . . . firing me?"

She shifted uncomfortably. She hated having to do this type of thing. "I'll pay you for yesterday and for a full day today —"

"You are firing me after *one* day?" His face was white with rage.

"I'd like you to gather your things and leave now."

Tristan shot to his feet, eyes like fire. "I don't *need* your money, you sanctimonious bitch!"

387

She heard a warning growl deep in Gabe's throat as he took a step to move in front of her. "It's okay," she said, placing a hand to the side. "Let me handle this.

"Nevertheless," she said, keeping her tone even, "I'll pay you. Either cash today, or I'll send you a check."

Tristan stormed toward the doorway. She stepped aside so he could pass. "You're going to pay," Tristan hissed as he passed her. The hatred on his face, the venom in his voice, caused the tiny hairs on the back of her neck and her arms to rise.

Gabe stood to her side, arms crossed, an immovable rock that forced Tristan to veer to his right in order to avoid crashing into him.

"Asshole," Tristan muttered under his breath as he stalked to the coat closet. He yanked his overcoat on, the hangers clattering, grabbed his umbrella, and slammed through the door.

Zelia watched him storm across the square, overcoat undone and flapping in the wind. He hadn't bothered to open his umbrella, even though the rain was still thundering down. He used it like a baseball bat to slash the hell out of the two pots of ornamental native grasses that flanked Twang and Pearl's door. Zelia made a mental note to reimburse Sasha for the cost to repair the damage as Tristan turned the corner and disappeared from sight.

"Thank God," Zelia murmured, feeling her fists unclench, grateful she was finally able to breathe deeply again.

"I know this might seem a little weird," Zelia said as she reentered her office and removed the partially burnt smudge stick, abalone shell, and matches from the bottom desk drawer. "But waving this thing around really does help. So, no laughter allowed."

"No laughter from this quarter. I've smudged on occasion. While you take care of that, I'm going to give my brother and Detective Mackelwayne a call. Ask them to look into Tristan Guillory as a possible person of interest."

SIXTY-ONE

Gabe tossed the last of the flattened cardboard boxes and packing material into the recycle dumpster and then shut the lid with a bang, his mind turning over the events of the morning. He was relieved Zelia had gotten rid of Tristan. There was no need for her to know that he'd come upstairs from the basement with the intention of sending the jackass packing. His alarm bells had been clanging overtime. Knew he'd be stepping on her toes and she'd be royally pissed off, but he was fully prepared to deal with the consequences if it kept her safe.

Luckily, his intervention hadn't been required. She'd handled the situation magnificently on her own.

Tristan had left, but Gabe still felt uneasy, on guard.

He reentered the gallery and locked the back door behind him. Experienced a slight jolt of alarm when he saw Zelia wasn't at the makeshift workstation.

"Zelia?"

"In here."

She appeared in the office doorway. "I needed the bigger screen." Ever since the Dropfile had arrived from Mitch containing the photographer's photos of the Feinstein & Co. event, Zelia had been going over them obsessively.

She rolled her shoulders as if she'd been hunched over the keyboard for a while. "Thanks for doing the dumpster run."

"No problem."

She smiled at him wearily, then moved back to her desk and sat down. He followed her in. She looked pale.

"You sure you're okay working in here?"

"Yeah. I'm used to this computer, and the bigger screen is better for zooming in. The energy in here is still jangly, but I'm pushing past it."

He watched her click from one photo to the next, then back to the previous photo again.

"What are you looking for?"

She scrubbed her face with her hands. "I don't know. I have a strong feeling that if I just *look* hard enough in the right place something important is going to pop out at me, but I don't know where to look or what it is I'm trying to find."

He wished he could scoop her up and take her far away from the source of her worry, wanted to eradicate the bruised look in her eyes, but he couldn't. He was not God. "Sometimes, when I'm writing and I get stuck, I print out the manuscript. There's something about seeing the words on paper that helps me see the flaws and what is missing better."

"That's it," said Zelia, nodding her head. "That's what I need to do." She reached down, her hand fumbling for the missing drawer. "Damn. I forgot the paper drawer is with the cops. No worries." She got to her feet and headed out of the office. "I've got a box of paper in the storage room downstairs."

SIXTY-TWO

Tristan was cold and wet by the time he arrived at his dinky motel room. The place was a shithole with paper-thin walls. He could hear a brat squalling next door. If he weren't on reconnaissance he'd have pounded his fist through the door and forced the mother to shut the kid up.

"The sacrifices I make for my art," he muttered.

He removed the paper he'd scribbled Zelia's home address on from his pocket. The rain had soaked through, but luckily the ink was only slightly smeared and the address was still legible. He gently laid the paper on the linoleum floor next to the baseboard heater to dry. Then he stripped off his wet clothes and stepped into the shower. There was mildew in the grout, but at least the water was hot and plentiful. He shut his eyes and pretended he was home in his pristine Calacatta marble shower with a thick stack of plush Egyptian cotton towels waiting to dry and caress his body. "Soon," he murmured. "Once I have the materials I need to complete my masterpiece."

In the meantime, he needed to make do. If that conniving bitch hadn't leapt off his yacht, he would have been able to set his trap in luxury. Instead, he'd been forced to send the boat and crew back to Seattle. Her body might be found, and connections could be made. No sense tempting fate.

Fredrick had begged him to come away with them, tears in his eyes, but Tristan had refused. He was not a coward, scurrying off at the first hint of danger. No. The risk made it more exciting and would fuel the muse like high-octane propane.

He lathered his body, his mind turning over plans. *Shower, sustenance, then swing by her place, gain access, bring tools and something to read, be prepared to wait.*

SIXTY-THREE

"Gabe! Come look at this." The urgency in Zelia's voice jerked Gabe's focus from his laptop and the plethora of crime scene evidence that his brother had sent him concerning the Richard Rye case.

By the time he reached her she was on her feet, her face alight with excitement. "Okay, look at this." She grabbed his arm. "Careful where you step. So, I used the photos and reconstructed the layout of Alexus's gallery. I cross-referenced with the brochure and flyers from her show and matched the placement of the art. See!" She strode among the pattern of photos lying on the floor, a piece of cellophane tape holding them in place, but still the papers fluttered gently as she passed. "Now look closely." She was practically vibrating with excitement.

What he saw were a lot of photos taped to the floor. In some he could see whole paintings and in some a partial view. He scanned the faces of the people in the photos, but nothing jumped out.

"What do you see?" she demanded, her face glowing.

"Photos of paintings and people."

"And what else?" She was clutching his arm, nodding as if that would send the information through the air to him.

"I got nothing."

"No Dattg!" she said triumphantly.

"No what?"

She started pacing again, her arms waving around excitedly, pointing at the layout of photos. "I re-created her entire gallery and there is not a *single* Dattg painting among the bunch! Now, she texted me the night she died, insisting that I hang his work. She sent me his CV and portfolio. Told me she had hung three of his paintings in that night's exhibition. But not one is gracing her walls. Why?"

She looked at him expectantly.

"Why?"

"Because she wasn't the one texting me! It must have been the artist. Dattg. We find the artist and I bet we find her killer —"

She slammed to a halt. "Wait a minute . . ."

She turned to him, her eyes wide. "The painting . . ." she whispered. "Oh my God."

She grabbed his hand. "Come on."

Zelia stared at the painting, her arms crossed, her stomach feeling the familiar clench. "There's something here. I know it. Maybe 'Insurance' isn't the title, but instead it's a message from her."

"Could be," Gabe replied. He gestured to the painting. "Do you mind if I look it over?"

"Be my guest." Zelia was relieved not to touch the thing. She watched as Gabe removed it from the wall and examined it.

"I think I'd better . . ." he murmured, deep in thought. Then he pivoted, strode to the office, flipping on the bright overhead lights as he crossed the threshold.

He laid the painting facedown on the desktop, rocked back on his heels, and crossed his arms. She could see the wheels turning as she watched him step to the desk with a faint frown on his brow. He carefully ran his fingertips under the cross braces. "Nothing there." He tipped the painting on its side and peered into the cracks between the inner and outer frame. "Ah . . ." He gestured her closer. "See there?"

"Uh-huh." Zelia stared at the slip of folded paper that had been tucked between the two slats of wood, her lungs seeming to constrict around the base of her throat.

He turned the painting over and attempted to dislodge the paper to no avail.

"I'll get my needle-nose pliers." Zelia ran to the maintenance closet, opened the toolbox, and snagged the pliers, telling herself not to get her hopes up. It could be an accidental, inconsequential piece of paper that had fallen there. Her heart was thumping like a rat in a trap.

The pliers were too thick to fit all the way in the gap, but she managed to snag the corner of the paper with the tips and gently extricate it.

She offered the folded paper to Gabe since he'd been the one to discover it. "Your friend," he said, shaking his head. "You do the honors." Even though she could tell he was dying to open it.

She unfolded the paper, and tears flooded her eyes, blurring her vision. "It's Alexus's handwriting." She blew out a breath long and slow, dragged her forearm across her eyes, and then began to read:

Zelia,
You know that new assistant I'd been raving about, Tristan? Turns out he's an artist. Eye roll. He's trying to pressure me into hanging his paintings. Ha! Good

luck with that. It's looking like I'm going to have to let him go. It's becoming uncomfortable, but I haven't found someone to replace him yet, so I'm limping along.

It's probably nothing but the midnight musings of my overly suspicious mind. However, just in case something untoward happens to me, I've sent this painting and letter as insurance.

I'm hoping we'll have a good laugh about this when I see you next.

Love, Alexus xo

She felt his arm settle around her shoulders.

"You okay?"

She nodded. Words were too difficult.

"How about we drop this off at the police station on our way to dinner, so they can follow up?"

SIXTY-FOUR

That was the beauty of a rustic island cottage, so damned easy to penetrate, he thought as he returned his neo-Gothic winged-demon dagger to the iron scabbard that was clipped to his belt. *Fire me, will you?* Tristan couldn't help the soft laugh that escaped. *And you felt Dattg was a little disturbing before . . . Just you wait.*

He lifted the screen he'd pried away from the window frame and tucked it behind a massive Douglas fir tree. The bathroom window had been left open a crack.

He slid his latex-clad fingers into the gap and hoisted up the window frame, his heart pounding. Within seconds he and his tools were safely inside. A triumphant sense of power surged through him as he shut the window and latched it behind him.

He relieved himself in her toilet. There was a ritualistic feeling about the act, hunkered down, voiding his bowels. Furthermore, he needed to be prepared for a long wait. *Where shall I hide out — the broom cupboard, a closet, or perhaps under her bed?* Once finished with his bodily housekeeping, he rose. For a split second he was tempted not to flush, to leave the mess as a calling card. *"Could you run a dust mop around the gallery,"* he mimicked in a high, mocking voice. But he didn't give in to his baser desires. It was important not to leave any evidence behind. He fished a DNA wipe out of his briefcase, cleaned the seat, flushed, and then exited the bathroom. Adrenaline coursed through him as he began his hunt for the perfect spot to lie in wait for his prey.

SIXTY-FIVE

Tristan Guillory awoke to the sound of footsteps tromping up the porch steps. Heard the jangle of keys, the dead bolt sliding open. Voices. Male and female. *Damn.* She wasn't alone. *Now what?*

He pushed his body to a standing position. His left foot had fallen asleep. Small wonder. He'd crammed himself into the back of her minuscule closet, tucked behind her hanging clothes. He hated being in such close contact with her things, surrounded by the vanilla-cinnamon scent of her clinging to the garments. Disgusting. Unfortunately, it was the only place he could find. Her bed was one of those boxed-in lowslung ones, and the broom closet was by the back door, too far to navigate from in the dark. Behind the sofa had been a possibility. The floor-to-ceiling curtains provided additional coverage, but the damned cat wouldn't leave him alone, meowing, winding around his legs. He was tempted to slit the creature's throat, but even if he'd been able to contain the mess, the fact that the cat was missing might have given him away.

He rotated his ankle, trying to encourage the flow of blood to his foot, ease the stinging pins and needles.

Footsteps were approaching.

Shit.

He slunk deeper into the far corner.

"Be just a sec," he heard her say. He sucked in a deep breath and held it a fraction of a second before the closet door slid open. He had a partial view of her as she flipped through a couple of garments. All she would have had to do was turn her head and their eyes would have locked. The jig would have been up. He had to exert masterful control over his impulses. He wanted to grab her arm, yank her to the floor, and plunge the syringe he had at the ready into her struggling body, watch her sink into unconsciousness, fear in her eyes. But her friend was there. So, unfortunately, he couldn't indulge in the pleasure of a struggle. He'd have to wait until she was asleep to make his move.

"Ah . . ." Zelia murmured. "This is comfy." Her arm exited the closet. He could hear her moving around, disrobing, redressing, and then she exited the bedroom. She hadn't closed the closet door, and from the sounds of it, she had left the bedroom door open as well.

Should I move to a different spot? I could stand behind the door. No. Too risky. Best to stay put.

SIXTY-SIX

"Thank you" — Zelia bent over and brushed her lips across his — "for your help today."

Gabe shoved his hands deep into his pockets in an effort to keep from reaching up and pulling her to him to claim her mouth and her body. "Does this mean" — his voice came out like gravel striking the undercarriage of a car — "that we're back on?"

She straightened, her hand rising to her mouth as if to keep the taste of him there. "I'm not sure," she said, her voice a soft moan. He could tell by the soft undulation of her hips and the flush high on her cheeks that her need for him was probably as intense as what he was experiencing.

"Well, when you're sure, let me know."

"Okay." She took a step back. "Sweet dreams." Another step.

"Good night," he said. "Call if you need

anything."

She smiled softly. "I will." She turned and walked into her bedroom.

"Damn . . ." he muttered.

She turned, resting her cheek against the partially shut door. "Did you say something?"

Yes. Let me strip off your clothes and devour you. "No. Nothing important."

"Okay, then. Night-night." She stepped farther into her bedroom and then closed the door behind her.

He exhaled slowly. Sometimes it sucked having a conscience.

Charlie leapt onto the sofa, then made his way to his preferred sleeping spot, nestled in the hollow between Gabe's arm and his chest, purring softly and kneading the duvet. Gabe tried to settle in, but his mind was racing. He'd felt uneasy all evening, probably on account of the events of the last few days. When they'd arrived at the cottage, they'd done a sweep. The doors and windows were still locked. Everything looked normal, undisturbed.

Gabe exhaled again, trying to disperse the tension in his body. *The police have a detailed description of Alexus's assistant and are on the lookout for him. All will be well.* Gabe petted Charlie absentmindedly and listened to the sounds of Zelia getting ready for bed. How he longed to join her. He heard the drone of her electric toothbrush switch off, water running in the sink. Then there were the soft sounds of her returning to her bedroom, disrobing, crawling into bed.

It was torture.

Finally, he made the executive decision to place the soft down pillow over his head instead of under it to tamp down the sounds of her warm body shifting restlessly in her bed.

Gabe had thought sleep wouldn't come. It had eluded him the previous evening. But the all-encompassing darkness, the sound of the soft wind rustling through the boughs of the ancient Douglas firs outside muffled now by the pillow, and the added comfort of Charlie's warm body and gentle purring lulled Gabe to sleep. To sleep and to glorious dreams of Zelia opening her arms and her body to him once again.

SIXTY-SEVEN

Zelia woke with a jolt, her heart pounding in her ears, the metallic tang of fear in her mouth. At first she thought perhaps a bad dream had awoken her, but then she heard it, the soft *shhsst* of a shoe. A shadowy figure loomed over her bed. Even with the darkness limiting her vision, she knew it wasn't Gabe. The scent of the intruder, plus an instinctual sense of wrongness, made the air thick and heavy.

She opened her mouth, but before a scream could escape, a hand slammed down to silence her, trapping the cry for help in her throat. He was on her now, straddling her hips, his weight pinning her down. His palm covered her mouth, his thumb and forefinger squeezing her nose tight, cutting off her air supply. *Oh dear God, please help me.* She clawed his hand, but she couldn't budge it. Slashed at his face, hoping to strike his eyes and blind him. She was using the force in her hips, twisting, arching in an attempt to buck him off, when she felt a sharp jab in the side of her neck, a burning sensation.

This is bad . . . This is really bad . . .

She could feel the effects of the drug he'd injected her with coursing through her veins, but she continued fighting, her lungs bursting from lack of oxygen. Clawing at his arms, face, neck, any inch of skin she could reach. Determined to do as much damage as she could before unconsciousness claimed her.

SIXTY-EIGHT

Tristan glanced at the bloated plastic blood bag lying on the bed beside Zelia like a redolent tick lolling after a feast. While he hummed softly to himself, his gaze followed the plastic tubing up to the sixteen-gauge needle he had inserted in her vein earlier that evening.

He trailed his latex-covered fingers gently down her arm, almost like a caress. When he reached her hand, he wrapped his fingers around it, curling her limp fingers inward into a fist. Squeezing as if he were performing CPR on her hand. The blood was coming slower now.

Maneuvering in the dark had added an extra challenge to the proceedings, but he couldn't risk switching on the overhead light. The illumination spilling under the door might draw unwanted attention.

He transferred the small flashlight he was carrying to his mouth. It was necessary in order to free up his hands. He applied a clamp to the plastic tubing, removed and sealed the blood bag. Then he placed the bag beside its brethren in his Italian leather briefcase, which lay open on the top of the dresser.

The harvest had been extraordinarily good. And there was something about having an unsuspecting witness sleeping just beyond the door that made the whole thing that much more delicious.

Tristan adored the whole ritual of the hunt, the letting of blood, the pomp and ceremony, but this final stage was perhaps his favorite, the pièce de résistance.

Lovingly, he removed the tools he had assembled earlier in his motel room: two test tubes, the spoon, the lighter, the ziplock baggie with the cotton, and last of all, the syringe. He placed the items on her bedside table. In one of the test tubes was thirty milligrams of heroin, in the other a few droplets of distilled water. The contents would soon be deposited into the center of his silver baby spoon — a gift from the grandparents on his mother's side — and heated. Such a lovely little spoon, all curlicues and embellishments, the bottom now blackened from his previous adventures.

A frisson of excitement shivered through

him. All was ready. What a glorious feeling. Standing over another smug, ball-busting bitch who hadn't bothered to give his beautiful art its due, with the assembled instruments of her death at hand.

He took a second to remove the flashlight that was slick with saliva and dried it on his slacks. "It's showtime," he whispered, smoothing her hair out of her face. *She is pretty, in a bovine sort of way,* he thought as he replaced the flashlight in his mouth, freeing his hands to prepare the — he couldn't stop the smile, had to grip the flashlight between his teeth so it wouldn't fall — *showstopper.* And who could blame him if he took a moment to indulge in a little "jazz hands" before picking up the test tube containing the heroin? All work and no play would make him a very dull boy indeed.

SIXTY-NINE

Gabe sat on the sofa, leaning forward, his hands clasped. He was wound tight. Felt like a boxer waiting to enter the ring. But he couldn't. He had given Zelia his word. She'd let him sleep on her sofa to keep watch over her, and as much as he wanted a future with her, he needed her to be just as certain she wanted the same things he did.

The sound of her moving around in her room earlier had jolted him awake. It was almost as if she'd tapped him on the shoulder and called his name. He'd shot to his feet, still half asleep but ready for action. Listened, every cell in his body insisting he run to her room, jerk the door open, but he didn't.

Wouldn't. Because it was possible his dreams and reality had gotten jumbled into a stew.

He waited for her to appear at her door, to make the choice to invite him to join her.

His heart was banging away as if he'd just completed the fifty-meter dash. He could hear her moving, shifting on her bed, then a muffled moan. And that's when he sank back down to the sofa, his heart suddenly heavy, shoulders bowed.

It was torture to sit there, listening to her. Was she secretly pleasuring herself?

He tried to lie back down, but his body wouldn't let him. All his senses seemed to be locked in overdrive, aligning themselves to the nightmarish quality he could taste in the air.

Then he noticed Charlie pacing in front of her door, agitated, his tail lashing.

The cat feels it, too. Something is off. The second that thought dropped into his solar plexus, he was on the move. She might hate him for barging in on her, but staying put was no longer an option.

He crossed the room like a rocket, slammed open the door. A beam of light slashed across his face, momentarily blinding him before the light source dropped with a *thunk,* spun across the floor, and disappeared from view. He sensed someone moving toward him fast.

Gabe veered to the side, swinging in the dark. His first fist went wide, but the second one made contact. He heard a grunt, a soft curse. Could feel the assailant shift toward where the blow had come from, but Gabe was already on the move, silently circling behind, listening hard.

Right there. A barely audible intake of air. The type someone would make as they set their body to charge.

Gabe launched his body low, again making contact, bringing the intruder crashing to the floor. Something sharp scraped across the surface of his bare shoulder. *A knife?* Gabe felt the assailant's muscles tense, knew whatever weapon was in the guy's fist would be coming down fast. He threw his body to the side and rolled to his feet, spreading his hand wide, sweeping it in an arc along the wall by the door.

He snagged the light switch on the second pass — the overhead lights flashed on, almost blinding in the sudden brightness. *Tristan,* Gabe thought, as the man charged toward him. *Son of a bitch. How did he get in here?* Blood was dripping down the man's face. Tristan was wielding a syringe in one hand, a dagger in the other.

Gabe had to make a snap decision. Which weapon posed the greatest threat? He whipped his leg in the air and smashed it down on Tristan's right collarbone. He heard the bone snap as the dagger in Tris-

415

tan's left hand slashed through his pajama bottoms and made contact with his thigh. Gabe pivoted on his standing leg and delivered a bruising side kick to Tristan's face, snapping pretty-boy's head back and decimating his nose. Blood splattered as Tristan staggered back with a hard *thump* against the dresser, the hand holding the syringe hanging limply at Tristan's side.

Snarling like a rabid dog, Tristan slammed the dagger into the holster on his belt. He grabbed the syringe from his useless right hand as he jerked his body upright. His gaze darted for a millisecond to Zelia sprawled on the bed, pale and still.

Tristan feinted charging Gabe again, but the flicker of his eyes had given his intentions away. Gabe lunged sideways, positioning himself between Tristan and the woman he loved, praying she was okay. Determined to do whatever it took to keep this madman at bay. Throbbing pain burned his left thigh as if a red-hot poker was sizzling his flesh, throwing his balance off. Liquid poured down his leg, his foot skidding in the blood.

He thrust his arms out and managed to snag Tristan's ankle as he crashed to the floor, bringing Tristan down with him. Half rolling, half dragging, he forced Tristan away from the bed, away from Zelia.

Tristan arched his back, noises coming out of his mouth — wild, animalistic noises — as he twisted his body around. Gabe saw light glinting on the syringe as it slammed downward. No time to roll to the side. His only hope was to change the needle's intended trajectory. Gabe delivered another punishing blow to Tristan's face as his other hand slammed to the side in a hard block. He closed his fingers like a vise around Tristan's wrist, controlling the direction of the syringe as he toppled Tristan backward and landed hard on top of him. Gabe wrapped his free hand around his other one and drove the syringe like a stake deep into Tristan's neck.

"Nooooo!" Tristan screamed. "Don't press the plunger! Dear God, please, I'm begging you, don't!"

The abject terror and panic in Tristan's eyes caused Gabe to hesitate. *Thou shalt not kill . . .* drumming through his brain. And yet Zelia wouldn't be safe as long as Tristan was in the world. *Maybe what's in the needle won't kill him. Maybe it will just incapacitate.* But even as Gabe thought it, he knew he was grasping at straws.

"I'll be good." Tristan sobbed. "I won't be bad anymore."

"I'm sorry," Gabe choked out, his own

eyes wet, too. "It's too great a risk." Heart-sick, he forced himself to depress the plunger, sending whatever concoction was in the barrel of the syringe into the blood-stream of the man struggling beneath him.

SEVENTY

Zelia awoke to a dimly lit room, monitors beeping by the side of her bed.

"You okay?" Gabe's familiar voice filled her with warmth and a sense of safety. Zelia turned her head. He was sitting in a plastic chair by her bed. He looked haggard and worn, as if he'd been planted there for a long time.

She nodded. Opened her mouth to speak. Wasn't sure if any words actually made their way out before she drifted into unconsciousness again.

"Hey there, sleepyhead," a woman's voice chirped.

Zelia opened her eyes to see her next-door neighbor Lori standing by her hospital bed. Big-eyed kittens frolicked across her nurse's scrub top. She was backlit by bright sunshine streaming through the partially closed plastic blinds across the window.

Zelia pushed onto her elbows. She felt so weak. The sun was high in the sky, so it must be around noon. "Where's Gabe?"

"Sent him home to take a shower. Hold on there. Let me help." Lori picked up a controller and pressed a button, raising the head of the bed until Zelia was in a seated position. "That better?"

"Yeah, thanks."

"How's it feel to be a famous crime-fighting sleuth?"

"A what?"

"Ah . . . that's right, you've been out. Blame my brain fart on a lack of sleep." Lori stifled a yawn. "We're short staffed. *Again.* So I'm pulling another back-to-back. Coffee is my friend." Lori switched out the depleted saline drip bag for a new one. "At least the excitement factor was off the charts. When things are slow, time seems to limp along. But last night?" Lori whistled through her teeth. "Honey, it's too bad you were unconscious. Picture this." Lori waved her spread-out hands in front of her as if they were revealing the sign above a movie marquee. "A smoking-hot guy comes tearing into ER in the middle of the night, you in his arms while he bled on our floor. Needed eighteen stiches. The man stayed by your side all night. Loyal as a dog." Lori poured ice water into a plastic glass. "Wish I could find me a man like that." She handed it to Zelia. "Here you go, sweetie."

"Thanks." Zelia gulped the water, grateful for the refreshing liquid. Hadn't realized how dry her mouth was.

"I've gotta confess, I've read Conaghan's books," Lori continued as she refilled Zelia's cup. "But I had no idea how gorgeous he was in person. Figured his author photo had been airbrushed, but *nooooo*." She fanned her face. "I mean . . . Wowza!

"By the way, I'd better give you a heads-up. The *media* has descended on our sleepy little island. There are reporters camped in the parking lot. One ballsy lady donned nurse scrubs and tried to sneak into your room to take photos. That might have worked in the big city." Lori chuckled as she smoothed the bed linens. "We run a tighter ship here. Tossed her out on her bony ass. The hospital switchboard has been lit up with inquiries from newspapers around the world. 'International Bestselling Author in Fatal Conflict with the Heir to the Guillory Fortune.' " Lori shook her head. "All that money must have messed up his mind. All kinds of wild stories flying about, kidnapping, attempted murder, a possible serial killer." Lori slid a look at her, clearly hoping Zelia would let a few tasty morsels fall, but a wave of weariness was breaking over her. Zelia placed the water cup on the overbed hospital table and sank her head back against the pillow. "I guess it's true what they say," Lori continued. " 'Money can't buy you happiness,' that's for sure.

"Anyway, back to business — we've been pumping you full of fluids, and the doctor would like to do a blood transfusion if you're agreeable."

"Why?" Zelia asked. Her mind was spinning with the flood of new information. Gabe had brought her in. Had stayed through the night, loyal and true, even though he had been wounded. Was he okay? She longed for the sight of his dear, trustworthy face. Tristan had been caught. How? Must have been Gabe. Last thing Zelia remembered was the struggle, Tristan plunging the needle into her neck. Media was in the parking lot. How crazy was that? The doctor wanted to do a blood transfusion.

"You lost a lot of blood, sweetie," Lori said.

"I did?" Zelia's eyes were feeling heavy.

Lori nodded her head emphatically, her ponytail bobbing, eyes wide. "Oh yeah."

"Well, then, sure. I guess. Blood transfusion would be fine."

"Good call. Here's a consent form. Read it over. The doctor will have you sign here and witness it once she's explained the various risks, et cetera." Lori tapped the X at the bottom of the page with her pen, then tucked the pen under the metal clasp of the clipboard and handed it to her.

The pager on Lori's belt buzzed. She glanced at it, made a face. "Gotta go. Be back in a jiff." She headed to the door. "Oh, hey," she tossed over her shoulder. "Your assistant, Mary Browning, is two doors down. Room 304. Close call. Poor thing nearly drowned . . . hypothermia. Imagine old Pete Wilkson's surprise, taking the rowboat out to pick up some Dungeness crabs for him and his missus's dinner. The man, as usual, was two sheets to the wind. Thought he was hallucinating when he found poor Mary, barely conscious, draped over his crab-trap float." Lori laughed, shaking her head. "Serves him right. Shouldn't be out there after dark with no lights. Anyway, Mary's responding well to treatment. Not a single visitor, though, aside from that crazy news photographer who doesn't count. Can you imagine, sneaking photos of someone lying in a hospital bed, hooked up to machines, bandaged and bruised? What kind of person does that?" Her pager buzzed again. "Yeah . . . yeah . . . yeah . . . I'm coming. Anyway, if you feel up to it later, poke your head in and say hello. I'm sure she'd appreciate seeing a friendly face." Lori turned to the door and banged into Gabe. "Oh. You're back already. That was quick." She smirked at Zelia and wiggled her eyebrows. "I think I'll shut the door on my way out. Give you two a little privacy."

SEVENTY-ONE

The door closed behind him, muffling the clatter in the hall from the lunch trolley that was delivering meals to the patients. "How are you doing?" Gabe stepped deeper into the room.

Zelia looked tired. Her face was pale. "Okay," she said.

"I brought you" — he lifted the brown paper bag in his hand and jiggled it temptingly — "some goodies from Intrepid, as hospital food isn't known for its culinary delights."

She smiled wanly. "Thanks."

"Maybe a bouquet of flowers would have been better?"

"No. Food from Intrepid is perfect. I'll eat some later." Her eyelids were drifting shut. She dragged them open again with considerable effort. "I'm a little sleepy still."

He nodded. "The drug probably isn't out of your system yet."

"That must be it." She rubbed her eyes. Reminded Gabe of a sleepy puppy. "Would you mind doing me an enormous favor?"

"Anything."

"I'm feeling kind of . . ." She looked embarrassed. "Shaky." Zelia shrugged, but he noticed now that she was trembling slightly. "Scared, I guess, from all the . . ." She exhaled. "Anyway, I was wondering if you would hold me for a while?"

"Of course." His eyes felt hot as he put the bag of food on her bedside table, bent over, and wrapped his arms around her, the relief of it choking his throat.

"More." Her arms tugged him downward. "Can you get on the bed with me?"

God, he wanted to. "You're attached to a drip."

"We'll be careful not to dislodge anything. I want . . . I need to be in your arms."

Gabe removed his shoes, and the soft smile of relief that bloomed on her face weakened his knees. "I know it seems silly, but . . ."

"Not silly at all," Gabe said, loving her so much he thought he would burst. She scooted over and lifted the blue sheet and the thin white blanket with a blue stripe that covered her. He climbed carefully onto her bed. Using his arms and right leg to

426

take the bulk of his weight, his left thigh on fire. Both of them mindful of the IV port, the lines running to the drip and the heart monitor. It was a tight squeeze, but it didn't matter. Once he was settled, she nestled in close, her head on his chest, his arm around her beautiful, silky-soft shoulders. And he was filled with a sense of peace, of coming home.

She was asleep within seconds. The muscles in the leg that she had draped over his and the arm that she'd wrapped around his chest grew lax and heavy.

Gabe lay in that narrow hospital bed with Zelia, drenched in sweat as he beat back the rolling waves of searing pain that had become a fierce drumbeat in his left thigh.

He held Zelia long after he'd lost feeling in his arm, unwilling to wake or release her. Hospital staff came and went and still she slept, her breath soft and steady on his chest as her heartbeat merged with his.

The scent that was uniquely hers, with a hint of vanilla and cinnamon from her soap or shampoo, soothed him. And he found if he focused on her smell, he could momentarily crowd back the images from the night before. Images, memories, and agonizing hot shame that threatened to devour him piece by piece.

SEVENTY-TWO

Zelia shooed the final guests through the gallery door and locked it behind them, heaving a sigh of relief. The March Madness art show had been a spectacular success. Record sales, with a huge surge in international buyers, and Zelia had a wait list a mile long to purchase works by the "overnight" sensation, artist Eve Harris.

She sighed with contentment, slipped off her heels, and then padded into the back room.

"Happy?" Gabe asked. He was already elbows deep in soapy water, washing wineglasses.

"The night couldn't have gone better," Zelia said, indulging in an exultant twirl before dropping her heels onto the coat closet floor.

She turned back to the room and watched Gabe and his parents puttering around and was filled with a quiet gratitude. "Thank you, so much." She walked over to Alma and gently removed the wastebasket from her hands. "I can finish up here. Seriously, I really appreciate all of your help setting up, but you and Fergus should go home now." Zelia wrapped her arms around the diminutive woman who had become so dear to her. "I have the cleanup routine down pat. It's going to take me fifteen minutes max."

"Many hands make light work," Alma said, but Zelia could see the weariness from the late hour was setting in.

"Gabe," Zelia called. "Your mom's being stubborn. Help me out here."

Gabe dried his hands. "Zelia's right," he said as he gathered his parents' coats. "I'll drive you home." He gave Zelia a quick kiss as he passed, herding his parents toward the door. "Be back in a jiff."

It wasn't until they'd left and the rumble of Gabe's SUV had been swallowed up by the night that the hole in her life created by Mary's absence made itself known once again. The two of them had always done this cleanup ritual together while chatting about the events of the night. Where was she? Was she safe?

The second Mary had been released from the hospital she'd packed her suitcase, swung by Zelia's, picked up her cat, and then was on the next ferry off the island.

"But what about all your things, your furniture? You've built a life here, Mary. I know you had a traumatic experience, but Tristan Guillory is dead. He can't hurt you anymore."

"I know." Mary's eyes had been dark with sorrow.

"Then why leave? Whatever it is, we can work our way through it. I'm your friend, Mary. Let me help. Please."

Mary didn't answer. Just gave her a fierce hug. Zelia could feel the thumping of Mary's heart. Mary's breath and body shook as warm, salty tears slid down the nape of Zelia's neck, soaking the polka-dotted white cotton fabric.

When Mary had finally straightened, her tear-stained face was resolute. She'd refused to give Zelia a forwarding address. "I can't," Mary had replied. "It's for your own safety." Another quick hug, and then she and Charlie were gone.

At least Mary had allowed Zelia to pay her the cash owed for hours worked. While Gabe gathered Charlie's belongings, Zelia had grabbed an envelope from her desk, then disappeared into her bedroom. She'd opened her lockbox, where she kept her passport and a stash of emergency cash.

She'd counted the bills, two thousand, five hundred dollars. She'd wished she had more. Then she'd seen Gabe's plump wallet lying on the dresser. "Gabe," she'd said, poking her head out the doorway. "Could you come in here for a second?"

A moment later he'd appeared, a multitude of cat toys in his arms.

"Can I?" she'd asked, pointing at his wallet.

"Absolutely," he'd replied. Understanding completely.

"I'll pay you back."

"No need." He scooped up a catnip mouse from the rug by the bed. "I'm gonna miss the little bugger," he'd said as he exited the room.

All in all, unbeknownst to Mary, she'd left with a little over four thousand dollars in a sealed envelope that Zelia had tucked inside the zipper compartment of her purse. Money, and half a loaf of Zelia's first attempt at homemade banana bread.

As she'd watched Mary's old rattletrap pull out of her driveway with all the money Zelia had at hand and half a loaf of warm banana bread, it still didn't feel like she'd done enough.

Life had gone on, however. The press finally departed, chasing the next hot headline, but not before Zelia and Gabe had been interviewed ad nauseam. The only caveats Zelia had insisted on was that all interviews must be held at Art Expressions Gallery. And any work of art that was featured in the background of a photo must be labeled in the photo description.

She had Gabe drive her straight from the hospital to Eve Harris's home, where Zelia loaded as many of Eve's paintings as the back of the SUV could hold. Once at her gallery she'd pulled an all-nighter. Got Eve Harris's work photographed and up on her website, chose which paintings to hang, labeled them. Gabe held paintings, hammered nails, made and consumed buckets of coffee. The two of them looked a right mess the next morning when the members of the press arrived for the conference. Gabe had zipped out, showered and shaved, brought back a change of clothes for Zelia. She'd figured he'd grab one of her business power suits, but he'd arrived with a jewel-toned velvet dress and boots. "It's my favorite," he'd said. So she had washed up in the bathroom sink and put it on. She had a spare powder and a tube of lipstick in the top drawer of her desk for emergencies, but even a dash of powder couldn't hide the dark circles under her eyes. No matter. The gallery looked *amazing,* and that was her number one priority.

The next night, Zelia hadn't needed to pull an all-nighter, but she had worked like a dog into the wee hours of the morn, rotating the artwork so that another of her artists would be featured. Also, after watching a few of the clips playing on TV, she'd redesigned temporary artwork labels. She removed the descriptions, the size, and left only the painting's title and artist's name. Instead of using the usual-size font, she blew the artwork title and the artist's name up to a massive size forty-eight.

Zelia gazed around the empty gallery, memories of Mary bumping gently against her. So she closed her eyes and sent a short prayer Mary's way, wishing her happiness, safety, and a peaceful resolution to whatever it was that had her on the run again. Zelia didn't know if it helped, sending these prayers Mary's way, but at least it eased the feeling of helplessness Zelia had whenever Mary popped into her mind. Once her prayer was completed, Zelia opened her eyes and began the tedious job of cleaning up the party debris.

SEVENTY-THREE

Zelia woke with a jolt, sat up in bed, panicked, darkness all around. "Gabe," she cried out. "Gabe, where are you?"

"I'm right here." His voice was gentle, groggy with sleep. "Don't worry. You're not alone."

"Thank God." She sank back onto the bed. Gabe wrapped his arms around her, snuggled her close.

"Don't leave me," she whispered, her voice hoarse. Her heart was still racing.

"Never," he replied, dropping a soft kiss on the top of her head.

They lay there like that, in the silence of the room, their bodies entwined. The accelerated pace of their hearts calming, like the ocean after a storm.

"It was him again. In my dream. He was in the room. Only I could see him approaching this time. It's like I was watching the whole thing unfold from where I was floating on the ceiling. Could see myself lying there, curled up on my side. Could see the shadow shape of him creep out of my closet, and I'm yelling as loud as I can, 'Wake up! Get out!' But the me in the bed doesn't hear." Gabe was moving his hand in slow, steady circles on her back. Grounding her to the present. She snuggled in tighter, needing the warmth of his body to chase away the cold. "I don't know why I keep having these dumb nightmares. It's frustrating. He's gone now. Can't hurt me anymore. So *why* am I still allowing him to terrorize my present?"

"Give yourself time, Zee. It was a traumatic experience. Since then you've been crazy busy dealing with the press, not to mention March Madness, as well as losing your assistant. The fact is, you've been running on fumes these last couple of weeks, so your body is using your dreamscape to process what happened the best that it can."

"Mm . . . you're right." Zelia could feel the tension from the dream draining out of her.

"I dream of him, too. Think of him often, of that night. Turning it over and over in my head. Wondering if there was anything I could have done differently."

"Was there?"

"I don't know. If there was, I haven't found it yet." She felt him shrug. He was talking in a matter-of-fact way, but she knew more was going on than he was showing.

"So, why don't we backtrack? Let's say when Tristan pleaded for mercy, you did the Jesus thing, released your grip on the syringe. Got off of him and let him go free. What do you think would've happened then?"

"Don't know."

"I do. The second you turned your back, he would have plunged that needle in you so deep, there would be no dislodging it. You'd be dead. Then he would've gleefully killed me, using the tortured-artist card to justify his deviant behavior. Yes, you'd have had a split second of peace knowing that you had refused to play judge, jury, and executioner. However, you'd also be dead, and so would I. And let's not forget, there are only two confirmed murders, *but* the police have now reopened OD cases involving gallery owners in Gstaad, Munich, and two in the UK." She hugged him tight. "You did the right thing. I know it's hard, and I'm sorry you've been forced to carry the burden, but I'm *glad* you did what you did. If that makes me a bad person, so be it. Who knows how many more people he would

436

have killed before he was apprehended?"

"I worried that perhaps you were repulsed by me, by the fact that I'm no better than him."

"God no. How could you even think such a crazy thought? You're a million times a better man than Tristan Guillory. I feel blessed and lucky that we found each other." She turned her head, placed a kiss over his heart, nuzzling her face into his chest, inhaling the scent of him. "I'm *with* you because I *love* you, Gabe." The second the words flew from her mouth Zelia felt lighter.

Gabe froze. She heard the breath catch in his chest.

"I don't know why I waited so long to tell you." Zelia continued. "Fear, I guess, plain and simple. I was terrified of being vulnerable, of loving again. It scared the hell out of me. So I shoved you away, using all kinds of bogus excuses, never mind that I believed them. It still doesn't make it right. The fact is, you repeatedly opened up to me and bared your heart, while I kept a fierce grip tight around mine. And I'm sorry for that, and I hope you'll forgive me, because I love you *so* much, Gabe. Truly."

"There's nothing to forgive," he replied, his voice gruff with emotion. "I love you, too. Always and forever."

Zelia smiled in the darkened room, reminded of a children's bedtime story her mother used to read. "I'm glad." She could feel the comforting thump of his heart underneath her outspread hand, and she was filled with gratitude. "Thank you for being so patient, giving me the space and time I needed."

"Wouldn't have had it any other way."

Zelia tilted her head upward, needing the taste of his mouth on her lips, and then needing more. Needing all of him surrounding her, inside of her, filling her completely. And Gabe, being the consummate gentleman, obliged her in a most satisfactory fashion.

SEVENTY-FOUR

Zelia stared at the blue plus sign that had appeared in the window of the white plastic stick. *Yes. Still there. Proof positive.* She gently laid it on a bed of tissue paper resting on the bathroom counter, unwilling to drop it in the wastebasket just yet. She washed her hands, her heart pounding, face flushed, then returned to the bedroom and eased her way back under the warm duvet.

"Morning," Gabe said, smiling sleepily at her.

She snuggled in close, jubilantly happy and yet a little bit shy.

He wrapped his arms around her. "Goose bumps in May?" he said. "That's what comes with having thin West Coast blood and a vintage cottage with unheated floors. What would a real man do under these dire circumstances? Can't have my woman catching a cold." He grinned happily. "Hm . . . I guess that means I'd better warm you." He nudged her onto her back.

She returned his smile. "Far be it from me to keep you from your manly duty," she replied, spreading her thighs.

It was remarkable how Gabe could go from zero to fully revved in a flash. Once he was embedded deep inside her, making slow, sweet, sweaty love, his warm breath fanning across her face . . . the time felt right.

"Honey," she said, humbled by the love she could see shining in the depths of his eyes. She slid her hand between them. Could feel her abdomen moving as he thrust inside her. Slid her hand lower, to encircle the slick girth of him moving in and out.

"Yeah . . . ?" His voice was a low, sleepy growl.

She slid her hand back to her abdomen, where she could feel him moving and also where invisible changes were taking place. "We're gonna have a baby," she said.

Gabe froze mid-thrust. "We are?" The look in his eyes, wide-open wonder.

She tried to speak, but it was impossible. An oceans-deep happiness was gobbling up her words. All she could do was smile, nod, and dash the happy tears that kept forming on her eyelashes. Not wanting to miss a moment of the slow-dawning rainbow of joy that was illuminating his face.

"Oh, Zee," he murmured, gathering her in his arms as if she were the most precious thing in the world. Holding her close he rolled the two of them to their sides, still deep inside her, kissing her face, her mouth, her throat, her shoulders, her face again. "A baby? You and me?"

She nodded again, words still too thick in her throat to speak them.

"What a blessing. What an undeserved blessing." Now there were tears in his eyes, too, as he gently laid his hand beside hers on her belly. "But I shall seize this good fortune like a thief in the night and do everything in my power to be worthy of this honor, of our child and you."

"Gabe, my love." She shook her head, couldn't help the soft chuckle that emerged. "You have no idea, do you?" She raised her hands to cup his dear, beloved face gently between her palms, wanting, needing him to see the truth shining out of her eyes. "I could have searched the whole world over and would *never* have found *anyone* more lovable, more loved, more worthy than you."

And then she kissed him, because she could. Arms and legs lashed around him tight. So close that she could feel the beating of his heart through the cage of his chest, through his flesh and bone and through hers. Still, she had the need to press even closer, until it felt as if the two of them had merged into one being. *And in a way, we have,* she thought, *with this beautiful, precious life that is growing in my belly.*

MEG'S TASTY BLUEBERRY LEMON-GLAZE MUFFINS

My sisters are in town as I write this. I got up early and worked on my edits while the house was quiet and everybody was sleeping. Then, as I heard sounds of life, I decided to take a stretch break, trotted downstairs, and whipped up some of my blueberry muffins with a lemon-glaze icing. I am munching on them now — piping hot, with a pat of delicious butter — as I type. And as I popped a tasty morsel into my mouth, I thought, *I bet my readers would like to have this recipe!* So here you are:

Ingredients:

For muffins:
1 1/2 cups unbleached flour
3/8 teaspoon salt
2 teaspoons double-acting baking powder
1/4 cup salted butter, softened
1/3 cup white sugar

1 egg
2/3 cup whole milk
1 teaspoon lemon zest
1 to 1 1/2 cups blueberries, fresh or frozen

For Glaze:
1/2 cup powdered sugar
Juice squeezed from 1/2 to 1 fresh lemon

Preheat the oven to 375 degrees Fahrenheit. Grease or place paper muffin liners in your muffin tin.

In a small mixing bowl, sift together the flour, salt, and baking powder. Stir the mixture with a fork to ensure it is well blended, then put it aside.

In a medium mixing bowl, cream the butter and sugar. Then add the egg, milk, and lemon zest. Once it is blended, add in the flour mixture. Important: do not over-stir! Stir only until all of the flour mixture is moist. Then sprinkle in the blueberries. (You can add more or fewer blueberries, depending on your preference.) Remember: minimal stirring. Just enough to get the berries spread relatively evenly throughout.

Spoon the mixture into the muffin tin and pop it into the oven. Bake for about 20–30 minutes. The cooking time will depend on your oven (as each oven is slightly different) and whether you used frozen blueberries or fresh ones. Frozen will add a couple minutes to your cooking time. To know your muffins are done, insert a toothpick in the center of them. The toothpick should come out clean, with nothing clinging to it. Also, the muffin should spring back if you gently pat it with your fingers.

While the muffins are in the oven, mix together the powdered sugar and lemon juice for the glaze in a small bowl until smooth. (The amount of lemon juice is the cook's call. If you like your glaze tart, add more lemon. For just a hint, use only half a lemon.)

Once the muffins are cooked, remove them from the oven and dip the tops into the lemon glaze, swirl so the whole top is covered, and then set them upright on a plate to serve.

I like my muffins piping hot and sliced with a pat of butter melting inside. My husband likes them hot or cold, sans butter. One thing you can be certain of, these muffins won't sit on your kitchen counter long!

ACKNOWLEDGMENTS

My thanks to my awesome editors, Kerry Donovan and Cindy Hwang. Collaborating with you is such a joy. I am also grateful for the skilled proofreading and copyediting provided that make me seem like a more refined writer than I actually am.

I feel blessed to be one of the authors who benefit from the talents of the design team at Berkley, who create such beautiful covers and interior designs. I am also lucky to reap the benefits of the marketing and publicity expertise of Erin Galloway, Jin Yu, Jessica Brock, and Fareeda Bullert.

I also want to give a shout-out to Nancy Berland at NBPR; Whitney Tancred at 42West; Cissy Hartley, Susan Simpson, and the Writerspace gang; as well as Kim Witherspoon and Jessica Mileo at InkWell Management for all that you do on my behalf.

Thank you, Linda Korn and Leeza Watstein, for your care and creativity with the audio versions of my books, and for the casting and sensitive directing of the talented audio actors Kendall Harper and Stephen Dexter, who brought my Solace Island series to life for the PRH Audio listener.

My thanks to my family and friends for your love and support, and to the romance community who have taken me under their wing. I've met so many wonderful people. I also wanted to let my fellow romance readers know that I have been floored by the kindness and generosity that have been shown to me by other romance authors, women whose books I have read and adored. They have reached out to me, shored me up, and offered advice. At the head of the pack is a woman whose books I have read and reread for decades, Jayne Ann Krentz/Amanda Quick/Jayne Castle! But she has not been the only one. Eloisa James, Lorraine Heath, Mariah Stewart, Lori Foster, Jill Shalvis, Elizabeth Boyle, and Kat Martin are a few of my favorite romance authors who have been so supportive, and I am so very, very grateful.

And last but certainly not least, I'd like to thank you, my readers, and the booksellers and librarians. Thank you for taking a chance on me, for passing my books on to other people who might enjoy them. Thank you to those of you who have taken the time to review, for letting me know that you enjoy what I write. That is the thing that keeps me returning to my keyboard day after day. To try, in my small way, to give back to the wonderful world of romance that has shored me up in challenging times by letting me disappear into one of my favorite author's books and come away feeling more hopeful once again.

Thank you!

Much love,
Meg xo

ABOUT THE AUTHOR

Meg Tilly may be best known for her acclaimed Golden Globe-winning performance in the movie *Agnes of God*. After publishing six standout young adult and literary women's fiction novels, the award-winning author/actress decided to write the kind of books she loves to read: romance novels. Tilly has three grown children and resides with her husband in the Pacific Northwest.

The employees of Thorndike Press hope you have enjoyed this Large Print book. All our Thorndike, Wheeler, and Kennebec Large Print titles are designed for easy reading, and all our books are made to last. Other Thorndike Press Large Print books are available at your library, through selected bookstores, or directly from us.

For information about titles, please call:
  (800) 223-1244

or visit our website at:
  gale.com/thorndike

To share your comments, please write:
  Publisher
  Thorndike Press
  10 Water St., Suite 310
  Waterville, ME 04901